N. A. Shenstone

Anecdotes of Henry Ward Beecher

N. A. Shenstone

Anecdotes of Henry Ward Beecher

ISBN/EAN: 9783337144890

Printed in Europe, USA, Canada, Australia, Japan

Cover: Foto ©Andreas Hilbeck / pixelio.de

More available books at **www.hansebooks.com**

ANECDOTES

OF

HENRY WARD BEECHER

BY
N. A. SHENSTONE.

PROFUSELY ILLUSTRATED.

CHICAGO:
R. R. DONNELLEY & SONS, PUBLISHERS.
1887.

CONTENTS.

ILLUSTRATIONS.

PREFACE.

Current literature has had much to say of the life and work of Henry Ward Beecher, and many interesting reminiscences and anecdotes have been given, the best of which, together with selections from various biographies, it is the purpose of this book to present in collected form. The work has been compiled from the following sources: "Lives and Deeds of Our Self - Made Men," by Mrs. Harriet Beecher Stowe ; "Successful People," by M. H. Smith; The Christian Advocate; Christian Herald; The Continent; Scribners Monthly; Contemporary Review; Atlantic Monthly; Appleton; Democratic Review; Harper's Magazine; the daily papers of New York and Chicago ; and the writings of Henry Ward Beecher.

THE AUTHOR.

APRIL 15, 1887.

ILLUSTRATIONS.

PREFACE.

Current literature has had much to say of the life and work of Henry Ward Beecher, and many interesting reminiscences and anecdotes have been given, the best of which, together with selections from various biographies, it is the purpose of this book to present in collected form. The work has been compiled from the following sources: "Lives and Deeds of Our Self - Made Men," by Mrs. Harriet Beecher Stowe ; "Successful People," by M. H. Smith; The Christian Advocate; Christian Herald; The Continent; Scribners Monthly; Contemporary Review; Atlantic Monthly; Appleton; Democratic Review; Harper's Magazine; the daily papers of New York and Chicago ; and the writings of Henry Ward Beecher.

THE AUTHOR.

APRIL 15, 1887.

ANECDOTES

OF

HENRY WARD BEECHER.

CHAPTER I.

ANCESTRAL TREE OF THE BEECHERS.

HENRY WARD BEECHER, the eighth child of Lyman and Roxana Foot Beecher, was born in Litchfield, Conn., June 24, 1813. From the days of Hannah Beecher, a widow who settled in New Hampshire in 1638, eighteen years after the landing of the Pilgrims, down to the present celebrated family of preachers and litterateurs, extends a long line of New England ancestors, nearly all of whom were remarkable for physical prowess or intellectual vigor.

No Beecher came over in the *Mayflower*. The first Americans of that name were part of a company who came to New England in 1638, eighteen years after the landing of the Pilgrim Fathers. This company, finding theological controversy rife in Massachusetts, resolved to form a new colony. They pitched upon a spot called by the Indians Quinnipiac, named Red

9

Mount by the Dutch, but to which they gave the name of New Haven on account of its good harbor. Of this company was Hannah Beecher, who, had become a widow just before they sailed. She was induced to go with the expedition by the assurance that she should receive her husband's share in the town plot. The first sermon preached to the company, after their arrival at their new home, was by Master John Davenport, under a great oak which stood on the widow's plot. The spot is marked by the "Old Beecher House," now standing in New Haven. Hannah Beecher lived a score of years, and died, leaving an estate valued at £55 5s. 6d. With her came her son John, who had already reached man's estate. His son Joseph, the first American-born Beecher, was mighty in hands and spine. He could lift a barrel of cider by the chines and drink out of the bung-hole — a feat which we commend to the trial of the strong men of our day. His son Nathaniel was a blacksmith, and his anvil stood on the stump of the old oak from which Davenport preached the first sermon ever delivered in Connecticut. He, too, was a strong man, though not so strong as his father; still he could lift a barrel of cider into a cart. He stood six feet high, and was the last of the tall Beechers. None of the race since have quite come up to the standard American height.

Next came David, the father of Lyman, a short, square-built man — blue-eyed, and a half Welsh by blood — strong enough to carry a barrel of cider into the cellar; a blacksmith, like his father, and also a farmer, who made famous hoes, and raised excellent rye and wheat. He kept, moreover, a boarding-house for the accommodation of Yale students and members of the Legislature. His table was a little more luxurious than was the custom of the country; consequently he was afflicted with dyspepsia and the consequent blues. Moreover, he had a sun-stroke while out soldiering toward the close of the Revolutionary war, which did not tend to improve his spirits. In his later years he always fancied himself bankrupt, and on the point of coming to want. Still he lived well; and when he died was found to have laid up four or five thousand dollars — a very fair estate for the times. He was a very well-read man, but notably careless and absent-minded — a trait which was transmitted to his more famous son.

David Beecher was five times married, and had a dozen children, of whom all but four died in infancy. Lyman Beecher was the only child of Esther Lyman, the third and best-loved of the five wives. She died of consumption two days after the birth of her son.

The motherless babe was almost from birth adopted by his mother's sister, the childless wife of Lot Benton, a well-to-do farmer of Guilford, a few miles from New Haven. Worthy Uncle Lot was a true father to the child, one of whose daughters long after described him under the name of "Uncle Lot Griswold." He was a tall, bright, dark-eyed man of pleasant countenance; always scheming, and contriving, and farming on the principle of making his land yield the most with the least outlay. The first sixteen years of the life of Lyman Beecher were passed mainly with Uncle Lot.

We get glimpses of the way in which well-to-do people in Connecticut lived two generations ago. Six mahogany chairs, in a shut-up parlor, were considered magnificent. Good David Beecher never got beyond cherry.

"We raised our breadstuffs," said Lyman, "and fodder for stock, and cut salt hay on the marsh. Raised an acre or two of flax, though it was impossible to keep Aunt Benton in spinning for the winter. In fall and winter there was wood to be cut and hauled. In June we went to Quinnepaug Outlet to wash sheep; a day or two afterward we sheared them. Then the fleece was salted, carded, and spun, all in the house; flax in winter, wool in summer. They made all sorts of linen work, table-cloths, shirting, sheeting, and cloths. Thrifty Aunt Benton and Annis — a bright thirteen-year old girl — got up very early in the morning and made breakfast, for which there was rye bread, butter, buckwheat cakes, and pie. After the dishes were washed Annis and I helped aunt milk. We dined on salt pork, vegetables, and pies; corned beef also; and always on Sunday a boiled Indian pudding. We made a stock of pies on Thanksgiving, froze them for winter use, and they lasted until March." Of the durability of these Connecticut pies a good story is told. It is said, on taking down the pantry of an old house, under it was found one of these pies, in perfect preservation, though the earthen dish which had contained it was entirely decayed.

None of this remarkable family have been more gifted nor more eccentric than Dr. Lyman Beecher. Yet his son, Edward Beecher, is well known as a theological writer, and his two daughters, Miss Catherine Beecher and Mrs. Harriet Beecher Stowe, have been women of rare abilities, and have made their mark on the times, and sad havoc with New England theology; while Henry Ward Beecher, the most distinguished of the sons, for many years occupied the foremost position among pulpit orators of America. They would seem, as a family, to owe their success partly to their audacity, but principally to a certain rough vigor and energy of character, and to their sympathy with the popular tendencies of their country, characteristics in a large measure the result of early experiences.

Fifty years ago, Lyman Beecher ranked among the first of living pulpit orators, and in his own country was without a rival. He was a graduate of Yale College, and he acquired in that institution an unusual reputation for fine speaking.

His first pastorate in 1799 was over a church in East Hampton, Long Island. This church had a bell and a clock, and was the largest and most splendid on the Island. The building, its interior quite altered, still stands, and bids fair to stand for another century.

Beecher's ministry at East Hampton lasted for a little less than twelve years. He preached earnestly, and in every way labored zealously in his vocation. Revival after revival rewarded his efforts. For rest, he fished some, and took good care of his five-acre plot, set out an orchard, the first known in the place, for the farmers had thought apples would not grow so near the salt water. His wife planted flowers and shrubs in the front yard of the parsonage—they say that a snow-ball and a catalpa of her planting are still living —and set out shade trees before the house. Others followed their good example, and set about beautifying their homes. Trees sprung up in the place of the old wood-piles, and now one can hardly find a more beautifully shaded place than East Hampton.

In 1804 he preached a sermon on the death of Alexander Hamilton, which drew to him the eyes of half the nation, and when, some years later, he gave his heart and genius to the temperance cause, six of the sermons that he preached touched the high-water marks of his unrivaled eloquence.

Many anecdotes are on record of Lyman Beecher's eccentricities. He was a very humorous specimen of the old time clergy, nor did he always keep his humor out of the pulpit. He was called "the fiddling parson," because he was so full of magnetism, and became so excited over his own discourses, that he could not sleep at night until he had calmed himself down to an ordinary level by playing "Auld Lang Syne" on the violin, and worked off his surplus enthusiasm by a double-shuffle on his kitchen floor.

He felt the need of exercise on Sunday. He would not work; he dared not ride; so he shoveled sand in the cellar, choosing sand because it made no noise.

An incident is told of a young man who came to town with an Episcopal ordination upon him. He tried to convince Dr. Beecher that he had no right to preach, because the bishop of his church had not laid his hands upon him.

"I will tell you a story,' said the Doctor. "There was a blacksmith in our town, and his father was a blacksmith before him, and his grandfather before him. He was a clumsy shoer, his tools were coarse, and his scythes without temper. A new-comer disturbed his peace and took the town custom. He regarded the new-comer as an interloper, and thought he ought to have the custom because of his descent from his father and grandfather. 'I care nothing about your father and grandfather,' said the new blacksmith; 'My scythes cut. I would rather have this brand on my tools than a certificate of descent from Tubal Cain.' "

Dr. Beecher came into the world for the purpose of seeing it. His eye was never closed, his tongue never tied. His speech was clear and sharp. He was a theological fighter by taste and instinct. His father was a blacksmith, full of sound sense and given to disputation. This habit Lyman Beecher inherited, and early in life he swung the sledgehammer of assault against all that seemed to him unworthy, until the country rang with the echo of his blows.

At one time he produced great excitement attacking Unitarianism with a vigorous hand. He had blows to take as well as blows to give. Some of the assaults on him were clearly libelous. His friends advised him to sue the maligners. He said, " No; when I lived in Litchfield, I wanted a book from the library of Yale College. In my return I walked up the hill with the folio under my arm. I saw a black and white squirrel before me, and I said, 'Shoo!' The squirrel did not run, but turned and looked at me. I shied a stone, and it missed. In my excitement I hurled the volume. The book was ruined, and I had to burn my clothes. Since that time I have never thrown a body of divinity at a skunk."

Out of the pulpit, Dr. Beecher was a somewhat impracticable and erratic person. His wife, who was refined and well balanced, had much of her time occupied in undoing the mischief her husband did. For instance, Lyman Beecher once bought and sent home a bale of cotton simply because it was cheap, without any idea or plan for its use. His wife, at first discomfitted, at once projected the unheard-of luxury of a carpet, carded and spun the cotton, hired it woven, cut and sewed it to fit the parlor, stretched and nailed it to the garret floor and brushed it over with thin paste. Then she sent to her New York brother for oil paints, learned from an encyclopedia how to prepare them, and then adorned the carpet with groups of flowers, imitating those in her small yard and garden. This illustrates at once the improvidence of the father and the useful and æsthetic turn of the mind of the mother, who seems to have had high ideals and great perseverance in attaining excellence under most unfavorable circumstances.

The people were astounded at the magnificence of
2

the pastor's parlor when the new carpet was laid down, for it was the first ever seen in East Hampton. Good old Deacon Tallmadge coming one day, stopped at the door, afraid to enter. "Walk in, deacon," said the pastor. "I can't," he answered, "'thout steppin' on't," adding after a moment's wondering admiration, "D'ye think ye can have all that and heaven too?" The good deacon in a breath got off a couple of mots which have since done good service in comic papers and religious tracts.

Lyman Beecher was passionately fond of children; his wife was not. They had thirteen, and the father, who married three times, chose his last wife after he was sixty years of age. Lyman Beecher was imaginative, impulsive and averse to hard study. His wife was calm and self-possessed and solved mathematical problems not only for practical purposes, but because she enjoyed that kind of mental effort. Lyman Beecher was trained as a dialectician and felt that he excelled in argumentation, and yet his wife, without any such training, he remarked, was the only person he had met that he felt was fully his equal in an argument. He had that kind of love for his children that moved him to caress and fondle them; she, on the contrary, did not care to nurse or tend them, although she was eminently benevolent and very tender and sympathetic. In other words, as the late Catharine Beecher

once wrote, "My father seemed by natural organization to have what one usually deemed the natural
traits of woman, while my mother had some of those
which often are claimed to be the distinctive attributes
of man."

LYMAN BEECHER IN 1803, AGED 28.
See page 13.

CHAPTER II.

Dr. Beecher's residence was a plain but substantial dwelling, characteristic of its State, standing in a broad inclosure upon a wide and grass-grown street and surrounded by tall and spreading elm trees. In the early days at Litchfield the doctor's salary was eight hundred dollars a year, and not always promptly paid, and the clothing and educating of his family became a dark problem. Young ladies attending a neighboring seminary were taken as boarders, and into this great bustling household of older people, all going their separate ways and having their separate interests to carry, Henry Ward Beecher was born. To be washed and dressed and sent to school in the morning and hustled to bed at the earliest possible hour at night was about all the attention the younger members received, and the child growing up in this busy circle had impressed upon it a sense of its own insignificance and of the necessity of obedience and non-resistance in regard to all grown-up people.

His own mother survived Henry's birth only three years. His early impression of her was that she was "the law of purity and the law of honor."

His sister, Mrs. Stowe, to whom we are indebted for most of the glimpses of his childhood and youth, · remembers his golden curls of that day and the little black frock that he wore "as he frolicked like a kitten in the sun, in ignorant joy." Though too young to attend her funeral or to understand all that the great change implied, that his mind had been busy with the problem is clear from this anecdote. He was told at one time that mother had been laid in the ground, at another, that she had gone to heaven; whereupon Henry, putting the two things together, was found one morning, digging with great zeal and earnestness under his sister's window. She called to him to know what he was doing, and lifting up his curly head with pathetic simplicity, he answered, "Why, I'm going to heaven to find ma."

The step-mother who came into Dr. Beecher's home was a lady of great personal elegance and attractiveness, of high intellectual and moral refinement, but with delicate health and, withal, such dignity that her influence was somewhat depressing upon children full of animal spirits and vigor. She had been much admired in general society, and in undertaking the care of a poor minister's family of ten children, combined with her attachment for a man of power and genius, an impulse of moral heroism. The children, Henry and Harriet (Mrs. Stowe), she found "as lovely children as she had ever seen, amiable, affectionate, and very bright," though of Henry she added that he "had no great love of books." She had a natural inclination toward extreme rectitude and propriety, with an unyielding conscience and habits of peculiar exactness. The absurdities and crudities of such childhood appeared to her as serious faults, and she conscientiously strove to instruct their young minds by reading and praying with them, until they came to view religion as cold and austere like herself.

Henry always felt when he went to prayer as though he were "going into a crypt, where the sun was not allowed to come," and he shrank from it. On his father's farm there was a poor man who, in his devotions, used alternately to sing, pray, and laugh, and in this method of worship the boy found great fascination. Upon his mind this poor man made a profounder impression than his step-mother, and though Charles Smith was many degrees below the boy in society, the boy learned to feel that he was the pauper and Smith the rich man. Years afterward Mr. Beecher said: "I would gladly have changed conditions with him, if, by so doing, I could have obtained his grace and his hope of heaven."

Henry was greatly influenced by her, although she was never able to impart any of her orderliness and primness to either him or his brothers and sisters.

When a little fellow, so small that his feet swung free from the floor of the old family chaise, he was once driving with his mother on an errand. As was the custom, the bell tolled for a death.

" Henry, what do you think of when you hear a bell tolling like that?" she asked. Filled with awe and surprise at having his thoughts inquired into, the child colored deeply and was silent, while she went on as in a revery:

"I think, was that soul prepared? It has gone into *eternity !* "

The impression on the boy's mind was of dread, like being turned out without clothing, in the icy fields of Litchfield's frozen hills.

Henry Ward's boyhood was innocent of children's literature, Sunday-school gatherings and the day of fétes and festivals that color the childhood of the present day.

Referring to this time in his autobiography, he says: "The only time that brought us any especial favor was Thanksgiving, when New England house-wives vied with one another in the composition of unique pies in limitless quantity.

"I didn't have any jumping-jacks, nor tops, nor marbles, nor toys of any kind. It doesn't seem to me that I knew any boys to play with, either. We lived

in a part of the village where there didn't seem to be
any boys.

" And so I was let alone.   My father was kept busy
with his pastoral duties, and my mother had so many
other children to attend to that little attention was
paid to me.   Still, I was not lonesome.   I was not
fond of reading, but I used to like to tramp about the
woods, and down by the brooks among the fens and
brakes.   I would go on a hunt for sweet-flag and sas-
safras, and I knew just where to find the squirrels.   I
found plenty to do.

"Occasionally the paternal government would reach;
sometimes my father would whip me.   I ˙remember
that he used to tell me that the whipping hurt him
more than it did me.   It was hard to believe, ,because
he was a strong man, but I believed it, and it used to
make me cry to be told so; then of course I had to cry
when the whipping began, and, all in all, these were
very doleful episodes."

The first steps in his education were taken at a
Widow Kilbourne's, where he was perched upon a
bench for several idle hours daily, only being called
upon twice each day to say his letters.   Of this time
his autobiography again gives us a picture: " A hazy
image of myself comes back to me—a lazy, dreamy
boy, with his head on the desk, half lulled asleep by
the buzzing of a great bluebottle fly, and the lowing

of the cows, and the tinkling of their bells, brought in the open door across the sunny fields and meadows."

When his lessons were learned he graduated into a little unpainted district schoolhouse near the parsonage, where he was exercised in reading the Bible and "The Columbian Orator," in elementary arithmetic and handwriting. But he avowed that he learned nothing there, for he did not feel any inclination to study.

The life of the minister's children, characterized by an almost Spartan simplicity, together with the winds and deep snows of the mountain town, developed ruggedness, energy, and self reliance. In Henry, these traits were especially strong. "At nine years of age," writes his sister, "in one of those winter draughts common in New England towns, he harnessed the horse to a sledge, with a barrel lashed thereon, and went off alone three miles over the bleak top of the town hill, to dip up and bring home a barrel of water from a distant spring. So far from considering this a hardship, he undertook it with a chivalric pride. His only trial in the case was the humiliation of being positively commanded by his careful step-mother to wear his overcoat; he departed, obedient but with tears of mortification freezing on his cheeks, for he had recorded an heroic vow to go through a whole winter without once wearing an overcoat."

At ten years of age he was a strong, well-grown boy, obedient, used, too, to hearing all the great theological questions of Calvinism discussed in his own home and to argue upon them himself.

His father's house was the headquarters of theological disputation, and many a battle was waged across the hospitable board, while the big-eyed children listened to that which no one could explain.

He entered a private school in Bethlehem, near Litchfield, under the charge of the Rev. Dr. Langdon. These schooldays were not such as to forecast a brilliant future, for he was deficient in memory, a poor writer and worse speller, the smoothness of his Latin exercises showing unmistaken signs of cribbing. He was painfully sensitive and diffident to the verge of stupidity. Partly from bashfulness and partly from an enlargement of the tonsils of his throat, his utterance was thick and indistinct.

"When Henry is sent to me with a message," said a good aunt, "I always have to make him say it three times. The first time I have no manner of an idea more than if he spoke Choctaw; the second, I catch now and then a word; by the third time I begin to understand." Who would predict for this lad the future of an orator?

CHAPTER III.

All of Mr. Beecher's boyhood as well as his later life was characterized by an intense love of nature and a fondness amounting almost to a passion, for being out of doors. The scenery around the parsonage fed this yearning,— on one side the fields of waving grain, and the lovely wooded slopes of Chestnut Hill; on the other, Mount Tom with its cover of steel-blue pines mirrored in the gleaming lake at its base. At Bethlehem, too, he spent hours wandering about old orchards or in the deep woods.

The melancholy which found the deeper side of the boy's nature was often lost sight of in an equally natural and constantly effervescing spirit of fun. When, after an unprofitable year at Bethlehem, he was transferred to his sister's school for young ladies at Hartford, he quickly gained the reputation of being " an inveterate joker and an indifferent scholar." One boy of eleven years has not much opportunity of making a lasting impression among thirty or forty girls, but we doubt whether any of his schoolmates ever forgot him. The school was separated into two divis-

27

ions for the study of grammar under leaders, and the grammatical reviews were contests where it was important that every member should be perfected. Henry was generally the last one chosen, being considered rather amusing than profitable on such an occasion. On one of these occasions a fair friend took him aside and endeavored to instill into his mind some of the definitions and distinctions on which the class honor depended.

"Now, Henry, A is a definite article, you see, and must be used only with a singular noun. You can say *a man*, but you can't say *a men*, can you?"

"Yes, I can say *Amen* too," was the ready reply. "Father says it always at the end of his prayers."

"Come Henry, now don't be joking; now decline He."

"Nominative he, possessive his, objective him."

"You see, His is possessive. Now you can say His book, but you can't say Him book."

"Yes, I do say Hymnbook, too," said the impracticable boy with a quizzical look in his merry blue eyes. Each of these sallies made his youthful instructor laugh, which was the victory he wished.

"But now Henry, seriously, just attend to the active and passive. Now, 'I strike,' is active, you see, because if you strike, you do something. But,

'I am struck' is passive, because if you are struck you don't do anything, do you?"

"Yes I do, I strike back again!"

Occasionally he offered gratuitously some of his

THE OLD BEECHER HOUSE, NEW HAVEN.
See page 10.

views on philosophical subjects. His sister in consideration of his frisky nature, placed him at her side while hearing recitations.

A class in Natural Philosophy, not well prepared, was stumbling through the theory of the tides.

"I can explain that," said Henry. "Well, you see the sun; he catches hold of the moon and pulls her, and she catches hold of the sea and pulls that, and this makes the spring tides."

"But what makes the neap tides?"

"Oh, that is when the sun stops to spit on his hands," was the brisk rejoinder.

At the age of twelve the whole atmosphere of his life was changed by the removal of the family from the dear old home in Litchfield to Boston. There Henry entered the Latin School. In a year of dry, hard study, with fear of disgrace, conscience and affection urging him on, he succeeded in mastering the Latin grammar so that he could give any form or inflection, rule or exception in the book. But he had become moody and restless. The restraint of life in the city, surrounded by high walls and confined for his sport to narrow streets, depressed his mind and distracted his feelings, so that in after years he believed that, had not a change occurred, he would have gone to destruction. Of this period he himself writes:

"My father let me read the stories of Nelson and Captain Cook. The adventure fever that often seizes boys took hold of me. I had all sorts of fancy-drawn pictures of what I might do in the jungles and deserts of the Orient.

"I used to lounge about the docks and wharves in Boston and listen to the shouts of the sailors and watch

the great merchantmen make ready for their voyage to
the Indies. At last I could stand it no longer."

He wrote to his brother of his resolve to go to sea,
with or without his father's permission. Dr. Beecher
read the letter, and for the moment said nothing, but
the next day asked Henry to help him saw wood.
Henry felt complimented by this invitation as imply-
ing a kind of manly companionship, for the wood-pile
was the Doctor's favorite ground for debate.

"Let us see," said the Doctor; "Henry, how old
are you?"

"Almost fourteen!"

"Bless me! how boys do grow! Why, it's almost
time to be thinking what you are going to do. Have
you ever thought?"

"Yes; I want to go to sea."

"To sea! Of all things! Well, well! After all,
why not? Of course you don't want to be a common
sailor, I suppose?"

"No, sir; I want to be a midshipman, and after
that a commodore."

"I see," said the Doctor, cheerfully. "Well,
Henry, in order for that, you know, you must begin a
course of mathematics, and study navigation and
all that."

"Yes, sir, I am ready."

"Well, then, I'll send you up to Amherst next

week, to Mount Pleasant, and then you'll begin your preparatory studies, and if you are well prepared, I presume I can make interest to get you an appointment.

But when the next week came, and Henry started for Mount Pleasant, Dr. Beecher said wisely to another member of his family, "I shall have that boy in the ministry yet."

The transfer to Amherst brought about an immediate change for the better. Under the mathematical tuition of Fitzgerald, a graduate of West Point, and for whom he conceived a genuine liking, inspired by a desire to please his friend and high ambition for his future profession, he worked laboriously and unceasingly, with his face toward the navy and Nelson as his ideal.

Thanks to Fitzgerald, his mathematical training gave him entire mastery of La Croix's Algebra, so that he was prepared to demonstrate at random any proposition as chance selected—not only without aid or prompting from the teacher, but controversially as against the teacher, who would sometimes publicly attack the pupil's method of demonstration, disputing him step by step, when the scholar was expected to know, with such positive clearness as to put down and overthrow the teacher. "You must not only know, but you must know that you know," was Fitzgerald's

maxim; and Henry Ward attributed much of his subsequent habit of steady unantagonistic defence of his
own opinions to this early mathematical training.

Here, also he was put through a systematic course
of elocution by Prof. John E. Lovell, which developed
his voice and taught him the use of gestures and the
proper management of his body. In later years, he
always considered that the removal of his natural disa-
bilities, without which he could never have attained
success as a speaker, was due entirely to Prof. Lovell.

At the close of the first year a religious revival
took place which crystallized into more definite form
the keen sensibilities and vague purposes—forming an
undercurrent of religious feeling which had been the
habit of his life and the result of his whole home education.

Going to Boston at his father's request, he there
united with the Hanover Street Church. Naval pro-
jects vanished and the pulpit opened before him as a
natural result, for Dr. Beecher was an enthusiast in
his profession.

For two years more Henry devoted himself to
classical studies at Amherst, with a view to entering
college.

At this time his love of flowers, which always
formed part of his enthusiasm for nature, found a
sympathizing helper in an old gardener who set apart
3

a plot of ground for Beecher's special use. This he filled with roses, geraniums, and other flowering plants, and tended with great devotion. The chaplain of Mount Pleasant Institute once finding Henry on his knees, bending over a little flower in wrapt contemplation of its buds and blossoms, said condescendingly :

" Oh, Henry, these things are pretty, very pretty, but, my boy, do you think that such things are worthy to occupy the attention of a man who has an immortal soul? "

Henry only answered with that abashed, half-stolid look, which covered so much from the eyes of his superiors, and went on with his attentions to his plants.

"I wanted to tell him," he afterwards said, "that since Almighty God has found leisure to make those trifles, it could not be amiss for us to find time to look at them."

In 1830 he entered the freshman class at Amherst, although the advanced state of his preparation entitled him to enter as a sophomore; his father deemed it best that he should have leisure during the first year to employ in planning and commencing a course for self culture in the college libraries, which he afterward systematically pursued, and in the study of oratory and rhetoric. As he himself said:

"I had acquired, by Latin and mathematics, the power of study. I knew how to study, and I turned it upon things I wanted to know. I studied what I liked and didn't study what I didn't like.

"Much of my time was spent in running about among the hills and gorges near the quaint old town. I was a powerful young fellow, with wind and perspiration up to high-water mark. I was a runner and a gymnast, and fond of kicking the foot-ball.

" And I was very fond of a good time; full of jokes and jollity of all kinds, and always ready for anything that promised fun."

In his Sophomore year he had the reputation of being the best writer and orator in his class, and was appointed president of the Athenæum society, though, owing to his neglect of the classics, he never attained class honors.

His classmates recall his mastery in debate and say that he had a power of ridicule and badinage that made him always a powerful advocate and a formidable antagonist. Although in maturer life he avoided controversies and taught the largest liberty in thought and action, while pursuing his studies, both in college and seminary he was quick to accept the gauntlet of discussions and prone to start a train of thought that was certain to provoke a challenge.

In this year another revival took place which, perhaps, marks the real starting point of his religious life. Of this period his sister wrote: "The only thing which prevented him from taking the first rank as a religious young man was the want of that sobriety and solemnity which was looked upon as essential to the Christian character. Mr. Beecher was like a converted bob-o-link, who should be brought to judgment for short quirks and undignified twitters and tweedles, among the daisy heads, instead of flying in dignified paternal sweeps, like a good swallow of the sanctuary, or sitting in solemnized meditation in the depths of pine trees like the owl. His condemnation from the stricter brethren generally came with the sort of qualification which Shakespeare makes,—

"'For the man doth fear God, howbeit, it doth not always appear, by reason of some large jests, which he will make.'"

Mr. Beecher, on one occasion, was informed that the head tutor of the class was about to make him a grave exhortatory visit. The tutor was almost seven feet high, and solemn as an Alpine forest; but Mr. Beecher knew that, like most solemn Yankees, he was at heart a deplorable wag, a mere whited sepulcher of conscientious gravity, with measureless depths of unrenewed chuckle hid away in the depths of his heart. When apprised of his approach, he suddenly whisked into the wood closet the chairs of his room, leaving only a low one which had been sawed off at the second joint, so that it stood about a foot from the floor.

He had made for himself at the the carpenter's, a circular table with a hole in the middle, where was fixed a seat. Into this table he crawled, and seated meekly among his books, awaited the visit.

LOT BENTON'S HOUSE.
See page 12.

A grave rap was heard. "Come in."

Far up in the air, the solemn dark face appeared. Mr. Beecher rose ingeniously and offered to come out. "No, never mind," said the visitor, "I just came to have a little conversation with you. Don't move."

"Oh," says Beecher innocently, "pray sit down sir," indicating the only chair.

The tutor looked apprehensively, but began the process of sitting down. He went down, down, down, but still no solid ground being gained, straightened himself and looked uneasy.

"I don't know but that chair is too low for you," said Beecher meekly; "do let me get you another."

"Oh no, no, my young friend, don't rise, don't trouble yourself, it is perfectly agreeable to me, in fact I like a low seat," and with these words the tall man doubled up like a jackknife, and was seen sitting, with his grave face between his knees, like a grasshopper drawn up for a spring. He heard a deep sigh, and his eyes met the eyes of Mr. Beecher; the hidden spark of native depravity within him was exploded by one glance at those merry eyes, and he burst into a loud roar of merriment, which the two continued for some time, greatly to the amusement of the boys, who were watching to hear how Beecher would come out with his lecture. The chair was ever after known as the "Tutor's Delight."

CHAPTER IV.

At this very time, when he was passing for the first humorist of college, the marks along his well-worn volumes of old English poets show only appreciation of what is earnest, deep, and pathetic. He particularly loved an obscure old poet of whom we scarce hear in modern days, Daniel, who succeeded Edmund Spenser as poet laureate, and was a friend of Shakespeare. Some lines addressed by him to the Earl of Southampton, are marked by reiterated lines in Mr. Beecher's copy of the old English poets, which showed enthusiastic reading. He says, " This was about the only piece of poetry I ever committed to memory, but I read it so much I could not help at last knowing it by heart."

"TO THE EARL OF SOUTHAMPTON.

" He who hath never warred with misery,
    Nor ever tugged with fortune in distress,
Hath no occasion and no field to try
    The strength and forces of his worthiness.
Those parts of judgment which felicity
    Keeps as concealed, affliction must express,
And only men show their abilities
    And what they are, in their extremities.

39

" Mutius the fire, the tortures Regulus,
  Did make the miracles of faith and zeal;
Exile renowned and graced Rutilius.
  Imprisonment and poison did reveal
The worth of Socrates, Fabricius.
  Poverty did grace that common weal
More than all Sylla's riches got with strife,
And Cato's death did vie with Cæsar's life.

" He that endures for what his conscience knows
  Not to be ill, doth from a patience high
Look on the only cause whereto he owes
  Those sufferings, not on his misery;
The more he endures the more his glory grows,
  Which never grows from imbecility;
Only the best composed and worthiest hearts
  God sets to act the hardest and constant'st parts."

These verses are so marked with Mr. Beecher's life, habits of thought, with his modes of expression, that they show strongly the influence which these old poets had in forming both his habits of thought and expression. His mind naturally aspired after heroism, and from the time that he gave up his youthful naval enthusiasm he turned the direction of the heroic faculties into moral things.

In this year, also, Mr. Beecher was led as a mere jovial frolic to begin a course of phrenological investigation which led to a broad physiological study and enquiry, and, collated with metaphysics and theology, has formed his system of thought through life.

When Dr. Spurzheim came over from Europe to teach the new science of phrenology there was much opposition to him, and after his death phrenology was fiercely discussed and ridiculed all over the country. In Amherst College it was sought to demolish the science by getting Henry Ward Beecher to take the negative side of the debate on the question, "Is phrenology entitled to the name of science?" But even then, a young student, Mr. Beecher was not a superficial one, and he resolved to study up the subject. So he sent to Boston by stage for the works of Spurzheim and Combe, intending to post himself from the opposition standpoint. But he found so much in the books that he asked for more time, and finally got the debate postponed two weeks. Then he delivered a speech in favor of phrenology that astonished the college and the town.

After the debate young Beecher asked a classmate named Fowler if he would not like to read his books on phrenology. The young man said he would, and from that time the name Fowler and Phrenology become wedded. Thus it was that Henry Ward Beecher gave the science in America one of its most ardent adherents.

Mr. Beecher's chief ability laid in the discussion of talent, character and disposition. In that field his knowledge of phrenology is the key to his power over men, for then he talks directly to faculty, and as he goes "from grave to gay, from lively to severe," men feel touched in their strongest and weakest points, and imagine that he knows them through and through.

Mr. Beecher once said to the late Samuel R. Wells, "If I were the owner of an island, and had all the books, apparatuses and appliances, tools to cultivate the soil, manufacture, cook and carry on life's affairs in comfort and refinement, and on some dark night pirates should come and burn my books, musical instruments, works of art, furniture, tools and machinery, and leave me the land and the empty barns and house, I should be, in respect to the successful carrying on of my affairs, in very much the same plight that I should be as a preacher, if phrenology and all that it has taught me of man, his character, his wants and his improvement, were blotted from my mind."

On another occasion he said: "All my life long I have been in the habit of using phrenology as that which solves the practical phenomena of life. I regard it as far more useful, practical and sensible than any other system of mental philosophy which has yet been evolved. Certainly, phrenology has introduced mental philosophy to the common people."

Through this study of phrenology Mr. Beecher got his first experience as a lecturer. With a classmate named Fowler he used to go to the little towns in the neighborhood and instruct the bumpkins in bump-science and its mysteries, Beecher delivering the lecture and Fowler examining heads.

In the last two years in college Henry taught district schools, beginning his library with the money obtained, preached and spoke regularly in religious meetings, lectured on temperance, and, as the anti-slavery agitation was just beginning, took his position boldly as an Abolitionist.

In 1836, he was graduated, without any marked honors or reputation, save that he was a jolly good fellow, a choice companion and the chief in debating societies.

" How did I come to be a preacher? " he once said. " It was fate, I suppose; that's all. I do not think that I can honestly assign any other reason. I took to preaching, as did all of my brothers, simply because nobody ever dreamed of my father's boys doing anything else.

" That's all there is to it."

His father, two years before this, had gone to Cincinnati, and thither the young man followed him, to find the abolition excitement at Lane Seminary, where his venerable father was president, just ended by the departure from its doors of an entire class of thirty students, with Theodore Weld at their head.

Here he was thrown into a life full of activity. Cincinnati, removed from slave territory only by the

width of the Ohio river, was convulsed with the contest between the slaveholders and the abolitionists.
Steamboats, the decks of which were covered with
chained gangs of slaves, passed daily by the wharves,
while the Ohio river where it passed between slave and
free territory was lined with the headquarters of Abolitionist societies bent on aiding slaves to escape.
The air was electrical with excitement, and the young
man, thrilling at the prospect of the coming fight, felt
his ardor redoubling before the obstacles and opposition that confronted all Abolitionists. In 1836 he
appeared first publicly as the champion of the anti-
slavery cause. The utterances of the Philanthropist,
an anti-slavery paper in Cincinnati edited by James
G. Birney, a slaveholder who had emancipated his
slaves, became offensive to the strong pro-slavery element. A riot broke out, and for a week Cincinnati
was overrun by a mob headed by Kentucky slaveholders. Young Beecher asked to be sworn in as one of
the special policemen, and, armed with a pistol,
patroled the streets. At this time, in the absence of
Mr. Brainard, he was for a few months occupying the
editorial chair in the office of the Cincinnati Journal,
the organ of the New School Presbyterian Church,
and his indignation over the Birney riot found vent in
some pungent editorials, which produced a marked
effect.

At this time, too, the fierce controversy of his father as the exponent of the New England new school theology and the doctrine of free agency, against Dr. Wilson, the advocate of the old school Calvinistic fatalism and the doctrine of the natural depravity of man, was going on.

Dr. Beecher's heart was in the war, and he waged it incessantly and with characteristic vigor.

No years of his life were more earnest and active than the first fifteen of those at Lane Seminary. "Never," said his son-in-law, "did he wheel a greater number of heavenly wheelbarrows at one and the same time."

Of Dr. Beecher's thirteen children, eleven were living; five were at home, the others widely scattered in various places, East and West. They had never been all together; some of them had never seen some of the others. A family meeting was at last arranged, and one Sunday morning the whole living family met for the first time under the parental roof at Walnut Hills, with smiles, tears, thanksgiving and sorrowing. One son filled the father's pulpit in the morning, another in the evening; the family occupied three pews. The family meeting lasted two whole days. On the morning of the third, after prayer, a farewell hymn, and a solemn blessing from the patriarch, they parted, never again to meet on earth.

In the seminary Henry made a deep impression on the faculty and his fellow students by his oratorical excellence. His father was surprised that he took so little interest in the battle of the Presbyterians, and looked with some doubt on the future usefulness of his son, Nevertheless he was proud of his abilities and did all he could to ground him in the faith of his fathers. This was a difficult task, and caused the old gentleman many an anxious night, for to him the doctrines were firm and steadfast, and any questioning that tended to unsettle them, or any one of them, was heresy, a little less than blasphemy.

Mr. Beecher had inherited from his father what has been called a genius for friendship. He was never without the anchor of an enthusiastic personal attachment for somebody, and at Lane Seminary, he formed such an intimacy with Prof. C. E. Stowe, whose roommate for some length of time he was, and in whose society he took great delight. Prof. Stowe, was a somewhat strict disciplinarian and disposed to be severe on his young friend, who was quite too apt to neglect or transcend conventional rule. The morning prayers at Lane were at conventional hours, and Henry's devotional propensities, of a dark, cold winter morning, were almost impossible to be roused, while his friend, who was punctuality itself, was always up and away in the gloaming. One morning, when the professor had indignantly rebuked the lazy young Christian, whom he left tucked in bed, and, shaking the dust from his feet, had departed to his morning duties, Henry took advantage of his own habits of alert motion, sprang from the bed, dressed himself in a twinkling, and taking a cross-lot passage, was found decorously sitting

YALE COLLEGE IN 1793.
See page 14.

directly under the professor's desk, waiting for him, when he entered to conduct prayers. The stare of almost frightened amazement with which the professor met him, was the ample reward of his exertion.

Mr. Beecher's first steps in preaching were taken while he was yet in college, and in all the years that followed he never preached what was regarded as a commonplace sermon.

During his course at Lane Seminary, he spent a week at his brother's house, and consented to preach for him. Mr. Beecher, in writing recently to the editor of the Brooklyn Magazine, thus refers to the incident: "My brother George wished to be away a Sunday and I was requested by him to supply his pulpit. Text, sermon, and all attendent circumstances are gone from my memory, *except the greenness—no doubt of that.*"

In his last theological term, the great question which had long been troubling him, of "what to preach," was solved. To present Jesus Christ, personally, as the friend and helper of humanity, Christ as God impersonate, eternally and by a necessity of his nature helpful and remedial and restorative, the friend of each individual soul, and thus the friend of all society; this was the one thing which his soul rested on as a worthy object in entering the ministry. He afterward said in speaking of his feelings at this time: "I was like the man in the story to whom a fairy gave a purse with a single piece of money in it, which he found always come again as soon as he had spent it. I thought I knew at last one thing to preach, I found it included everything."

On leaving the seminary he was selected to deliver

the commencement oration. This oration was an attack on the absurdities of the then preachers, their manners, customs, habits—particularly their attire. The point that he made was, that the clergy should dress and address like other men—that they should be careful to avoid all strong marks that would distinguish them from others. The oration was full of humor; and to cause himself to correspond with his teachings, his dress was with an open throat, with a very narrow cravat, and more in the style of a sailor than a clergyman of the time.

This oration at Lane Seminary might be said to be the key to his whole public life. It began there with combatting the peculiarities of the clergy—and thus he has been a combatant the whole of his career. He was never so happy as when in the midst of a fierce combat.

4

CHAPTER V.

In 1837 Mr. Beecher concluded his theological studies and married Miss Eunice White Bullard, a daughter of Dr. Bullard of Worcester, Mass., to whom he had been engaged for seven years. She was slightly older than himself, well born and bred, and educated at Worcester and Hadley, Mass. While Mr. Beecher was at Amherst her brother invited him over to spend his vacation, and here she met him.

When Mr. Beecher applied for a life insurance policy thirty years ago he was asked the usual question as to the health of his heart. His answer was: " Experienced a peculiar feeling about the heart during the days of my courtship." He was not rejected.

To an unusually acute wit Mrs. Beecher united physical and emotional power of rare development. Her energetic nature was a needed complement to the careless dreaminess of the young preacher, and in all his early life she was the spur and director of all his affairs.

When ready to enter upon active ministerial work, Mr. Beecher went over to Covington, Kentucky, and

50

preached in the Presbyterian church for several Sundays and expected to form a church and remain; but a call from Lawrenceburg, Indiana, was made and he was soon settled there.

Lawrenceburg was a scanty town of the Miami Valley, some twenty miles west of Cincinnati, and in the State of Indiana. It was not an attractive place in those days. The houses were cheap and flimsy of construction, without yards or gardens, and the population was of the kind that has no local attachment and merely make a temporary sojourn that shall last so long only as enough money can be made to sustain life.

In writing of the town, Mr. Beecher said: "It doesn't occur to me now that Lawrenceburg was remarkable for anything but a superabundance of distilleries. I used to marvel how so many large distilleries could be put in so small a town. But there they were, flourishing right in the very face of the gospel that my little flock and I were preaching in the shadows of the chimneys.

"My thoughts often travel back to my quaint little church and the big distilleries at Lawrenceburg.

"The church edifice was a low, broad, plain structure, very like the ordinary Quaker meeting house, entered from a broad uncovered wooden platform which was approached by a flight of wooden steps.

It would seat one hundred and fifty people. There

were twenty members; in his own words, "Nineteen of them were women, and the other was nothing." With the exception of two, every one was dependent for her livelihood on her industry. He and Mrs. Beecher lived in two rooms over a stable, and studied economy on four hundred dollars a year, of which only two hundred and fifty dollars could be relied upon with certainty. The balance was supposed to be given in provisions by the people of the church.

Referring to this period, Mr. Beecher observed: "I remember the days of our poverty, our straightness. I was sexton of my own church at that time. There were no lamps there, so I bought some; and I filled them and lit them. I did not ring the bell, because there was none to ring. I made the fires and swept the building. I opened the church before prayer-meeting and preaching, and locked it when they were over, in fact, doing everything, but coming to hear myself preach—that they had to do. We were all poor together, and to the day of my death I never shall forget one of those faces or hear one of those names spoken without having excited in my mind the warmest remembrances. Some of them I venerate, and the memory of some has been precious as well as fruitful of good to me down to this hour."

The following is a graphic sketch of his hardships during those years: When he needed a house to live in, he hauled the logs himself. His neighbors aided him to put it up. The whitewash and paint he attended to himself. Children followed in quick succession, as they did in the family of Dr. Lyman Beecher; poor pay, hard work, cheap living, and the malarial condition of the section in which he lived, broke the strong constitution of his wife, and as they were unable to pay a servant, threw on him the domestic drudgery. He chopped wood, drew the water, peeled the potatoes, cooked the food, served it, washed the dishes, and cleaned up the house. When sickness necessitated frequent washings of soiled clothes, it was he who did the work. Part of the time he did double duty, and rode twenty miles through the woods and across the prairies to the log schoolhouse in which service was held, preached, rode back again, cooked the dinner, preached in his own church, returned to nurse his sick wife and attend to the children, got the supper, and spent the evening in the prayer-meeting. At times he was so poor that an unpaid letter, on which eighteen or twenty cents were due, remained in the postoffice, with news from the East, uncalled for, because he did not have the money with which to pay the postage. Yet in these days was laid the foundation of his greatness, for there he learned how to enter into the lives of his people, making their cause his own, sharing their sorrows as well as their poverty, imbuing his kindly nature with that great charity for others that so strongly marked the sympathies of his later years.

In the two years of his Lawrenceburg pastorate Mr. Beecher made his mark. As a preacher he was eloquent; as an orthodox teacher he was not over zealous; as a sympathizing pastor he was of average merit only. His meetings were well attended and he made himself felt. His personal magnetism was great, the flush of vigorous health was in his veins, and he stirred up the dry bones of his neighborhood to such a degree that the attention of a wider circle was attracted.

"The first time I heard Henry Ward Beecher preach," writes an ardent admirer, "was when he once occupied the pulpit of his father, who was then nearing the close of his ministry as pastor of the Second Presbyterian Church in Cincinnati, perhaps in the year 1843, forty-four years ago. Mr. Beecher was then a settled pastor over the Presbyterian Church at Lawrenceburg, Ind., twenty miles away. As young people sometimes do, I left the church when the preacher was through his sermon. I had been quite stirred up and entertained, but was so impressed with the remark of a lame elder of the church, who descended the steps and went. in my direction, up Fourth street, eastward, as I passed to my boarding-house, that I have never forgotten the remark. It was this: "There was a good deal more of Henry Ward Beecher in that sermon than there was of Christ." This seemed to me thoroughly true, and altogether apposite, and at this distance of time I may say that the observation was made by a man of great integrity, and uprightness, and intelligence, too — Isaac G. Burnet, an own brother of David G. Burnet, not long after President of Texas, and a half-brother of Judge Isaac Burnet, of Cincinnati, a special friend of Dr. Lyman Beecher and family. From that hour to the present I have never ceased to be interested in Henry Ward Beecher, his doings and sayings. I soon after came to know him personally and always have held him in the highest regard for his warm-heartedness and noble manliness."

While in Lawrenceburg he narrowly escaped being switched off on another and very different track. A new railroad was projected and a superintendent was to be chosen. A bank president, who was one of the chief directors, had been greatly affected by the go-ahead manner and zeal of the young parson, and, concluding that he was possessed of the qualities that would make him a first rate railroad official, proposed his name. The contest was close; Beecher lost by one vote, and thus the railroad interest of the West was spared the disgrace of pulling from the American platform the man who has done the most to make that platform famous.

Not long since Mr. Beecher declared that for the first three years of his ministry he "did not make a sinner wink," and he almost made up his mind to abandon the pulpit; but as his field grew larger he had more faith, and was persuaded to go on with his work, "From that day to this," he added, "I have been in hot water." How much he meant by such a statement we can in large part only surmise. But enough is known of his signally active, aggressive, and tempestuous life to justify the belief that, in spite of his notably sunny and optimistic teaching, he has had sore need at every step of one fond and immovable soul to lean upon for comfort, sympathy, and inspiration, and that in his wife he has uniformly found a helper of that description. If we could know the whole truth it would very likely appear that but for her robust and indomitable faith, her power of encouragement, and her gift of smoothing rough places he would have faltered and missed his chance many times when he went boldly and grandly forward; or possibly, but for that assistance, he would have given up his appointed career, thus depriving the world of the greatest preacher of his time. There must have been not a few occasions when he was tempted to choose rest and safety instead of the strife and peril into which he plunged;

and we may be sure that his wife's advice was always a potent force on the side of such a conclusion.

Mr. Beecher's stay at Lawrenceburg was, however, brief. A larger field of usefulness opened, after several applications in 1839, by a call to Indianapolis, then a town of about twenty-five thousand inhabitants. Here he lived and labored for eight years, and here his influence as a speaker, writer, and thinker began to make itself strongly felt. As the son of Lyman Beecher he was accorded a courteous welcome, but it was not long ere he was esteemed and followed for his individual merit.

CHAPTER VI.

A member of the church brought Mr. Beecher and his family to Indianapolis in his own carriage, and on the 31st of July, 1839, the first sermon was preached. For nearly two years the congregation worshipped in the old seminary. It then moved into the building now standing at the corner of Circle and Market streets—a structure of the ordinary country church type, with round columns in front and a square belfry rising from the roof in front. The building was long since abandoned as a church, and has served successively as a schoolhouse and a public hall. When Mr. Beecher left it the congregation and membership of this church was the largest possessed by any church in Indianapolis.

The members of his church were dissenters from the First Church, the only organization in the city at that time, and which had been violently disturbed by the new and old school discussions. Fifteen members from the First Church had organized a Second Church, one of them being Samuel Merrill, President of the State bank. Mr. Beecher was their first pastor. It

58

was Mr. Merrill who had discovered him, being at the time on a tour of inspection of the branch banks throughout the State.

His salary was now six hundred dollars per annum, but the nominal increase was of no real advantage to the young minister and his wife; for, on the one hand,

EAST HAMPTON CHURCH.
See page 14.

their regular expenses were larger, and, on the other, he was the city minister, and was expected to entertain the country clergymen.

"I had a more considerable congregation, though I was still far from rich in the world's goods."

His life at Indianapolis was in two senses of a pas-

toral kind. The house he occupied was on the outskirts of the town, and was a one-story dwelling of
four rooms with a roof sloping to the street and surrounded by barns and sheds.

His life was of Arcadian simplicity. He cultivated
a garden, and gathered around him all that wholesome
suit of domestic animals for which he had been accustomed to care in early life.

He subsequently dwelt in a larger and finer house,
which he built himself, and the painting of which he
did with his own hands.

"I remember very well," he wrote afterwards, "how
I borrowed a paint-pot and brushes and gave my house
a fresh coat—it was yellow, I believe."

Added to the poverty of his pocket, the incessant
drain of his sympathy at home, the continuous
necessity of physical toil in the house, the garden
and the woodshed, and the preparation of his sermons,
was a doubt, an uncertainty in his beliefs. The
little cloud, small as a man's hand, that frightened
him when a boy, made him gloomy when in college and
shadowed him in his first charge, now assumed vast
proportions. He was all afloat. All that kept him
from sinking—humanly speaking—was his own honest
expression of doubt. Had he kept it to himself and
brooded over it in secret he might have been carried over the falls of infidelity or gone to the fool's

refuge—suicide. But Beecher was then, as always, open mouthed. What he felt, thought or knew he told. Secretiveness was never fairly developed in his nature. He never could keep a secret. He made friends easily, and the last person with him invariably knew his mind. He was easily deceived, for, although he had constant experience in human strengths and human weaknesses, he was by nature confiding and trustful. Truthful himself, it was next to impossible to persuade him that any would be false in speech or inference to him. He knew all about wickedness in general, but special cases bothered him. When doubts assailed him, instead of taking them to his study he used them as illustrations in the pulpit. If he questioned the possibility of forgiveness of sin, he became the example. It was his breast that he beat, his doubt he asserted, his fears he expressed. In picturing the estate of a lost soul the imagery lost nothing of its power by a personal application. Enthusiastic in everything, from the culture of a flower to the worship of his Savior, Mr. Beecher carried his zealous search for remedies in this state of doubt to the extremity of his passionate nature.

Crowds attended his preaching. Waves of religious feeling carried all classes of people before them. The State of Indiana was in an uproar. The Presbyterian churches looked on amazed. Dr. Lyman

Beecher thanked God that he had given him such a son, and in the same breath he beseeched Him to guide him lest he should fall. The Legislature sat in Indianapolis, and in its train followed the evils that generally accompany the camp followers. Intemperance, gambling and kindred vices were rampant in the place. Everybody knew it. The sores affected the entire body politic. The members of the Legislature knew it as well as the rest, and winked at it like the rest. This seemed to Beecher a fair target. He announced a series of lectures to young men, and delivered them in his church. The feeling engendered by them was intense. Those who were hit were indignant. All classes went to hear them, and before they were concluded a revival arose that swept the city.

A member of his church wrote of him: "It is not improper, however, to speak of the pastor in that revival as he is remembered by some of the congregation, plunging through the wet streets, his trousers stuffed in his muddy boot-legs, earnest, untiring, swift, with a merry heart, a glowing face, and a helpful word for every one, the whole day preaching Christ to the people where he could find them and at night preaching still where the people could find him."

He always preached twice on a Sunday, and in various districts of the city held an average of five other meetings a week. During three months of every year, by consent of his people, he devoted himself to missionary work throughout the State, making the journeys on horseback and preaching at some place every day. His fame spread throughout the whole country, until finally his arrival in any town was sufficient to attract a multitude of people to hear him. About the third year of his ministry, a great revival of religion took place at Terre Haute, followed by a series of revivals elsewhere in the State, in all of which Mr. Beecher was unceasingly active.

The following anecdote illustrates Mr. Beecher's love of humor and drollery. He was naturally cut out for a great actor. Once he was returning from Terre Haute to this city in a stage coach. Mr. Graydon, a prominent member of the congregation, got into the coach at Greencastle. It was dark, and after jogging along a little way in silence Mr. Beecher disguised his voice and began making inquiries of Mr. Graydon as to where he lived. When he learned it was at Indianapolis he began to ply his fellow traveler with all manner of questions; inquired about Beecher's church and congregation, and finally about Beecher himself. Mr. Graydon was loyal, and eulogized Beecher greatly. The hoax was discovered at the next stopping place.

Meantime the uncertainty of young Beecher increased, and with it grew his power. He was maturing mentally and physically. His head expanded as

he read the books of nature and of humanity all about
him.   He felt the necessity of supplementing his
sparse education by such means as were at his disposal.
Books were rare and costly.   Newspapers were in their
infancy.   He read all that he could borrow or obtain
from the public libraries, and felt inexpressible gratitude when the choice volumes of a wealthy friend were
placed at his service.   The West, and especially that
section of it, was full of quick witted men and growing women.   Both sought comfort in the preaching of
this man of the people.   Instead of scoffing at their
doubts he boldly proclaimed his own.   This made him
the friend and spokesman of the wavering,   He pictured
in vivid colors the unhappiness of his thoughts, the
terror of his fear, and produced in their minds the
impression that Beecher and they were one and the
same.   When he found relief they participated in his
joy.   When he sang the song of salvation they joined
in the chorus.   He became immensely popular in his
parish and in the State.   He was not the ideal parson.
He wore no distinctive garb.   His face was round and
jolly.   His eye was full of laughter.   His manner was
hearty and his interest sincere.   It was often said that
Beecher could have attained any desired distinction at
the bar or in politics.   He was importuned to stand as
candidate for legislative honors, but invariably refused
even to think of it.   At this time, when he regarded

himself spiritually weak, he was eloquently strong.
He preached without notes and talked as if inspired.
His prayers were poems. His illustrations were constant and always changing. He kept his people wide
awake and made them feel his earnestness. His acting
power was marvellous. Those who knew him well will
remember that when talking he could with difficulty
sit still. He almost invariably rose, and in the excitement of description or argument acted the entire subject as it struck him. Oftentimes in his most solemn
moments an illustration or an odd expression would
escape him that sent a laugh from pew to pew. Waking suddenly to the incongruity of the scene and the
subject, it almost seemed as if the rebuking spirit of
his dead mother stood before him, for with a manner
that carried the sympathy of the audience he would
drift into a channel, tender and deep and full of tears,
along which the feeling of the people were irresistibly
borne. There as here the chief topics of his repertory
were the love of God and the dignity of man. He
rarely preached from the Old Testament. The thun-
ders of Sinai and the flames of hell had no power over
him. It would puzzle an expert to find in all his published sermons — and for more than a generation every
word he spoke was reported as he spoke it — a sentence of which threats or fears were the dominant
spirit. He preached the love of God and the sympa-

5

thy of Christ first, last, and all the time. He knew
the politicians of the West thoroughly, and the gam-
blers, who were a powerful fraternity, made up their
minds that it was folly to interfere with the robust
preacher, who was not afraid to push their bully aside
when he stood in front of the ballot box, and who met
them eye to eye on the street as well as in his pulpit.

There was then a feeling in the church almost
throughout the country — which was especially strong
in Indianapolis — against discussions on slavery from
the pulpit. Some of Mr. Beecher's most prominent
parishioners were bitterly opposed to the subject being
even publicly named by a Christian minister. But he
emphasized his position by early introducing into the
synod a resolution declaring that every minister should
preach a thorough exposition and *condemnation of
slavery.* Thereupon, he preached three sermons upon
the life of Moses, the bondage of the children of Israel
under Pharaoh and their deliverance. His hearers,
who had comfortably settled themselves to listen to a
rebuke of the Old Testament culprits, were electrified
by a searching and merciless expose of the horrors of
American slavery and a scathing denunciation of the
whole institution. There was talk and excitement, of
course, but Mr. Beecher persisted in openly attacking
the great wrong, and through his persistence his

church became one of the strongholds of the anti-slavery cause.

Mr. Beecher never engaged in controversial strife on points of doctrine. Ministers of every denomination were welcomed at his home—a cottage on the outskirts of the town—inspected his beloved garden, or shared his rides over the rolling prairies.

There were in Indianapolis, Baptists, Methodists and an Episcopal minister, but he stood on kindly social terms with them all. His humorous faculty gave him a sort of universal coin which passed current in all sorts of circles, making every one at ease with him. Human nature longs to laugh, and a laugh, as Shakespeare says, "done in the testimony of a good conscience," will often do more to bring together wrangling theologians than a controversy.

A Methodist brother once said to him:

" Well, now, really, Brother Beecher, what have you against Methodist doctrines?"

"Nothing, only that your converts will practice them."

" Practice them?"

" Yes, you preach falling from grace, and your converts practice it with a vengeance."

One morning, as he was sitting at table, word was brought in that his friend, the Episcopal minister, was at the gate, waiting to borrow his horse.

"Stop, stop," said he, with a face of great gravity, "there's something to be attended to first," and, rising from the table, he ran out to him and took his arm with the air of a man who is about to make a serious proposition.

"Now, Brother G——, you want my horse for a day. Well, you see, it lies on my mind greatly that you don't admit my ordination. I don't think it's fair. Now, if you'll admit that I'm a genuinely ordained minister, you shall have my horse; but if not, I don't know about it."

Mr. Beecher has always looked back with peculiar tenderness to that Western life, in the glow of his youthful days, and in that glorious, rich, abundant, unworn Western country. The people, simple and strong, shrewd as Yankees, and excitable and fervent as Southerners, full of quaint images and peculiar turns of expression, derived from a recent experience of backwoods life, were an open page in his great book of human nature.

"How are you, stranger?" was the usual simple salutation, and no one thought of any formal law of society; why one human being might not address another on equal terms, and speak out his mind on all subjects fully.

In his leisure hours his love for nature found scope for enjoyment. He edited a horticultural paper, read books on gardening, farming and stock raising, imported and set out roses and fruit trees, and in his note books of this period, among hints for sermons, come memoranda respecting his favorite Berkshire pig or Durham cow.

"I always had a fondness for journalistic work,

BEECHER'S HOUSE AT EAST HAMPTON.
See page 14.

especially if it was of an agricultural nature, and found it pleasant and remunerative.

" I suppose, though, that all newspaper work is like that.

" That, at any rate, was my dearest recreation—I thoroughly enjoyed it."

Mr. Beecher was for many years a trustee of Wabash College, Crawfordsville, Ind.

It was in the forties—'44 or '45,—that he first attracted general public attention as a member of the Presbyterian General Assembly in session at Buffalo, N. Y. A reporter of the proceedings of that body, remembers very well his first appearance on the floor. A young man—Mr. Beecher always had a younger look than his age would indicate—with ruddy face, abundance of hair, glowing eyes, but with attire not up to the ministerial pattern, rose in his place, in the back part of the house, and the very first words he uttered —" *Mr. Moderator* "—attracted attention. There was an important question under consideration—an overture relating to slavery, as we recollect. He had not proceeded far before heads were turned and all eyes bent upon the speaker. " Who is that young man," was whispered and heard audibly. Scarcely anybody knew. But the fervor, enthusiasm, originality, and eloquence of his address carried the house with him, and Henry Ward Beecher was known after that to the representatives of the denomination of the Northern states, at least. The reports of his speeches on that and subsequent occasions attracted the public attention as something new and more vigorous than people had been accustomed to in these discussions of the theologians. Out of the recognition, undoubtedly came his call to Brooklyn which followed within a year or two, and which has since been the scene of his life-work, so remarkable and productive of such grand results for forty years.

The commencement of the college year brought the Presbyterian ministry in large force to Crawfordsville. At an evening party where the two most noted guests were Mr. Beecher and United States Senator E. A. Hannegan, of Covington, Ind.—the one American the other Irish, the latter was noted for intellectual and oratorical brilliancy. That the two should drift together in the early evening was but natural. Pious as the preacher was, and humble follower, he did not willingly allow any one in a social gathering to put him in a state of eclipse. Never did two contestants in a ring, each the darling of his particular friends and backers, ever watch each other more closely than did the preacher and the politician.

The former was in his happiest vein of rollicking humor. The latter was all sentiment. The two seemed for the time to have exchanged places. The preacher's coruscations of wit fell swift and thick as sparks from a blacksmith's anvil, while the politician, in a voice that was melody itself, let fall from his lips a very torrent of imagery that fascinated as it fell. For two hours those intellectual gladiators carried on their wordy contest with no sign of weariness. The

hundred others present were crowded in the large parlor or eagerly listening from the adjoining rooms.
Those two for the time being had wielded a monopoly
of entertainment, and were thoroughly conscious that
their display of *intellectual pyrotechnics* was brilliant
and all satisfying. It was only when the lady of the
house, worried into a fever of impatience, laid her hand
on the preacher's shoulder that he ceased talking.

"Mr. Beecher, you and Mr. Hannegan must be
weary after so much argument, and my coffee is
spoiling!"

It was a drawn battle and Hannegan arose and taking the preacher's hand said:

"Well, Brother Beecher, you certainly promise to
achieve fame as a minister of the Gospel, but if you
had been bred to politics, you would have captured the
country."

"And you, Brother Hannegan," replied the preacher,
"with the grace of God implanted in your heart, and
a pulpit at your command, would have captured more
souls for Christ than ever I can hope shall fall to my
lot!"

Yet, while in the height of his popularity in the
West, Mr. Beecher was hampered as few men would
care to be. He was hungry for books and papers, but
could not afford them. He had a royal physique and
every vein throbbed with superabundant health, but

his home was a hospital. His ambition was great, but he was tied to a stake in a contracted field. He strove to live outside of himself, made many pastoral calls, talked with men about their business trials and sympathized with women in their domestic woes. At his own home his hands were full. His wife was broken in health and discomforted in spirit. She did not like the West and the West was unkind to her constitution. It was a serious question whether she could much longer endure the strain on her physique, and this wore on the sympathetic nature of her husband. He was entirely unselfish, but the attrition of years of complaint worried him. He did the best, all in fact he could, but to no use. Finding himself depressed, Mr. Beecher resolutely set to work to drive his fits of despondency away. He became interested in trees and flowers. Aided by friends he started an agricultural paper and posted himself from books on floriculture, and read the fat and prosy volumes of London. His fresh and novel mode of treating these subjects won him fame, but not fortune. His own garden gave evidence of his skill, and the fairs were not niggardly in premiums to the amateur gardener. Eight years swiftly wore away, and in the often recurring excitements of revivals, public meetings, home trial and personal bewilderments, the young man passed from the first period of his career to the second.

CHAPTER VII.

In the year 1847, Plymouth Church was founded by advanced Congregationalists. The Congregationalism of New York and Brooklyn was a modified Presbyterianism. The pastor and standing committee stood for the minister and elders in the Presbyterian Church that ruled everything. The Plymouth brethren proposed to have a church in which the laymen should come to the front. The preacher was to be simply a layman in all church matters, and to-day the pastor can not preside at a church business meeting unless he is formally elected. For many years the pastor was not allowed to conduct the Friday night meeting. The church has never belonged to any organization, though in fellowship with other churches, and it is absolutely as independent as though there was not another church in the world.

May 8, 1847, David Hale, of New York, Ira Paine, John T. Howard, Charles Rowland, David Griffin and Henry C. Bowen met at the house of the latter, resolved themselves into an association of trustees of the new church, and decided to begin holding services at once.

They had purchased in June, 1846, for $20,000 the ground upon which now stands Plymouth Church, and which already contained an edifice of worship. They had paid outright the sum of $9,500, giving a mortgage for the remainder. The money for this payment was furnished by Henry C. Bowen, Seth B. Hunt, John T. Howard and David Hale, the first three being members of the Church of the Pilgrims.

A peculiar minister was needed for so peculiar a church. Among the many merchants who from time to time returned to their New York homes to report the singular sayings and Pauline preachings of the Western orator, was one who lived in Brooklyn and had incidentally learned of these plans. He called the attention of Mr. Bowen to the rising young man, a son of Lyman Beecher.

Early in the spring of that year a committee from the church organization went to Indianapolis to learn something more of the author of the "Lectures to Young Men," copies of which had found their way to Brooklyn.

How Plymouth Church was to hear him was a question. The church did not wish to hear him as a candidate, and did not wish to call him until they knew something of his metal. Bowen urged the Home Missionary Society to invite young Beecher to come on and preach the annual sermon. The society did not know enough of Henry Ward to invest the expenses of his visit. Mr. Bowen offered to be responsible for the cost, and paid out sixty dollars that the church, in this roundabout way, might hear Mr. Beecher.

The invitation was accepted, Mr. Beecher never suspecting that during his visit he would be on trial.

Even then Brooklyn was known as the City of Churches, and men of mark in divers denominations were drawing audiences to their feet. Among others at that time were Dr. Bethune, of the Dutch Reformed Church; Dr. Constantine Pise, of the Roman Catholic Church; Dr. R. S. Storrs, Jr., of the Congregational Church; Dr. T. L. Cuyler, of the Presbyterian Church, and *facile princeps* Dr. Samuel Hanson Cóx, of the First Presbyterian Church, one of the oldest organizations in the country. Obviously to bring an untried man to a place like Brooklyn was venturesome, to say the least.

Mr. Beecher was, at this time, thirty-four years old. Mentally he had become broader and looked over wider fields than when he began to labor. Morally he was as sincere, as truthful and as ingenuous as when he opened his big blue eyes with astonishment at the Bible stories he heard at "Aunt Esther's" knee. Physically he was a picture of vigorous health. He stood about five feet eight inches high. His large, well-formed, well-developed head sat defiantly on a short, red neck, that grew from a sturdy frame, rampant and lusty in nerve and fibre and blood and muscle. He had no money, owned no real estate. His capital was in his brains, and they needed the culture procurable in the metropolis alone, where libraries and bookstores, art galleries and men of thought were to be met at every turn.

A career in the East was far from Beecher's thoughts, and yet his sick wife seemed to need a medicament not to be found in the West.

Mrs. Beecher was overjoyed at the prospect of a trip that might benefit her health and enable her to see her Eastern relatives and friends, and Mr. Beecher was more than glad of anything that would relieve the monotony of a sick-room and bring him in contact with a side of the world that was as truly Greek to him as — well, as Greek itself. With scanty wardrobe, old fashioned and rusty at that, the couple started Eastward. The difference in their appearance may be inferred from a remark made by an old lady on the cars. Mr. Beecher had jumped from the train to the platform at one of the stations to get "Ma," as he always called his wife, a sandwich. "Ma" sat gloomy and sad-faced, and attracted the attention of the old lady, who approached her and said, sympathizingly, "Cheer up, my dear madam, cheer up.

Surely, whatever may be your trial, you have cause for great thankfulness to God, who has given you such a kind and attentive son."

That settled Mrs. Beecher for the remainder of the journey, and made her cup of misery more than full. However, though the lady knew it not, she was rapidly nearing the haven in which she was to find a glowing welcome, reinvigoration of mind and body and an anchorage of safety for life. Mr. Beecher was a success from the moment he opened his lips in the Broadway Tabernacle. In those days "Anniversary Week" was an institution. The great men of the nation spoke from their platforms. The evangelical expeditions against the heathen, intemperance and slavery were organized, equipped and started then and there. Each year the respective advocates returned with their reports. The Tabernacle was always crowded, and some of the best thoughts of the churches' best men were uttered in speeches from that pulpit. Henry Ward Beecher, *per se*, was unknown; but his father and his elder brother and sister were known to every one at all familiar with affairs. Consequently, when the sturdy son of Lyman Beecher rose to speak he was greeted by a friendly audience, and soon found himself at home, although his garb was not in accordance with the fashionable cut of his hearers.

BEECHER'S HOUSE AT LITCHFIELD.
See page 19.

On May 16, he attended the dedication of Plymouth Church, but was as innocent as a lamb of any knowledge that he was ever to become part and parcel of it. He felt hampered here. His heart was in the West, and he longed to be home again. He was invited to remain and preach a few Sundays. That meant $25 and a welcome each week in the house of one of the churchmen. The health of Mrs. Beecher seemed to improve, and her husband reluctantly consented to continue awhile.

Twenty-one persons united in the formation of the new Plymouth Church, and on June 13 the church was publicly organized, the Rev Richard S. Storrs preaching the sermon for the occasion.

Mr. Beecher took part in the ceremonies, and made so deep an impression upon the members of the new church that they unanimously decided to "call" him. They offered him $1,500 per year. The amount was at that time a princely salary in his eyes, and he at once accepted.

An amusing theological examination preceded his installation. "Do you believe in the Perseverance of the Saints?" asked Dr. Humphrey. "I was brought up to believe that doctrine," replied Mr. Beecher, "and I did believe it until I went out West and saw how Eastern Christians lived when they went out there. I confess since then I have had my doubts."

The council that assembled to examine the young candidate soon found that their task was no ordinary one. They asked the set and formulated questions, but received very strange and unexpected answers. On the broad ground of God's supremacy and man's responsibility they found him sound, but he seemed to put more faith in the love of Christ, in the doctrine of charity and in the oneness of the Father and His children than in the time-honored dogmas and doctrines of the churches. The wise heads doubted, and for a while it was by no means certain that they would take the responsibility of seating him in the pulpit. They might have saved themselves their trouble. If every man of them had voted "no" it would have made no difference. Then as now, then, as through the dark days of outspoken abolitionism, then, as in the perilous period of the war for the Union, then, as in the sickening scandal, Plymouth Church believed in Henry Ward Beecher first, last and all the time. He was adopted and settled in spite of the protest of his venerable father.

"Don't, I beseech of you," he wrote to Mr. Howard, "don't induce Henry to leave the West. He has a great field here, and is brought in contact with men of influence and all the members of the Legislature. He will be buried in the East." There is no doubt that the son shared the father's apprehension.

"I came East," he said, "with a silken noose about my neck and did not know it."

That the benefit his wife would derive from a residence here was a great point with Mr. Beecher is well known to his friends. He felt that she had been overtasked in all her early married life, and desired that she should now begin to enjoy the advantages of civilization. At all events, he sold out his few effects and came to Brooklyn.

His wardrobe was in a sad condition and that of his wife was worse. His hat was shockingly bad, his coat seedy and his pants darned; his boots and his shirts equally out of repair. Mr. Bowen purchased for him an entire outfit; purchased the cloth and

6

had a suit of clothes made up so that the pastor of Plymouth Church could be presentable on Sunday.

The new pastor wore his hair long, no beard was permitted to grow, a wide Byron collar was turned over a black silk stock and his clothes were of conventional cut. His hair was thick and heavy. His eyes were large and very blue. His nose was straight, full and prominent. His mouth formed a perfect bow, and when the well developed lips parted they disclosed regular, well set teeth. There was nothing clerical in his face, figure, dress or bearing. He was more like a street evangel—a man talking to men and standing on a common level.

At the first services on Oct. 10 the church in the morning was about three-quarters full; in the evening it was completely full, and in a short space of time the edifice was found to be inadequate to the constantly increasing congregation.

The first thing he insisted on was congregational singing. The organ was not a very fine instrument, but it did its duty, and a large volunteer choir led the singing—at first. At first, but after awhile the congregation was the choir and the organ, the leader. Mr. Beecher had the pulpit cut away and on the platform placed a reading desk. In this way he was plainly visible from crown to toe, and whether preaching or sitting, every motion was in full view of the

crowded assemblage. Instead of resting a pale forehead on a pallid hand and closing his eyes as if in
silent prayer while his people sang, Mr. Beecher held
his book in his red fist and sang with all his might.
Although not a finished singer, he had a melodious
bass voice, and he sang with understanding. As he
did so his eyes would take in the scene before him,
and it needed no wizard's skill to detect its power over
him. Ever impressible and as full of intuition as a
woman, he felt the presence of men and women. Time
and again the tenor of his discourse was altered at the
sight of a face. Incidents of the moment often shaped
the discourse of the hour. He laid great stress on the
influence of congregational singing. It brought the
audience to a common feeling. It made them appreciate that they were not only in the house of worship,
but that they were there as worshippers, part of their
duty being to sing praises to the Most High.

His prayers, too, attracted great attention. The
keenest eye, the most sensitive ear never detected an
approach to irreverence in Mr. Beecher's manner in
prayer. He prayed, it is true, as a respectful son
would petition a loving and indulgent father. It was
noticed that he addressed his prayers very largely to
the Saviour. In his sermons it was the love of Christ
on which he dwelt. It seemed as if he delighted to
put away all thought of the Judge, and to keep always

present the tenderness of the Father and the affection of the Elder Brother. The little church was always overcrowded. Hundreds applied in vain for seats. It became the fashion to "go to hear Beecher." Thousands went to criticise and ridicule. Thousands went in simple curiosity. It was soon the affectation to look down upon him. He was called boorish, illiterate, ungrammatical, uncultivated, fit for the common people only and a temporary rushlight. Dr. Cox, an old friend of Lyman Beecher, to whom the new comer expected to turn for advice as to a father, said,

"I will give that young man six months in which to run out."

After a few months the church took fire from a defective flue, and, although not entirely destroyed, was badly damaged, and the trustees concluded to pull it down and build anew. Meantime they put up an immense temporary structure on Pierrepont street, near Fulton, which they called the Tabernacle. There, every Sunday, immense crowds of strangers and visitors from other parishes assembled to listen to Mr. Beecher. Already the journals had discovered the pith of the preacher and made him noted in the land. His utterances were never commonplace, his manner was always fresh, his illustrations ever new. He never avoided issues. Indeed, it was charged that he was sensational because he talked and taught about the topics of the hour. He rarely preached a doctrinal sermon, and when he did there was a kind of explanatory protest with it, as much as to say, "I don't really believe I know anything about this, but it can't do any harm." At first he dealt largely in practical lessons to the young men who formed a large part of his congregations. It was often remarked that while the proportion in other churches was five women to one man, in the Tabernacle, and later in Plymouth Church, the proportion was reversed. This is accounted for by two facts—young men, clerks, students and those who lived in boarding houses felt at home in that church, and the hotels of New York sent over hundreds every Sunday, who considered hearing "Beecher preach" one of the essentials of their business in New York. At all events there they were, and Mr. Beecher made it a rule of his lifework to address himself to them. He never bombarded the Jews, he left the heathen to their normal guardians, he avoided a decision of questions raised in the Garden of Eden, and left the sheep and the goats of ancient history to follow the call of their shepherd. His flock was before him. His duty was to care for the men and women who sat in the pews of his church and thronged its aisles and packed its galleries. He was human and avowed his love for man. Their weaknesses were his, and he called on them to seek a common physician.

The clergyman of fashion was pale and fragile; he of the people was florid and muscular. He had no attendant to remove his hat and cloak. He had no comfortable study in the church building where he smoothed his hair and arranged his cuffs. He declaimed before no full length mirror, and never wore a pair of patent leathers in his life. When he ascended the platform, threading his way through the men and women on the steps and patting the curly hair of boys perched on the ledge, he slung his soft felt hat under a little table, put one leg over the other while he removed his rubber, threw back his cloak, settled himself in his chair and gave a sigh of relief as he drew a restful breath after his quick walk from home. In other words, he was a man bent on man's duty. If the air seemed close he said so, called an usher and had the windows lowered. If he desired a special tune sung to the hymn he gave out, he turned to the director and told him so. If he forgot a date or a name, he asked one of the people near him what it was. If strangers sitting close to the platform were unprovided with hymn books, he leaned forward and handed them several from his desk. As he said, "I am at home; they are our guests. What is proper in my house is eminently proper in the house of the Lord."

The practice of adorning the pulpit with flowers, now generally adopted, was one of Mr. Beecher's ideas, and was followed at all seasons, when these beautiful productions of nature and the God of Nature could possibly be brought and placed on the altar.

CHAPTER VIII.

PERSONALITY SANS PARSONALITY.

When Mr. Beecher came to Brooklyn forty years ago, all of the City of Churches lay within a mile of Fulton Ferry; boys picked blackberries from hedgerows within a quarter of a mile of the present City Hall; all of Brooklyn Heights, now covered with costly residences, was a grassy bluff, and the great flat below the heights, now crowded with great warehouses, was occupied principally with sheds, in which were stored what to the juvenile eye seemed millions of barrels of tar, pitch and other unsightly items included under the general head "naval stores."

Then, as now, the busiest part of the city was in Fulton and other streets very near the City Hall, but not all the business was done indoors. The leisurely, rural style showed forth in the country village habit of the forefathers of the hamlet (and all the town loafers beside), sitting on barrels, boxes and bales in front of stores and shops to talk business, politics, theology and gossip.

Mr. Beecher's ways were quite like those of his new parishioners and neighbors, and many a time was

HANOVER CHURCH, BOSTON.
See page 33.

he a member of such a group. He never seemed to have any faculty or inclination as a proselyte, but he seemed determined to know all he could of the town's people and their doings — this purpose he afterward admitted in conversation.

In those days nearly all the men who gathered to chat chewed tobacco vigorously as they swung their legs and whittled splinters split from the sides of boxes. Beecher did not use the weed, but he had a habit that to some good people seemed still more un-dignified — he ate peanuts, and as a distributor of

shells of these esculent tubers he could equal any
newsboy.

At first the natives regarded with a watchful, half-
suspicious manner the new-comer who was drawing
such large congregations every Sunday. As soon as
he arrived there would be a sudden change of manner,
such as usually occurs when a clergyman drops upon a
party of men engaged in general chat; but those who
expected or feared that a sanctimonious turn would be
given to the conversation were always disappointed,
for the young preacher talked only as a public-spirited
citizen, and he gave many a man more insight into
points and purposes in architecture than they ever had
before. Among the men with whom he talked most
frequently were an undertaker, a grain merchant, a
grocer, an old English tavern-keeper, and an Irish cartman. Not one of these belonged to his church, either
then or after; indeed, none of them were members of
the same denomination with him, and as denominational feeling was far more intense then than it is now,
it was amusing to observe their efforts to occasionally
work doctrinal points into conversation and see Beecher
dodge the subject. These men—all but one are now
dead—afterward became his enthusiastic friends, after
.which they admitted that he strengthened their own
faith by the ardor with which he clung to the great essentials on which all professing Christians agree, and

all of them have told, again and again, of how they depended upon him to help them when they were striving to reclaim some poor estray from their own spiritual fold. Said the Irish cartman one day: "That's a quare man, is Mr. Beecher. When I tell him of a friend of mine that's doin' wrong he niver tells me to sind him to his church; he tells me to thry to coax him to go to confession."

When in later years Mr. Beecher's great trial came upon him, from no class did he receive more numerous and hearty letters of sympathy and encouragement than from Catholic priests.

Another thing that endeared Beecher to the people of Brooklyn was the immense fund of general and practical information which was always at the service of everybody. He could tell a man what to do for a cold in the head, or a smoky chimney, or a bad boy, or a sick horse, or a sterile fruit tree—for there were fruit trees in Brooklyn in those days; he always had a piece of thick string in his pocket with which to help a man mend a harness that broke on the road; he gave villagers points on raising chickens, knew what were the best varieties of vegetable seeds, and knew more about nursing sick folks than half the doctors in town. Few of the present generation knows that Brooklyn once had a big fire, but it did; about half the buildings on Fulton street, between the river and the City

Hall, were burned in 1849, and the town was very gloomy about it, but Beecher went about with a heart full of hope that found its way to his lips, and did an immense deal toward reviving public spirit and confidence.

It has been said that Mr. Beecher was coarse and vulgar, and that he had no appreciation of the delicacies of life or the proprieties of place. It would be a waste of time to multiply instances of proof to the contrary. He was cheerful and robust, and in some sense awkward, but he was innately gentle and sensitive to a degree. A remark may illustrate the feeling he had about the conduct of service. In 1878 a friend was narrating an awkward mishap that attended a baptism, and Mr. Beecher said: "Well, in all my ministry, I have never had the slightest accident of that kind. I have never spilled a drop of wine nor dropped a piece of bread. The only approach to a *contretemps* that I recall was when I miscalculated the distance in sitting down on a newly upholstered chair. I expected to go down several inches further than I did, and the sudden bump I received startled me and sent the blood in torrents to my cheeks. It was with the greatest difficulty I refrained from laughing outright. If I had caught a contagious eye anywhere I certainly should have roared."

That he was a great mimic and a natural panto-

mimist is well known. When he described a long faced
hypocrite he saw him and unconsciously pictured him.
If he pictured the love of Christ and His tenderness
to the broken ones of life, he felt the love and tenderness, and unconsciously portrayed them in manner and
gesture.   Satire and ridicule were weapons always
ready to his hand. In those days, people hidebound in
prejudice could not understand that a preacher was
right in using all his powers in the service of his Master, so they inveighed against Beecher, pronounced him
a mountebank and left him to die an easy death.

He continued, however, and a great revival occurred.
It grieved Mr. Beecher greatly that some of the clergy
of Brooklyn allowed their prejudice to outweigh their
love for their fellows; but accepting the bitter with
the sweet, he kept on. His Tabernacle was too small
for the crowds. His congregation included families
that stood high in social circles, merchants of the first
repute, judges and literary men of renown, but, chief
of all, an army of young men who, like himself, were
bearing the burden and the heat of the day. Professor
Phinney took him by the hand and worked with him
for weeks. Morning meetings were held and the entire
city was filled with religious enthusiasm. Gradually
the personal habits of Mr. Beecher changed. He was
always a great walker. He wandered along the river
front. He visited studios and read about painters and

their art.   He was proficient in pottery and knew the varieties, and where and how they were made.   Arboriculture and horticulture and agriculture were specialties with him.   He was known in the great foundries of this city as a searcher into affairs.   He visited shipyards, and with one of his dearest friends, who was building steamers for several years, he studied the art of shipbuilding.   He was versed in the lore of the pole and line.   He had rare fowling pieces and the most fanciful facilities for field and river sports.   That his people benefited by this habit let his illustrations attest.   From birds and flowers and all manner of mechanics, from industries of every name and nature, he drew pictures, arguments and convincing assertions in analogy that clinched the nail of his discourse already driven home by the power of his eloquence.

In about one year and a half after the arrival of Mr. Beecher the corner-stone of the present structure was laid.   In January of the following year (1850) it was opened for worship.

When the new church was built it faced on Orange street, where the old lecture room stood.   On Cranberry street a supplemental building was erected; on its ground floor the lecture room, on the next the Sunday school rooms and what one then called the Social Circle parlors.   Forgetting that Brooklyn was not exactly a rural township Mr. Beecher was pained to observe that while Mr. A. knew Mr. B. Mrs. A. had not the pleasure of knowing Mrs. B. and that while in the church every one was a "dear brother or sister," out of the church such social distinctions existed as utterly precluded any real Christian feeling. This he thought was all wrong and subversive of genuine brotherly love.

So he resolved to change it.

Without much consultation he announced on Sunday that on a specified evening the parlors would be thrown open, and all the people were invited to appear and make each other's acquaintance. He said he and his family would be there, and he thought it high time that the brethren and sisters of his church knew a little something of each other.

The Social Circle assembled. A few of the old families of Brooklyn responded because they wished to please their pastor, but the attendance was mainly such persons as had everything to gain and nothing to give in return. Young men and young women went for fun and had it, but the attempt was Quixotic and the scheme impracticable. Oil and water in a tumbler would mix sooner than social elements in a metropolitan city. It was entirely proper in theory, but it didn't work in practice, and Mr. Beecher was compelled to abandon the idea.

Success, however, attended him on every other line.

His pews were rented at high rates, his regular congregation was large and respectable, his church membership grew rapidly and the influx of strangers was so great and so constantly increasing that their accommodation was an utter impossibility. The liberality of the Plymouth pastor was a sore point with his critics. He always contended for his right to beliefs of his own, and as vigorously defended the right of others to beliefs of their own. His church membership soon became eclectic. Presbyterians and Congregationalists were not so far apart that their union caused remark, but presently a few Baptists joined the church. Mr. Beecher said, "You must believe and be baptized and it's for you to determine how you will be baptized. I am content with any symbol, however slight, but if you prefer to be immersed and we have the conveniences for it, it's your faith, not mine." In other words, the fact was essential in his mind; the form was of no consequence. A baptistry was built beneath the pulpit platform, and he often immersed those who desired to be baptized that way. Swedenborgians, Spiritualists and even Quaker and Episcopalians joined the communion of Plymouth Church. Indeed, one of the pleasantest features in Mr. Beecher's experience was the favor he found with clergymen of other denominations. Father Pise, the learned and devout Constantine Pise, for many years the loved and honored pastor of the Catholic Church of St. Charles Borromeo, in Sydney place, Brooklyn, was a warm friend and admirer of Mr. Beecher, and many of the Episcopal, Baptist and Methodist clergy were bound to his heart with ties of love and tender sympathy.

His ministry did much to soften intolerance and promote brotherly love and charity.   Not indifferent to creeds, he urged the higher value of a theology

BEECHER'S HOME, WALNUT HILLS, CINCINNATI.
See page 45.

7

based on the moral uses of the Bible as a practical
book, and a belief in the direct inspiration of the Holy
Spirit in noble aims and endeavors.   His intuitive
grasp of subjects and his marvelous fluency of thought
and force of expression gave him power over the intelligence of men, as his deep humanity, tenderness,
sympathy, ruled their affections.   He was veritably a
hope-bringer.

His theology grew into the religion of love, of
benevolence, of infinite goodness, putting away the
idea of an implacable judge, the theory of endless tor-
ture.   This spirit was the guiding influence of his life
and of his work, and this it was made him one of the
most manly of zealous anti-slavery teachers, and
taught him to regard that institution not only as a
political evil but as a moral wrong, a deep sin against
humanity.   He was enabled thereby to stand firmly
and bravely against the opposition of prejudice and
the strong force of custom and though he lived to
triumph in the cause, it was not to glorify his own
acts but to rejoice in the inflow of Christian light.

CHAPTER IX.

POLITICS IN THE PULPIT.

People who did not know, thirty or forty years ago, where to class Mr. Beecher as a theologian, had no difficulty in fixing his status in political agitation. At a time when many of the foremost preachers and teachers and leaders of the country were hesitating over the fugitive slave law Mr. Beecher was saying, "When we have ceased to pray—when we have rooted out the humanities, which since our connection with the gospel have been growing within us; when we have burned our Bible and renounced our God—then we will join with those whose patriotism exhibits itself in disrobing men of every natural right, and in driving them from light and religion into gross heathenism."

While he was becoming the greatest preacher of his time he was, says John G. Whittier, "As a life-long friend of freedom, gaining what Milton calls 'a freehold of rejoicing to him and his heirs' in the emancipation of the slave."

When this influential manhood began, our Nation was divided into two very hostile sections. The

South had become so alarmed regarding its peculiar property that a Northern man, having a known love of liberty, did not dare travel in the South. The Northern merchants were so anxious to retain the cotton and sugar trade of the South that they all frowned upon any politics which numbered freedom among its ideals, and they would mob or burn a church which contained the disciples of a Christian liberty and equality. The students in Dartmouth College mobbed free-soil speakers; the President sympathized with the students. Churches, schoolhouses, asylums, and homes of colored people in the North were burned to check the spread of hope among the Africans in the South. Twelve buildings were burned in New York, one large church and many homes in Cincinnati, forty houses and two churches in Philadelphia. Pennsylvania Hall, built for anti-slavery meetings, was burned down, along with its valuable library, while Mayor and Council offered no protection and no word of sympathy. White men were imprisoned in Boston for preaching abolitionism. In 1837 a slave had been burned to death over a slow fire in St. Louis, and for denouncing such atrocity the Rev. Elijah Lovejoy of this State was mobbed to death.

It was in such days, reaching from 1830 to 1860, the hot oratory of Mr. Beecher was fabricated, like the bolts of Jupiter in the infernal shop of Vulcan.

Thence came also the equipment of Dr. Cheever, Phillips, Parker, and Sumner. The age sharpened their speech, condensed their style, and poured in the heroism and passion which make martyrs. Of all these men Mr. Beecher was the most visible, because his pulpit brought him each week before the people. His logic, his simple style, his illustrations, his pathos, his hope, made his words fly straight as arrows to the heart. This vast plea for universal freedom was well sustained for twenty years, and beginning in our West it reached its zenith in England, when, in 1863, he had to teach the horrors of slavery to the nation which had produced Cowper and Wilberforce, but had forgotten them. He embodied the new genius of the United States. He had lived in 1840 the life our Nation reached thirty years afterward. Boston railways built a mean, plain car for negroes to ride in. It was called the "Jim Crow" car. Charles Lennox Redmond, an educated colored man, entertained in England by persons of rank and fame, and commissioned by O'Connell and Father Mathew to bear greetings from liberty in England to liberty in America, found, on going from Boston to Salem, his home, that he must not take the good car, but must ride in the "Jim Crow" car. In such a time Mr. Beecher began to ask the colored men to sit on his platform in his church, and thus the "negro car" was met in equity by the refuge of the greatest pulpit the world possessed. In 1835, while Mr. Beecher was looking out of his soul-window with his powerful vision and tender nature, he saw in the Charleston Courier a notice of a public sale of slaves to satisfy a mortgage held by the Presbyterian Theological Seminary of South Carolina. He read, also, that the estate of the Rev. Dr. Furman was to be sold at auction— "the farm, a large theological library, twenty-seven negroes (some of them very prime), two mules, one horse and an old wagon." In those days the Episcopal Bishop of Virginia, Dr. Meade, had published some sermons to slaves. One great thought was that they must bear well correction, and even if corrected when not guilty of the offense, they must bear the flogging in meekness, and assign the whipping to some other transgression which had been concealed from their masters in the Lord.

It was high time for religion to reach out its hand to the slave.

Mr. Beecher at once announced his determination to preach in the Plymouth pulpit Christ as an absolute system of doctrine, by which the ways and usages of society should be judged, and further gave notice that he regarded temperance and anti-slavery principles as a part of that gospel.

There was no need for him to wait in order to prove

his words by his deeds, for the storm burst almost immediately. In the North were irresolution, weakness, and a desire for peace at any cost save the disintegration of the Union. But Mr. Beecher's fighting-blood was up, and he threw himself into the thick of the conflict on coming to Brooklyn.

Wide as was the platform of Plymouth Church a wider plane was now preparing for Mr. Beecher. In the early days of anti-slavery agitation he sounded the bugle call of danger to the Union in the West. When he came East and began to teach man how to live, rather than how to die, he stirred up several hornets' nests. He enraged the dead-and-alive clergy because his methods were a virtual rebuke of their laziness, and he angered the mercantile community because he hurt their trade, while the politicians, who had for years endeavored to smother the sin of the century, were maddened at the idea of a mere minister's daring to arouse the nation from a stupor and indifference. As he went on the agitation increased.

The excitement caused by the fugitive slave law and Webster's seventh of March speech brought him forward into the arena of practical work. From the pulpit he went into the lecture field, and visited various parts of New York and the New England States.

"Beecher developed from a local into a national character," said Thomas G. Shearman, "in the year

1850. The slavery question was causing great excitement, and Clay had proposed his compromise, while Calhoun, on the part of the South, was strongly opposing all compromise. So also was the Northern anti-slavery party, and it was just at this time that Mr. Beecher became decidedly famous. The Journal of Commerce had published an article threatening that the clergymen that meddled with slavery would have their coats rolled in the dirt. That aroused all the spirit that was in Beecher. He challenged the editor of that paper to a debate in the newspapers, which was carried on for some time, Beecher writing in the Independent, which was at that time edited by Dr. Storrs and Dr. Leonard Bacon, under the famous star (*) signature."

His articles were so felicitous and effective that they attracted universal attention, and John C. Calhoun had them read to him aloud while on his death-bed, and pronounced them the ablest articles on the subject ever written, saying repeatedly, "That man understands the subject. He has the true idea." Of course he did not mean to approve Beecher's views on slavery, but that he heartily approved of his argument that it was impossible to compromise the question. This occurrence was published soon afterward in a very graphic manner by Calhoun's private secretary, and it gave Beecher a really national reputation, making him known as well in the South as he had been in the North.

When Mrs. Stowe's "Uncle Tom's Cabin" was published, in 1852, Henry Ward Beecher had become so well known that thousands of people in the country were foolish enough to believe that he had written the book for her. On the other hand, Mrs. Stowe's name became so familiar in England that for many years, when the English papers spoke of Mr. Beecher, they were accustomed to mention him as Mr. Beecher Stowe,

Garrison and Phillips and Wade welcomed this zealous champion to their ranks, and he assumed the lead—where McGregor sat was the head of the table.

At the anniversaries Beecher was the popular speaker. In his own church he never allowed the fire of hostility to die out. The dignity of man was his constant topic. Man, as made in the image of his Maker, was sold as a chattel—that was his never dying grievance, day in and day out; year after year he rang the changes on the glory of manhood and the degradation of slavery until the abolitionists became a party to be feared and dreaded. When the mob said that Wendell Phillips should not speak in Brooklyn Mr. Beecher said, "He shall, and Plymouth Church is open to him." In the midst of his usefulness he fell ill and for weeks hovered between life and death. His strong constitution pulled him through, and his people

breathed again.   He resumed his teaching, and Harper's Weekly, then a strong pro-slavery journal, published a page illustration of Beecher refusing the
communion wine to Washington because he was a slaveholder.   He was denounced, lampooned, and vilified.
His doorsteps were smeared with tar and filth, and
scurrilous communications came daily by mail.

For all this he cared nothing.

His heart was in the fight, and believing he was
right he was bound to win or die.   It was about the
time Mr. Beecher first began to deliver set lectures
out of town for $50 and his expenses that Charles
Sumner was knocked in the head in the Senate Chamber by Brooks, of South Carolina.   The entire North
was fired with indignation, and the solid merchants of
New York thought that was going too far.   A mass
meeting of protest was called in the Tabernacle, and in
order to make it significant no one was invited to
speak who had ever countenanced the anti-slavery
movement.   It was entirely in the hands of conserva-
tives.   The chief speakers, resolution readers and
fluglemen were Daniel D. Lord, John Van Buren and
William M. Evarts.   The Tabernacle was packed with
an earnest, enthusiastic audience, which, in point of
numbers and respectability, culture and influence, has
rarely been surpassed.   For some reason Mr. Beecher,
who had been advertised to lecture in Philadelphia

that evening, was in the city. He had dined with his
his friend Mr. Howard, and together they went to the
Tabernacle to hear the speaking. As the meeting was
about to be closed some one in the audience called out
" Beecher." The people took up the cry and
" Beecher, Beecher " resounded through the church.
Mr. Evarts, evidently annoyed, advanced to the front
of the platform and said, " The programme of the
evening is concluded and the meeting will adjourn.
(A voice—" Beecher!") Mr. Beecher, I am told, is
lecturing in Philadelphia this evening." " No, he
isn't," called out one of the reporters; " there he is
behind the pillar." The greater part of the audience
had risen and prepared to leave. Beecher was recognized and half led, half forced to the platform from
which Mr. Evarts and his friends precipitately retired.
John Van Buren, with the instinct of a gentleman, advanced, took Mr. Beecher by the hand and led him to
the speaker's place. The audience reseated themselves, but for fully five minutes the house was in an
uproar of enthusiastic greeting. With a wave of his
hand Mr. Beecher secured silence and attention. For
an hour he delivered the speech of his life. Every
eye glistened. Such applause was never given before.
The occasion was an inspiration. The opportunity
was one he had never had before. But it is doubtful
that he thought of either one or the other. He had

the scene in the Senate Chamber in his eye. It was the culminating outrage in a series of horrors. He felt it. He foresaw its end. He made that audience feel what he felt and see what he saw, and when he closed he glowed like furnace, while the people cheered with their throats full of tears. Such scenes occur once in a lifetime. The next day's papers reported Beecher verbatim and gave the others what they could find space for.

From that time on the printed and spoken utterances of Henry Ward Beecher were taken as the keynote of the great campaign against slavery and its extension into the free Territories of the Northwest. Some of his people objected strenuously to their pastor's course. They thought it lowered the pulpit and brought religion and politics to a common level. Mr. Beecher met their objections good humoredly but seriously. That any man worthy the name could contemplate the slavery of his fellow and seriously defend an institution whose corner-stone was the defilement of the image of God seemed to him an abasement of human intelligence. "Tell me," he said, "that you mean to hold on to slavery because it is profitable or because you love power and I will respect at least your truth, but if you attempt to justify your infamy by scriptural quotations or specious arguments about rights I spew you from my friendship." The "silver-

DR. LYMAN BEECHER.

gray " merchants who demurred at his constant agitation of this subject and who affected to regard him as
a mountebank he bombarded without mercy. They
were rich and in positions of influence, therefore they
were the more dangerous and he spared nothing that
would convict them of treachery to the Master whose
children and servants they professed to be.

Finally, after years of agitation, from the labors of
the little coterie was born the republican party. Mr.
Beecher was one of its few fathers and tended it carefully from its birth. When John C. Fremont was
nominated as Presidential candidate he took great
interest in the campaign and addressed great audiences
in Massachusetts, New York and Pennsylvania. He
was then forty-three years old and in perfect health.
With the exception of several months in 1849, when he
was so seriously ill as to prevent his preaching from
March until September, and three months in 1850,
when he made a convalescing trip to Europe, he had
not been absent a Sunday from his pulpit. The
national peril in 1856 seemed so great that he was
induced by his political friends to accept a leave of
absence from his church and travel through the Middle
and Western States on a kind of oratorical pilgrimage. Wherever he went his fame preceded him, and
in that memorable fight he added laurels of imperishable renown to those already won.

The defeat of Fremont, by Mr. Beecher and many others believed to be the work of Pennsylvania tricksters, consolidated the republican party, intensified the growing hatred of the sections and afforded the extremists both sides of Mason and Dixon's line a never ending theme of discussion.   Plymouth pulpit had become a national institution.   The streets of Brooklyn leading from the ferries were busy with processions of men from New York looking for " Beecher."   The policeman never waited for a stranger to conclude his his question, but invariably interrupted him and said, " Follow the crowd."   That hundreds heard Mr. Beecher preach from Sunday to Sunday who hated him and his doctrines is undoubtedly the fact.   Some of the "best people" in the city refused to speak to him, and all over the land he was vilified and abused. All this made no impression on him.   As he said after he had been twenty-five years in Plymouth Church:— " In the first sermon that I preached on the first Sunday night after I came here was a declaration that those who took pews in the church and attended my preaching might expect to hear the gospel applied faithfully to questions of peace and war and temperance and moral purification and liberty, and that there should be no uncertain sound on these subjects.   During the earlier periods of my ministry here, and perhaps for the first twelve years, I made it a point, just preceding the renting of the pews, to show my hand with all the power that I possessed, to declare my opinions on the subject of slavery, in order that no man might be deceived and that it might not be supposed that popularity or seducing sympathy had changed the intense conviction of Plymouth Church in respect to the great and fundamental truths of human liberty."

8

CHAPTER X.

The overwhelming defeat of the Free Soil party in 1852 was followed in May, 1854, by the repeal of the Missouri Compromise, and slavery was allowed to enter where it had once been excluded. Mr. Beecher was among the first to express the indignation of the Northern States at this breach of good faith. But the march of events moved on with almost bewildering rapidity. In Massachusetts and Connecticut companies were incorporated to aid emigrants in settling the new territories. From the Northwestern States came likewise sturdy children of the Puritans in search of homes and freedom. But on the fertile plains of Kansas they met rampant slaveholders from Missouri, with their gangs of slaves and hostile defenders of " the institution " from the Southern slave States, eager to force the Territory at the muzzles of their rifles into the shackles of a pro-slavery despotism. Standing in his church, Mr. Beecher declared that the innocent must be protected by force, if need be, against the guilty. And the practical result was the starting of a subscription in Plymouth Church to supply every

114

Eastern family going to Kansas with a Bible and a rifle. When, June 17, 1856, at Philadelphia, the Republican National Convention declared for the maintenance of the principles of the Declaration of Independence embodied in the Constitution, for the preservation of the Constitution, the rights of the States, and resolved that Congress should prohibit slavery in the Territories, Mr. Beecher at once gave this platform his unreserved and enthusiastic support. More than this, he openly "took the stump" for Fremont at mass meetings in New York and elsewhere, and unceasingly advocated the Republican cause with his pen through the columns of the Independent and other publications. And yet, during this period, he was a voluminous reader, and a student and collector of artistic treasures. One of the most popular of his lectures was on "The Uses of the Beautiful," and much as he lived in public at this time he was devoted to his home and social relaxations.

Disappointed in the election of 1856, he watched with absorbing interest the border warfare, the debates in Congress, John Brown's attack on Harper's Ferry and his tragic death, and the movements toward secession, which culminated in the withdrawal of South Carolina from the Union Dec. 20, 1860, and of other States soon after. With pen and voice he labored for the success of Abraham Lincoln in the campaign of

1860, urging the preservation of the Union and of National honor. When, April 12, 1861, the first shot fired at Fort Sumter smote the Northern heart, Mr. Beecher sprang to the aid of his country. From Plymouth pulpit came the ringing words of patriotism, cheering the timid, encouraging the downcast, denouncing traitors, but hopeful of the future, pointing out clearly the path of right and duty for those who love their country. His church, prompt to answer, raised and equipped a regiment, the First Long Island, in which his eldest son was an officer. Before this regiment went into actual service, Mr. Beecher often visited the camp and preached to the young soldiers, many being "my own boys," as he used to call them.

It was in 1856, when the slavery excitement was more intense than ever, that the famous Sharp's rifle scene took place. The people of Kansas had been left to fight out the question of slavery among themselves. The Missourians were naturally the first on the ground, and brought their slaves with them, but a number of colonies were organized in New England, Ohio, and the West, who, of course, were strongly opposed to slavery. The Missouri emigrants regarded the Northern ones as intruders, and, being accustomed to the use of arms, proceeded to drive them out. The Northern men thereupon appealed to their friends to send them arms for self-defense. A colony was being or-

ganized in Connecticut, and a great meeting was held
at New Haven, to raise subscriptions with the avowed
purpose of providing the colonists with rifles.   Mr.
Beecher was there and made a very stirring speech,
insisting on the right of Northern men to stand up in
self-defense.   A subscription being called for, the
Senior Class of Yale College announced that they
would subscribe $50 to buy one rifle.   Henry Killam,
a carriage manufacturer, gave his name as a subscriber
for another rifle.   It was then that Mr. Beecher said,
" Killam! That's a significant name," a remark which
brought out great laughter and applause, and which
was the origin of many fierce attacks upon him for
years afterward.

Early in the same year Beecher gained a great triumph over ultra-conservatism in the anti-slavery ranks.
A meeting had been called for the purpose of denouncing the outrageous attack made by Preston S. Brooks,
of South Carolina, upon Senator Sumner, and Mr.
Beecher had not been invited to speak by the highly
conservative men who were in charge.   He was present at the meeting as a listener, and had no intention
of interfering, but the audience clamored for him and
shouted until they became hoarse, so that finally the
chairman of the meeting was obliged to invite him to
speak. He did so, making a speech which quite
eclipsed all the others and aroused the people to the

utmost enthusiasm. It made so deep an impression that when Fremont was nominated, soon afterward, the Republican managers insisted on having Beecher make a canvass through some of the Northern States. Wherever he spoke he was received with enthusiasm, and, except in New York City, the Republican majorities were very large.

The courage, based upon principle, of the man showed to fine advantage in 1850, when Captain Rynders had brought about a riot in the Broadway Tabernacle on the occasion of Wendell Phillips speaking there. This incident alarmed the owners of the Tabernacle building so that they refused to allow Mr. Phillips to speak there again. Mr. Beecher immediately called upon the Trustees of Plymouth Church and demanded that Mr. Phillips should have the use of that building. The Trustees were not unfriendly, but some hesitated from a fear that the church might be burned by a mob. Beecher declared that he would rather preach over the ashes of his church than in a comfortable church that could not be used for the maintenance of free speech. The Trustees agreed to consent. Some years afterward, when another riot was threatened in New York, and when the use of nearly every building was refused, Mr. Beecher again insisted that Plymouth Church should be offered for a similar purpose, and, although the city was then under the government of a party not at all in sympathy with Beecher or his views, the effect of his public appeal to the citizens to maintain the right of free speech was so effective that police were sent to guard the church, and the scattering mob which came with the intention of creating a riot was speedily dispersed.

Again, in 1860, party spirit having risen very high, serious threats of a mob were made, and a crowd of hostile people surrounded Plymouth Church one Sunday evening, but the volunteer guards protected the building throughout the service, and no more harm resulted than the throwing of one stone through a window.

Plymouth Church, meanwhile, grew steadily stronger in membership, and though dependent entirely for support on the sale of seats, Mr. Beecher made it clearly understood that the buying of a seat would make it necessary for the holders to hear the gospel uncompromisingly applied to the practical issues of the time. When Kansas was being settled, he fearlessly took the ground that emigrants should go out well armed, and caused a subscription to be raised in his church to supply every family with a Bible and a rifle.

At his prayer meeting at Plymouth Church one evening, a day or two after Horace Greeley had gone to Virginia and become bondsman for the release of

Jeff Davis, the topic of Mr. Beecher's remarks was
"The effect of temperament on a man's religious
creed," and toward the close of his talk he said something very much like this: "Recently a prominent
Northern man has gone to the relief of a noted male-
factor, and an avalanche of abuse has been heaped
upon him. But, in my opinion, his act is worthy of
commendation." When he had finished a hymn was
sung, and then the usual discussion by the congregation began. Tommy Shearman led off, and respect-
fully but warmly, and almost tearfully, condemned the
remarks of the pastor. He was followed by a dozen
more, all in the same strain, Mr. Beecher getting more
nervous all the time. The last speaker told about a
Quaker farmer who had given directions to his servants about a sheep-killing dog that had devastated his
flocks, and who told them to catch that dog and cut off
his tail close up to his ears. "That," said the
speaker, in his last sentence, and with a venomous
gesture, "is what I would do with Jeff Davis." As
these words were uttered, Mr. Beecher gave an impatient hitch in his chair, and said, "Jeff Davis never
once entered my head, in what I said." This astonished but quieted the people, and so the meeting
closed. The next day the newspapers were filled with
accounts of the rumpus, and loudly called on Mr.

HARRIET BEECHER STOWE.

121

Beecher to tell what case he really did have in mind, but Mr. Beecher never told.

Some of his people left his ministry, but where one went twenty new ones came. He demanded a free platform for himself and accorded it to others. His people did not servilely believe anything because he said it, for they often maintained opinions different from his to the end. Fortunately Mr. Beecher was a many-sided man. His superabundant health and exuberent flow of spirits made him fresh and full of life. Cares, troubles and work seemed but to inspire him. The more he had to do the easier he did it. The habits of his life were regular. For years after he began his Brooklyn work he slept an hour or two every afternoon. He ate sparingly. At first it was his habit, after the evening service, to go with his wife and a few friends to the house of a parishioner and eat a hearty supper—cold roast beef, roast oysters, cold fowl or whatever—but as he grew stout and older he gave that habit over. So far as the public were concerned he was equable in temper. He always bore himself good naturedly, and from the first met strangers, old or young, with a frank look and a pleasant smile. At this period—1856 and on—he was writing for the Independent, lecturing two or three times a week, preaching twice every Sunday, lecturing in his chapel Wednesday evenings, and talking with his people in the prayer meetings of Friday. This, in addition to pastoral calls, funeral services, weddings, and the thousand and one importunities to which popular men of all professions are liable. But even this did not seem to be enough. Throwing his heart into the work, he endeavored, in spite of great national excitement, to turn the thought of his people heavenward, and, in 1858–9, the most "extraordinary works of grace were in progress" in his congregation. In the early summer of 1858, a perfect harvest of young people was gathered into the church, the total number being 378.

Meantime Mr. Beecher, in his pulpit and by his pen, stirred the depths of the heart of the nation, and although to many it appeared as if pastor and church were monomaniacs, it must be admitted that they stood together in stormy and troublesome times, faithful witnesses to the great truths of human right and human liberty. Later on, when, as the result of such agitations, discussion broke out into a flame of war, they did not flinch, but gave their sons and daughters, sending them to the field and the hospital. He kept a vigilant eye upon affairs, and was one on whom men in authority leaned for counsel. He had worked hard to elect Abraham Lincoln, and often thanked God that He had raised such a man from the level of the people. As the nation hesitated in its first step the clarion cry

of Beecher recalled it to its duty.   Later on, when disaster and defeat sent the thrill of dismay through the
North, the voice of Beecher warned the people of the
danger of neglecting duty and the infamy of desertion.
He wrote and spoke and urged and worked without
rest. He counselled the President, cheered the troops,
and encouraged the people.

"I first saw Mr. Beecher," said General Horatio C.
King, "in 1857, when I was a student at Dickinson
College, and a number of us clubbed together and
chartered a stage to go to Harrisburg and hear him
lecture. He was then already noted, but excited very
diverse sentiments as to his religion and patriotism.
The college was largely recruited from the Southern
and border States, and there was quite a hot discussion
among the boys as to going to hear this abolitionist
who had counselled Sharp's rifles for 'bleeding Kansas.' But curiosity and good sense prevailed, and we
went. There was a feeling of disappointment when
the orator came upon the platform. He was then in
the prime of his physical vigor, with well-knit form,
long dark hair, careless apparently in demeanor and
with little appearance of the clergyman or public
speaker about him. But he had not proceeded far in
his discourse before he revealed his power, and we
found ourselves frequently applauding sentiments we
didn't believe in and were completely carried away by

his masterly eloquence. He seemed to be regardless
of the ordinary rules of oratory, restless, impatient of
restraint, moving across the platform impetuously,—in
a word, the highest exponent of what we supposed to
be natural oratory. Mr. Beecher told me years later
that it required three years of the most arduous study
and practice, mostly in the wood, where he wouldn't
disturb any one, to acquire this natural style. I can
see him as if it were but yesterday, with impassioned
speech, throwing his head back to get rid of the rebel-
lious lock which would fall over his forehead and
obscure his vision."

In 1860 or 1861 a beautiful octoroon girl, raised
and owned by a prominent citizen of this country, Mr.
John Churchman, attempted to make ⸲her escape
North. She was arrested and brought back. Her
master then determined to sell her, and found a ready
purchaser in another citizen, Mr. Fred Scheffer.
Shortly after this the late owner was impressed with
the belief that the girl intended to make another effort
to go North the first opportunity that presented. To
meet the emergency and save trouble Mr. Scheffer
proposed to Sarah that she should go North and raise
enough money from the abolitionists to purchase herself. This proposition she eagerly accepted, and,
being furnished with means by Mrs. Scheffer to pay
her fare, she started. A few days after her arrival in

New York she was taken to Mr. Beecher, and on the
following Sabbath morning was escorted to his pulpit
in Brooklyn. She was a woman of commanding presence, rounded features, and winning face and long jet
black hair, and of course, under the circumstances,
attracted most eager attention and interest from the
large and wealthy congregation assembled. She was
requested to unloosen her hair, and as she did so it
fell in glistening waves over her shoulders and below
her waist. Robed in spotless white, her face crimsoned and form heaving under the excitement of the
occasion, she stood in that august presence a very
Venus in form and feature. For a moment Mr.
Beecher remained by her side without uttering a word,
until the audience was wrought up to a high pitch of
curiosity and excitement. And then in his impressive
way he related her story and her mission. Before he
concluded his pathetic recital the vast audience was a
sea of commotion. Tears ran down cheeks unused to
the melting mood, eager curiosity and excitement per- .
vaded the whole congregation, and as the Pastor announced that he wanted $2,000 for the girl before him
to redeem her promise to pay for freedom, costly jewelry and trinkets and notes and specie piled in in such
rapid succession than in less time than it takes to
write this down enough and much more was con-

tributed than was necessary to meet the call that had been made.

   "After she was free the ladies of the church wrote a little book, in which a full account of her life was given. With the money that was obtained from the sale of this they bought a little place for her at Peekskill, where she raised fowls and sold eggs and butter for a living. She is living there still, but is now an old woman about fifty years of age. Sarah was known as both Sarah Scheffer and Sarah Churchman. She never married, and was never tired of talking about how good Mr. Beecher and his family had been to her.

CHAPTER XI.

These incessant and exhausting labors finally under-mined Mr. Beecher's strength, and his voice began to fail. It was decided that he should go abroad for temporary rest. His health once before had been broken. This was in March, 1849, when he was severely ill and unable to preach between March and September, and in the following June, under a leave of absence, he went abroad. Another leave of absence was granted in 1856, but this was not on account of ill health. Eminent clergymen and others had requested it " in order that he might traverse the country in behalf of the cause of liberty, then felt to be in peril." On going abroad a second time, in June, 1863, he had no idea that he was going in behalf of the cause of liberty, and the many entreaties that were made on his arrival for him to speak in England were uniformly declined. He remained in that country but a short time, going thence to Wales, to Paris, Switzerland, Northern Italy, and Germany. He received in Paris the news that Vicksburg had fallen and that the Union Army had won at Gettysburg. Returning to England

9   129

he was again asked to speak. He again declined, and on the same ground as before, that this was a quarrel which the Americans must fight out, and which could not be talked out. Requests were, however, still pressed upon him, and he was at last made to see that he owed a duty to that small but devoted party which had been holding up the Northern cause in England against heavy odds. A series of engagements was accordingly formed for him to speak in the chief cities of England and Scotland. It was very easy to arrange. The task was for the speaker.

In order to fully comprehend the magnitude of the work on which Mr. Beecher had entered, it is necessary to recall the state of feeling in England at that time. Oliver Wendell Holmes wrote after Mr. Beecher's return: "The Devil had got the start of the clergyman, as he very often does after all. The wretches who have been for three years pouring their leprous distilment into the ears of Great Britain had preoccupied the ground and were determined to silence the minister if they could. For this purpose they looked to the heathen populace of the nominally Christian British cities. They covered the walls with blood-red placards, they stimulated the mob by inflammatory appeals, they filled the air with threats of riot and murder. It was in the midst of scenes like these that the single solitary American opened his lips to speak in behalf of his country."

Stirred by long nursed hatred of the man and his principles, the Southern agents, aided by their English friends and blockade runners, organized gangs of roughs to attend and, if possible, to break up the meetings. Howling mobs crowded into Mr. Beecher's meetings, fighting and picking pockets by way of relaxation, and sought in a fury of blind and unreasoning rage to drive the preacher from the platform.

Fortunately, Beecher had entirely recovered his health. He was in prime condition. He knew his subject and his whole heart was in the work.

His opening address was made in Free Trade Hall, at Manchester, to an audience of 6,000 persons.

The largest hall was engaged. The largest hall was packed. When the orator appeared at once there rose so wild a yell, such a storm of hisses and such an outburst of opprobrium that braver men would have been justified in declining to face them.

Not so Beecher.

He advanced to the front of the platform and benignantly smiled. He was the embodiment of good nature — fat, round and jolly. His bump of humor was erect and took in the situation. Of physical danger — and there was plenty of it — he had no fear. All he wanted was silence and attention.

Notwithstanding the roar and fury which was raised in order to prevent his being heard, he bravely pushed ahead and completed his address. On the following day the London Times published the whole of it, along with a column of severe criticism. Four days later he spoke in the City Hall, at Glasgow, and the next day at Edinburgh. At Liverpool he had a great struggle with a noisy throng that filled the public hall. It was at Liverpool that Clarkson was mobbed and nearly drowned after being thrown off a wharf, and it was little that Mr. Beecher could expect from its brutal population. Printed reports of his speech contained many parentheses describing wild uproars, hootings, cat calls, clamorous denials, and other interruptions, but in spite of all the tumult Mr. Beecher told the men of Liverpool all that he had to say. He afterward said of this experience: "I had to speak extempore on subjects the most delicate and difficult as between our two nations, where even the shading of my words was of importance, and yet I had to outscream a mob and drown the roar of a multitude. It was like driving a team of runaway horses and making love to a lady at the same time." Mr. Beecher, we are assured by his sister Mrs. Stowe, has always felt this pleading for the cause of his country at the bar of the civilized world to be the greatest effort and severest labor of his life.

HENRY WARD BEECHER AT 25.

See page 50.

October 13, Mr. Beecher was invited to a temperance meeting in Glasgow, which assumed a political character. His speech was almost conversational in character, and appears to have been entirely unpremeditated. The quietest meeting that he addressed was in the Free Church Assembly Hall at Edinburgh on the next day, October 14. But the mobs of Liverpool were in waiting for him, and his address in that city was the stormiest struggle that he passed through. By dint of cheerful perseverance, fearlessness, and a powerful voice Mr. Beecher said his say. " I stood in Liverpool," he wrote in a letter, "and looked on the demoniac scene without a thought that it was I who was present. It seemed rather like a storm raging in the trees of the forests, that roared and impeded my progress, but yet had matters personal or willful in it against me. You know how, when we are lifted by the inspiration of a great subject, and by a most visible presence and vivid sympathy with Christ, the mind forgets the sediments and dregs of trouble and sails serenely in an upper realm of peace as untouched by the noise below as is a bird that flies across a battlefield. O, my friend, I have felt an inexpressible wonder that God should give it to me to do something for the dear land. When sometimes the idea of being clothed with the power to stand up in this great kingdom against an inconceivable violence of prejudice and mistake and clear the name of my dishonored country, and let her brow shine forth, crowned with liberty, glowing with love to man, O, I have seemed unable to live, almost. It almost took my breath away! I have not in a single instance gone to the speaking halls without all the way breathing to God unutterable desires for inspiration, guidance, and success; and I have had no disturbance of personality. I have been willing, yea, with eagerness, to be myself contemptible in man's sight if only my disgrace might be to the honor of that cause which is intrusted to our own thrice dear country."

Speaking of these times, an Englishman writes: It was my privilege to hear him when he addressed an audience of Englishmen in Exeter Hall, London, on the then all-absorbing topic of the "American War." Never shall I forget the scene. The masses of the English people had already taken sides in favor of the Southern Confederacy, and only a few, such, for instance, as the Rev. Newman Hall, the Hon and Rev. Baptist Wriothsley Noel, and a few other nonconformist clergymen of the same stamp, had the courage to defend the North, and this at the hazard of mob violence, when Mr. Beecher suddenly appeared, and, fighting his way from Manchester to London, dared to face the howling and vicious mobs who assailed him, and by his indomitable courage succeeded in gaining at least a respectful hearing, which, at Exeter Hall, culminated in a grand triumph on behalf of liberty and justice. On that occasion his grand eloquence carried his audience until burst after burst of deafening cheers greeted his every period, and the scene at the close of his address can never be fully realized, except by those who were eye witnesses of this grand event.

Tuesday, Oct. 20, Mr. Beecher's series of addresses culminated in his last and greatest effort at Exeter Hall, London. Mr. Beecher had won the sympathy of his hearers at last. He wrote home the next day: "Even an American would be impressed by the enthusiasm of so much of England as the people of last night represented for the North. It was more than willing, than hearty, than even eager; it was almost wild and fanatical. I was like to have been killed with people pressing to shake my hand; men, women, and children crowded up the platform. I was shaken, pinched, squeezed, in every way an affectionate enthusiasm could devise, until the police actually came to my rescue and dragged me down to the retiring-room, where gentlemen brought their wives, daughters, sons, and selves for a God bless you! England will be enthusiastically right provided we hold on and gain victories. But England has an intense and yearning sense of the value of success."

One passage in this last speech should be remembered: "Standing by my cradle, standing by my hearth, standing by the altar of the church, standing by all the places that mark the name and memory of heroic men, who poured their blood and lives for principle, I declare that in ten or twenty years of war we will sacrifice everything we have for principle. If the love of popular liberty is dead in Great Britain you will not understand us, but if the love of liberty lives as it once lived and has worthy successors of those renowned men that were our ancestors as much as yours, and whose example and principles we inherit to make fruitful as so much seed-corn in a new and fertile land, then you will understand our firm, invincible determination — deep as the sea, firm as the mountains, but calm as the heavens above us—to fight this war through at all hazards and at every cost." The splendor of these words swept even the phlegmatic Englishmen off their feet. The enthusiasm of an audience spell-bound by oratory can not, of course, be taken as a fair example of the result of Mr. Beecher's work in England, but, in this moral embassy, preaching the great universal truths of humanity, he certainly influenced greatly the English middle classes and affected somewhat the tone of public thought.

To him alone should be attributed the credit

of having turned the tide of English opinion, and
of having succeeded in laying the foundation of
that better judgment which prevented the government
of that day from officially recognizing the Confederacy
as an accomplished fact. As a theologian, Mr.
Beecher can hardly be classed as belonging to any
known school, but as the representative of that higher
and nobler range of religious thought which soars
above, and breaks through the narrow limits of all
theological systems. Creed he had none, but he possessed that which is better than creeds, a love for his
fellow men, which made him the friend of all. To him
his pulpit was the platform from which he delighted
to scatter broadcast the truths which were dear to his
heart, irrespective of denominational formulas or colle-
giate restrictions. With an instinctive love for the
human race, he delighted to so deal with religious
truths that his utterances might help upward and
onward the thousands who flocked to hang upon his
lips and listen to his peerless discourses. Throughout
the length and breadth of this land, thousands to-day
are thankful at the remembrance of the fact that it
was their privilege at some time or other to sit at his
feet, and in the revelations of the great beyond he has
doubtless already met many who recognize in him the
honored one whose privilege it was to lead them out of
darkness into light.

As a citizen of the United States, he was a thoroughly loyal and devoted son, believing most profoundly in the Republican form of government, and ready to trust an educated and enlightened democracy to the fullest extent. But although preferring his own above every other land, and its form of government above every other, he had no unkind words for constitutional monarchies, and no grander sentences have ever been uttered by living man in praise of the stability and permanence of British institutions than by Henry Ward Beecher. Long before the war, and before his visit to England in 1863, when he could have no possible object to serve, he spoke as follows:

" Which is the strongest throne on the globe to-day? Why, the English unquestionably. Partly because a noble, virtuous, illustrious woman sits upon it. An everlasting answer to those who say that a woman ought not to speak and vote is the fact that the proudest sovereign in the world to-day is Queen Victoria. She dignifies womanhood and motherhood, and she is fit to sit in Empire. That is one reason why the English throne is the strongest, but that is not the only reason, it is the strongest also because it is so many-legged. It stands on thirty million people. It represents the interests of the masses of its subjects. Another cause why England is the strongest nation is, because it is the most Christian nation —

because it has the most moral power. It has more than we have. We like to talk about ourselves on the 4th of July; but we are not to be compared to-day with Old England. I know her sturdy faults; I know her stubborn conceit. I know how many things are mischievous among her poor, common people, among her operatives of the factory, and among her common serfs of the mine; but taking her up one side and down the other, there is not another nation that represents so much Christianity as Old England. If you do not like to hear it, I like to say it, that the strongest power on the globe to-day is that kingdom. It is the strongest kingdom, and the one that is least liable to be shaken down. England should have been destroyed every ten or fifteen years, from the time of the Armada to the present day, in the prophecy of men. * * * And yet she has stood, as she now stands, mistress of the sea, and the strongest power on the earth, because she has represented moral elements."

Speaking afterwards in the Free Trade Hall in Manchester, he said: "There is not reigning on the globe a sovereign who commands our simple, unpretentious and unaffected respect, as your own beloved Queen in America." For continental despots he had no respect, regarding them as the enemies of all true progress, but for Britain's Queen, he had nothing but lavish praise. On every fitting opportunity he held her up as a pattern for imitation in all that gives glory to Christian womanhood!

Speaking of this fight of the great preacher, single-handed, against the British public, the Rev. Dr. Peter MacLeod, of Glasgow, said: "The British people began to see the case more clearly; the press became more subdued as it prepared to wheel round, and the Alabama and blockade runner building on the Mersey and the Clyde were suddenly stopped by the government by orders from Whitehall. Had Mr. Beecher only come two years sooner, there would have been little sympathy in Britain for the slave-holding South."

Theodore Parker once spoke of Beecher as the "preacher of the Plymouth pulpit whose sounding-board was the Rocky Mountains."

At another time he said: "He is eternally young, and positively wears me out with his redundant, super-abundant, ever-recovering and ever-renewing energy."

Mr. Beecher returned from England in the winter of 1863-4. He came so quietly that he had reached his own house in Brooklyn before the facts of his arrival became generally known. A few days later a great mass meeting was held in the Brooklyn Academy of Music, and when Mr. Beecher rose to speak, he was, as Harper's Magazine said, "next to Abraham Lincoln, the most honored man in the country." He told his audience that it was aristocratic, commercial, and voting England that was against us, and declared that non-voting England was our friend. Mr. Beecher was much exhausted by his English labors. All the strength he had acquired by his rest abroad was poured out in the battle he waged with English preiudice on the eve of his departure.

CHAPTER XII.

When he returned to America the close of the war was near at hand, and then, with the penetration which characterized him, he perceived the need of a different message. Now it was not opposition to the South that he labored to arouse, but peace, forgiveness, and magnanimity. It mattered nothing to him that such teaching might be unwelcome.

Immediately after the surrender of Richmond he expressed in strong terms his desire for a complete reunion of the people of the North and South and his opposition to any scheme of punishment other than the mere abolition of slavery, which he really did not look upon at all as a punishment, but as a benefit alike to master and slave. A majority of his people had become so excited at the events of the war as to receive this advice with disfavor, and, upon the assassination of Abraham Lincoln, which happened while Beecher was at Fort Sumter, and therefore could know nothing about it, the feeling on the part of his friends became quite intense—was especially so among those who had not been known as abolitionists before the war. Many

144

of them informed him on his return that they would
not consent to his advocating a general amnesty as he
had intimated his intention of doing. This was the
first time that any of his friends had thought him too
conservative. It made but little difference to him.
He persisted in opposing the execution of Jefferson
Davis, the confiscation of rebel property, and every
other form of punishment. For more than a year this
difference of opinion between him and a majority of
the church continued, producing the only instance of
what might be called alienation between them ever
known in the history of the church.

He spoke the message that was in him, whether
men would hear or whether they would forbear. Men
listened, and Beecher's popularity grew with marvelous
rapidity. The streets of Brooklyn leading from the
ferries were busy with processions of men from New
York looking for "Beecher." The policemen never
waited for a stranger to conclude his question, but invariably interrupted him with, "Follow the crowd."

An interesting incident occurred at the Academy of
Music in Brooklyn on the occasion of the celebration
by the negroes, of the passage of the XVth amendment.
The vast building was packed with whites and negroes
in about equal numbers. Mr. Beecher was called
upon to introduce Senator Revel to the audience, and
as, at the conclusion of his remarks, he grasped the

latter by the hand, saying, "As the representative of
one race I extend to you, the representative of another,
the right hand of fellowship," the great audience rose
in a perfect frenzy of enthusiasm.

With the fall of slavery Mr. Beecher's activity in
regard to public questions did not cease.   He was
among those who, with William Lloyd Garrison, went
down to raise again the national flag above the ruins
of Fort Sumter.   He had many exciting experiences
in the South, one of the most touching and characteristic being a great meeting in one of the largest
chuches in South Carolina, at which he preached to a
congregation of liberated slaves.

The first time Mr. Beecher lectured in the South
was on the evening of January 31, 1865, at the Mary-
land Institute.   There was considerable objection to it
among the timid.   Chief Justice Chase, Mr. Stanton
and others sat upon the stand with him.   A telegram
was received while he was speaking announcing the
passage of the constitutional amendment abolishing
slavery.   This created what is known among men of
the world as a "high old time."

On returning home he was met by the news of Lincoln's death.   Not long afterward he preached in Plymouth Church a sermon which led to great discussion
and in which he expounded the crisis of the time as a
great and rare opportunity for the forgiveness of inju-

ries. Plymouth Church continued still to be the center from which radiated much political activity on the part of Mr. Beecher. It was his idea that a Protestant church ought to be a congregation of faithful men and women seeking to apply to human life and society the principles of Christianity. It was always distinctively a temperance and an anti-slavery society, and in this line of action it continued after the war to prosper financially and to be a source of wide moral influence. Its revenues in 1868 amounted to $50,000 a year. The debt had been entirely extinguished and the church was devoting its surplus to missionary operations in the neighborhood. A new organ had been purchased at a cost of $22,000. It was the largest church organ in the country. These were years of astounding financial prosperity. What is known as the Bethel had been organized in 1841, and came under the care of Plymouth Church in May, 1866. Mr. George A. Bell was made superintendent in the following year, and a plot of land was purchased in Hicks street for the erection in the following summer of the present edifice. The attendance at the school in 1866 had been 220. In two years it increased to 373, and several years ago the average attendance was about 600. The entire cost of the Bethel was about $75,000, of which sum $20,000 was raised by voluntary subscriptions, $6,250 by a church fair, and the remainder by the surplus from pew rents in Plymouth Church. On the Mayflower mission at the navy yard $25,000 had been expended ten years ago. Some interesting statistics of the internal work of Plymouth Church may here be given. During the thirty-five years that had elapsed in 1882 since Mr. Beecher began his work, 4,500 persons had been received into the church, or an average of 130 for each year of the whole period. The membership in 1882 was 2,491, of whom 878 were men and 1,613 were women. The audience room will contain 3,000 people, and 3,200 have been known to get within its door. Six hundred of the sittings are free, and if pewholders do not fill their pews by five minutes before the service begins it is a printed rule that the ushers may fill them with strangers. Pews are sold each year at auction, and each has a fixed rental. They are sold to persons who bid the highest premium in addition to the rental. For a period of thirty years the total receipts from pews have been $1,139,633, of which sum $554,855 were received during the ten years (1872–1882), $423,209 in the ten previous years (1862–1872), and $161,569 in the next previous ten years (1852–1862). This is a yearly average of nearly $38,000, the lowest average having been about $11,000, and the highest about $69,000. For benevolent and charitable objects about $500,000 has been collected in the church building, which sum does not include either the collections made by committees of ladies or the individual gifts to colleges, schools, and sufferers by fire, pestilence, and famine, all of which have been very large. The assistant pastor of the church, Mr. Halliday, in one of his recent yearly reports, stated that he had made 2,000 visits, had attended more than 300 religious services, nearly 150 funerals, and had married twenty-two couples. During a period of eleven years the number of his visits had exceeded 20,000, the funerals he had attended were about 1,400, and the couples he had married were about 200.

General Horatio C. King gives the following anecdote of the large organ: "It would be impossible, in a brief space, to give any adequate idea of Mr. Beecher's many-sided character as manifested in daily intercourse with him. I became connected with the church in 1865 under very happy auspices, my wife, who was then soon to be, being the daughter of Mr. Howard, the first member of the church, and probably Mr. Beecher's oldest and closest friend in the commission. It was thus I was brought into continued intercourse with him. His great fondness of music was also a special bond of sympathy with me, and with that faculty he had of winning friends to him and making them do his will cheerfully, he soon had me in harness in the musical world. The church had just before expended an unusually large sum for a new organ. While it was being put together, Mr. Beecher was as much interested as a boy with a new toy, now going around the workmen, asking questions without number, studying the mechanism, cracking jokes on all sides, and, finally, immortalizing the largest of the pipes of the thirty-two foot diapason by crawling through it. He was not so large then as in the last few years of his life, but he was big enough to fill the great tube and have a pretty hard struggle to crawl through. The pipe still bears in lead pencil an inscription of this exploit."

These were years of astounding financial prosperity, and Plymouth Church and its pastor were matters of national pride.

"After the war," writes another admirer of Mr. Beecher, "I came to Brooklyn and became a member of Plymouth Church. He speedily made me most welcome, and it was not long before he had me in harness and ready to help him in any of the work of the church. Music had always been a hobby with him, and when the great organ was put up in the church he cast about for some means to make it useful for other than mere Sunday work. So the organ concerts were instituted at his desire, and for several years, during the larger part of each year, the church was thronged every Saturday with interested listeners, and organists were secured from all parts of the country and Canada.

"In this he took great satisfaction. It was a worthy succession to his successful efforts in congregational singing, for it was through his instrumentality, backed by arduous personal effort, that the first hymn and tune book combined (the Plymouth Collection) was introduced into the churches. This was only a little over thirty years ago, and now nearly every Protestant denomination has its own particular hymn and tune book and the compiling of new ones, continually going on. It is a matter of history, by the way, that, although the sale of the Plymouth Collection has probably exceeded a hundred thousand, neither the compilers nor the church ever received a cent of income from it, but the revenue from this source, which was intended for the church, was improperly diverted into other channels.

"In this connection I may as well speak of a project which is known to very few. During the life of John Zundel, now deceased, who was organist of the church for twenty-five years, Mr. Beecher made up his mind that he wanted a new hymn book. When the old collection was made the use of certain copyrights was refused, and some of the most beautiful hymns were wedded to tunes so unsatisfactory that they were rarely if ever used. So there were many

hymns which advanced thought had left far in the
rear, and for these and other reasons the work was
undertaken. The details were intrusted to Rev.
Samuel Scoville, his son-in-law, Mr. Zundel and
myself.

" We went heartily into the work, and much earlier
than was expected, we had a dummy hymn book ready
for his examination. My residence was then on
Columbia Heights, two or three blocks below Mr.
Beecher's, so the examination was conducted at my
house, the tunes being usually played over by me,
while Mr. Beecher, as chief critic, passed upon our
work. No pleasanter duty ever fell to my lot, for at
each sitting, every hymn almost was the occasion for
some historical reminiscence full of interest, pathos,
wit and humor, as the case might be, and before we
got through we had received a pretty thorough disqui-
sition on hymnology, ancient and modern, and an endless fund of anecdote touching the inception, preparation and publication of the original volume. Thus
far all went smoothly, and we had gone even to the
extent of securing a publisher, when we ran against
an obstacle in the shape of a name for the new publication. The copyright of the Plymouth Collection had
not then expired, and Mr. Beecher declined to permit
any encroachment upon the name, even with the modi-
fication of the ' New Plymouth Hymnal,' nor would he

allow us to call it 'Beecher's Collection.' So, after drifting about for a while, the whole matter was indefinitely postponed."

To portray the ideal Henry Ward Beecher requires that he be taken as he stood before the public eye at the close of the Civil War. He was then about fifty-two years of age, perfect in health, robust, not clumsy, —his complexion like that of a vigorous young woman, his voice strong, clear, and of great compass,— a commanding voice, his body the willing and complete servant of his mind and heart, every gland and muscle responding to his changing moods. He had come of an ancestry so famous in American ecclesiastical history that he was introduced in England by one who thought to do him the greatest honor as "the son of the great Dr. Beecher, of America." In personal presence he was remarkable, chiefly by the great transformation of his countenance under the play of emotion. On the platform of Plymouth Church he was as a king upon his throne or the commander of a war ship in victorious action. His manners in private life were most ingratiating. His good fellowship put children and servants and the most distinguished, reserved and cultivated persons alike at ease, and served as a center of union for every company of which he was a part.

Did Mr. Beecher go to the theatres?

"I remember," said a friend, "when he first went to Irving Hall. A billiard match was in progress somewhere in the sixties, I should judge, about 1865. The room was fringed on three sides with amphitheatrically-arranged seats, the large central portion being reserved for the tables, the players, the judges, and the members of the press. Mr. Beecher entered the room attended by a young friend about half-past eight in the evening. He was not then known so universally as in late years, but he was tolerably well known even to the class of men there congregated, and when some fellow, half in fun and half earnest, proposed 'three cheers for Henry Ward Beecher' they were given with a will.

"The dominie took his seat near the head of the reporters' table and watched with unfeigned interest the progress of a particularly interesting and exciting contest. About ten o'clock he arose to go, and again the audience saluted his retreating form with three tremendous, hearty, manly cheers, which he acknowledged with bow and smile, and not a suggestion of an unpleasant incident occurred until, as he neared the door, that vulgar brute Isaiah Rynders confronted him in the aisle with 'Beecher, what will you have to drink?'

"'Nothing, sir,' replied Beecher, with characteristic dignity, and left the hall."

HENRY WARD BEECHER IN 1863.

In those days going to the theatre by clergymen
made much talk, and in speaking of an early lecture
delivered when he was a very young man in the West
for a particular purpose against theatres and theatrical
entertainments generally, Mr. Beecher said: "I have
no doubt I would be instructed, entertained, edified by
witnessing a good play, but it would take months of
explanation and years of weary controversy to explain
the why and the wherefore, so I say to myself it is not
worth while even to gain so much good to go through
so much more worry."

And he was entirely right.

I saw him once in Burton's Chamber Street
Theatre. Burton was a famous farceur, and he had
a great company with him. But it wasn't to see
Burton nor to see his famous company that Mr.
Beecher went to his theatre. It was on the occasion
of an initial revival meeting, where he was invited as
one of the clergymen of the vicinage, and into the pro-
cedure of which he entered with all the enthusiasm
and spirit then so eminently characteristic of him, and
which, in spite of all the glowing obituaries that are
printed here to-day, I must say were largely toned
down in the last ten years of his useful and exacting
life. When abroad he went several times to the
theatre. He went to see Rip Van Winkle as played
by Joe Jefferson, and enjoyed it heartily. He was

much sought by Henry Irving and by Ellen Terry, and he reciprocated their courteous civility by attending and enjoying their peculiar performances. He wanted to see Booth's Hamlet, but whether he went or not I can not say. He had accepted a box for Daly's Theatre Wednesday night of this week, and had invited some friends of forty years' standing to go with him. He felt a natural diffidence about going into any public audience, because he was instantly recognized wherever he went and became a target for the glasses and gossip of the occasion, as he did subsequently for the carping criticisms of the outside world.

Did this indicate lack of stamina, lack of independence?

Not at all.

And if it did, if there was any man on the face of God's footstool who could afford to meet the charge of a lack of independence, surely it was Henry Ward Beecher, the man who fifty years ago grappled the monster intemperance by the throat, who forty years ago electrified the world and put himself in the pillory of commercial and social contempt by challenging the beast of slavery to a life-long combat. O, no, it wasn't that. It was precisely what he said it was—a disinclination to gain a little good at too heavy a cost, a cost which meant mental bother and physical worriment of no small dimensions.

The dramatic profession had in him a sincere and intelligent friend. He was always ready to defend it against fanatical attacks and to pay tribute to its virtues of charity and fraternity. An English guest who recently visited Mr. Beecher found himself invited to spend the evening, not at a church conference, but at a performance of "Othello." The oration of Mr. Beecher at the Irving banquet last year was a masterpiece of criticism as well as of eloquence. When the Elks dedicated their cemetery at Long Island Mr. Beecher said that he was glad to accept the invitation to deliver the dedicatory address, and his speech was a logical demonstration of the sympathy between the stage and the church. Later, he took an active, personal interest in the dramatization of his novel "Norwood," and, in or out of the pulpit, he was never chary of his praises of deserving professionals.

11

CHAPTER XIII.

Many anecdotes of these years are told of the great Brooklyn divine.

One of Mr. Beecher's hobbies was jewelry. He never wore jewelry, but he had a great taste for it, and had more than one cabinet full of unique and curious gems and pieces of jewelry. At one time he had a habit of carrying loose diamonds and other precious stones in his vest pocket, wrapped up in the tissue paper in which dealers usually carry them. Mr. Beecher had excellent taste also in the selection of engravings, of which he was quite as fond as he was of jewelry. He had his house at Peekskill papered with old and rare engravings; even the walls of the halls and the backs of the doors were covered with them. Mr. McKelway thought that the collection of old engravings was probably the finest in the country, and that it would bring $20,000 at a sale. He valued Beecher's gems at $15,000.

" Once," said a well known sporting man, " I thought, like most people who have a penchant for gems, that opals were unlucky. Henry Ward Beecher con-

verted me out of that superstition. I was in Washington at the time, flat broke, and scarce knew which
way to turn for a dollar. A friend invited me to go
and hear the great preacher deliver a lecture. Under
ordinary circumstances I suppose I should have refused the invitation, since I was never much of a hand
at sitting still and being talked at, but I went, and my
attendance that evening proved the turning point of
my ill luck. Mr. Beecher was in one of his happiest
moods. He alluded to his fondness of jewelry and
precious stones, and said that, although he rarely wore
them, he never traveled without some rich and rare
gems in his pockets. 'They exercise a soothing influence over my mind when it is troubled,' continued the
great divine; 'they bring joy and inspiration to my
heart. I remember once when traveling in Germany
of being gloomy and distressed to an unusual degree.
I thought I had not a friend in the world. The future
seemed dark, dreary and dismal, and do what I would
I could not dissipate the gloom which overshadowed
my heart. Unconsciously my hands went deep into
my trousers' pockets, where I had some very fine opals.
I at once felt a pleasant sensation flash across me. I
drew forth the opals, placed them on the table and
looked at them contemplatively. In a moment my
dejection vanished, the blues were dispelled and I was
happy and contented as a lark. Do not ask me to

explain this mysterious influence. All I know is that precious stones of all kinds wield a potent influence over my moods and temper, and that opals, perhaps beyond any other gems, bring comfort and solace to my soul.' This incident made a great impression on me. The day after the lecture I came unexpectedly into the possession of a respectable sum of money, and my first act was to buy this opal, which I have worn ever since. I can not say that I feel any magic influence from it such as Mr. Beecher described, but one thing is certain, that I have never known a day's real bad luck since I started to wear it."

Henry Ward Beecher earned several fortunes during his lifetime, but did not keep any of them. He spent his princely income generously in trying to make himself and others happy, and he came as near realizing the fulfillment of this desire as it is possible for human weakness to do. Out of his own purse he paid for two years the entire interest on the mortgage under which struggled the Park Congregational Church, at Sixth avenue and Seventh street, Brooklyn. The members of that church having thus been enabled to start in on raising money to clear the debt of $17,000, raised $11,000 and could do no more. Mr. Beecher submitted the case to his Trustees and said if they didn't pay the remaining $6,000 he would do it himself. They agreed to do it, and he contributed generously for that purpose, thus clearing off the debt.

He was forever aiding his friends, lending them money, indorsing their notes, getting them out of troubles, and bearing their burdens. He was indiscretion itself in the management of his pecuniary affairs, and, although he was comically "careful at the spigot, he was largely lavish at the bung." In fact, Mr. Beecher seemed to have no idea of the value of money except what he could get for it. He once said in his pulpit that if he had $100 in bills he could not count it and make it come out twice alike. When he saw anything he wanted, whether it was a picture, a precious stone, a book, or a piece of bric-a-brac, and he had the money, he bought it. Then, if any one took a fancy to it, he would give it away. No one ever knew how much money he gave away in private benefactions, and many persons miss his unobtrusive charity. One of his acts was to send two barrowsful of books from his library to the church as the nucleus of a collection for the benefit of the Western branch of the Soldiers' Home at Leavenworth, Kansas. He would never have saved anything if it had not been for his wife, who looked after his affairs. When in Brooklyn since the house in Columbia Heights was sold they boarded with their eldest son. The summers they spent at Peekskill. Mr. Beecher used to say that his farm there cost him more than it paid, and one summer he told some visitors that the potatoes they ate cost him a dollar apiece to grow.

Writing to a friend Mrs. Beecher alludes to the " two or three bushels of letters " that had accumulated during Mr. Beecher's vacation, and exclaims:

" O, that the whole world could know that we are poor, poor—poor in everything but the ability to grieve for woes we have not the power to aid. From the letters I have classed as genuine I find that the sums so pitifully pleaded for aggregate over $30,000."

Referring to this subject in another letter, she says:

" What can I do but half break my heart over sorrows that my dear husband could not alleviate were they known to him. It would make him ill to read the letters. This suffering I can spare him."

Mr. Beecher was wonderfully fond of children, and he always carried oranges and candies in his pockets to help entertain them on the cars. If he saw a poor mother with a baby crying in her arms he would go and comfort it and make it stop its crying where others failed. In coming up from Washington one time a characteristic incident occurred. There were two little children, boy and girl, eight or nine years old in the car, and they huddled close up together and appeared to be very fond of each other. He had breakfast at Wilmington, but the children did not get off the car, and they had evidently traveled all night without anything to eat. When Mr. Beecher came back from breakfast his arms were laden with good things for the children. Then he talked to them. He found that they were from the South, that their parents had died, and that they were on their way to this city to find an uncle whom they expected to meet them. The train was late; what if the uncle should fail to meet them? When the train arrived in Jersey City Mr. Beecher got out of the car with the children, walked slowly along, looking around to see if he could discover any one looking for the children, and got out between the two ferries and stood there waiting until both boats had gone. Soon a man came hurrying along in great distress and saw the two children, but as he expected to find them unaccompanied, he stopped in doubt. Mr. Beecher suspected that he might be the uncle and asked him what he was looking for.

"Two children."

"Well," said Mr. Beecher, "I guess they're here. These look like two children, don't they?"

It was the uncle, and he was indeed grateful. Thanking Mr. Beecher, he said:

"Will you kindly give me your name?"

"My name is Beecher."

"Where do you live?"

"In Brooklyn."

"What! Can you be the Rev. Henry Ward Beecher?"

"I am inclined to think I am."

Tears came into the man's eyes, and he explained to the little ones who it was who had befriended them. The two children soon after were seen in Plymouth Church, and they have since then listened to Mr. Beecher's sermons frequently.

Major Pond's attention was called to the statement which had been published, and which has been received with general credence, that Mr. Beecher never wore a silk hat. Mr. Beecher's manager smiled and then quickly exclaimed: "Only once. I must tell you about that. I was at Mr. Beecher's house one afternoon, and we were to leave the house at 4 o'clock in order to catch a train. Mr. Beecher, according to his custom of an afternoon, had laid down for a nap. I was in the library, when, as the hour approached, Mrs. Beecher called my attention to the fact and asked where Mr. Beecher was. I went up to call him, but he was not in his room. I went down stairs and thought I would get my hat, which was a silk one. I could not find it where I had left it, in the hallway. Just then Mrs. Beecher called my attention to the front of the house. Mr. Beecher had a cardigan jacket, which he used to wear around the house at times, and you can imagine that it was not particularly

PLYMOUTH LECTURE ROOM.—TWENTY-FIFTH ANNIVERSARY.

becoming to his form. I went to where Mrs. Beecher
stood and looked out. There in the middle of the
street, with a lot of children around him, was Mr.
Beecher in his cardigan, my silk hat on his head, and
a stick in his mouth, with strings attached, as children
make bits. and he was prancing up and down and back
and forth, and playing horse with the youngsters.
You would have died a laughing seeing that sight.

" 'Henry,' exclaimed Mrs. Beecher, 'what on earth
are you doing? Do you know what a sight you are?
You will lose the train.'

"Mr. Beecher stopped, drew out his watch—he
always carried a first-class timekeeper—and, replying,
as he put it back.

" 'No, I won't; I've got two minutes yet,' off he
galloped, with the children at his heels in high
glee. He used up the two minutes, and we just
caught the ferryboat in time. Many a time have we
barely caught the last boat; but Mr. Beecher's watch
was as true as steel, and he always calculated apparently to the second. When he got on the ferryboat he
never stopped until he landed in the pilot house. He
had the key to them, and every pilot knew him, and
there he would go and stay until the boat had got to
her landing."

There were few sharper men at *repartee* than Mr.
Beecher. There were few livelier places than Plymouth

Lecture Room on Friday nights. Mr. Beecher treated his people as he did his family. He sat in his chair as cozily as he did at his fireside, and said any racy, jolly thing that came into his mind. When any one bored him with a long speech, he brought them up with a round turn. If they retorted, he brought the laugh upon them, and they sat down covered with confusion. Very few Plymouth people tried a retort with their pastor.

A very venerable and solemn deacon was one night pronouncing a funeral oration over the past members of the church.

"I was recalling," he said (and this was uttered in a very whining and solemn tone), "the large number of people who used to take part in this meeting, who are now dead. I have the names of thirty or forty at home, written in a hymn book, I think, Mr. Beecher, by yourself." Mr. Beecher sprang up, and said: "There! I missed that hymn book, but I did not think, Deacon ——, you had stolen it. Won't you send it back?"

A general laugh ran around the room, and the deacon suddenly terminated his funeral oration.

One Friday night, while the congregation were singing a beautiful hymn, in which Mr. Beecher was joining heartily, the assistant minister came up, arrested the pastor's attention by pulling his pants, and handed him a note.

At the close of the hymn Mr. Beecher rebuked the irreverence that grew out of a defective education, which did not regard singing as a part of devotion, which took the time of song for opening and shutting windows, rushing round and doing chores generally.

Even ministers would use that time to scribble their notes, look over their sermons, or call up the sexton and send him around the church on errands.

He then read very impressively two verses of the hymn they were singing when he was interrupted, to show that it was really a prayer.

"Had I been making a prayer, and Brother —— had come and twitched my pants and handed me a note, the whole congregation would have been shocked."

To ward off the blow, Brother —— said, "Mr. Beecher, I hadn't any hymn book."

"And you hadn't any prayer book," was the quick retort, which the people relished keenly.

Mr. Beecher kept a reporter in his church. The form of Mr. Ellenwood was as well known as that of the Plymouth pastor. He sat for years at a little table in front of the platform, and took down everything that Mr. Beecher said—his notices, prayers and sermons. These Mr. Beecher revised before they were published. Sharp, racy, humorous utterances, keen remarks, sentences thrown off in the heat of speaking, witticisms that shook the Plymouth audiences as the forest leaves are shaken by the winds, were often missed in the public report.

Many of the illustrations lost much of their point, because no reporter could take down the manner of their utterance.

His familiar illustrations were drawn from his own family, and these were constant.

One Sunday morning he brought his stepmother on to the platform by describing her as a woman of great excellence, but as a great martinet, strict in her religious practices and teachings, and, like the mistress of Dotheboys Hall, she gave her children weekly a stiff dose of the catechism. She was the pink of propriety, and held in abhorrence all vain and trifling amusements.

Dr. Beecher had a weakness—that of playing on a fiddle. He mixed up "Yankee Doodle," a round country dance, and "Old Hundred," and he did not exactly know where the one began and the other ended.

One day he was amusing himself on his favorite instrument, and struck up a genuine jig, which, unsanctified, had been running in his head ever since he was a boy.

Just at that moment the mother came in, and, catching the inspiration of the tune, placed her hands on her hips and actually danced a minuet.

Mr. Beecher described the scene. He stepped back on the platform, placed his hands on his hips, and showed the audience how his mother did it. He described the consternation of the children. He clasped his hands, rolled up the whites of his eyes like a regular maw-worm, opened his mouth, drew down his lips, and stood the personification of rustic horror.

The whole scene was irresistibly comic. He wound up with the moral that, if his mother had danced more and plied the catechism less. he would have had a happier childhood.

On one occasion a stranger, upon meeting Mr. Beecher, and doubtless feeling awe-struck in having spoken to a man who seemed to know so much about the hereafter, said: " Mr. Beecher. do you really know our Lord? "

" Well," Mr. Beecher replied with twinkling eyes, " I have had occasion to speak favorably of him from my pulpit."

" Mr. Beecher was preaching one day about the mercies of God toward all penitent men, when suddenly there was heard the chink chink of falling glass and the patter of a stone that had been thrown through the window. Mr. Beecher was interrupted in his preaching at the words, 'Let the mercies of God come to all good men '—and, as he heard the noise of the shattered glass, he added, 'and to miscreants, too.'"

According to Mr. Edward R. Ovington, of Brooklyn, Mr. Beecher was a great admirer of beauty in bric-a-brac, although he never leaned toward marble or bronze statuary.

"I don't know why it was," said Mr. Ovington, "but Mr. Beecher would never look at a statue. I reckon it was too cold. He loved pictures and vases and articles of the smaller decorative style. He would come into my store nearly every day and take in a stock at a glance. There was no use trying to persuade him that a thing was lovely. He would know at once whether he liked it or not. And everybody loved him. He would sit for ten and fifteen minutes at a time and talk with the salesman. A dozen other ministers might have come in and not have been noticed. He would never allow a purchase to be wrapped in paper, and would carry home whatever he bought under his arm. Sometimes he would go home with some big, bulky thing that he could hardly carry."

"Being a somewhat elderly man, I became a little prominent in the Bethel Sunday school," said Professor Brainerd Kellogg, of the Polytechnic, "and it got to

Mr. Beecher's ears, that I was a little too radical. Mr. Beecher came to me and said:

"Kellogg, don't pull off more shingles than you can replace."

Mr. Beecher was not particularly happy in addressing Sunday schools, and I believe the reason of that to be that he felt the necessity of brevity, and preparation with him demanded foundation, division and subdivision. He believed in the root and the trunk and the twig before he got to the leaf. The root might be recondite, the trunk short and sturdy, the branch thin and brittle, the twig a simple film, but the leaves were for the healing of the nations. He absolutely blossomed with illustrations. He thought in figures. He reasoned in pictures. Why, I remember distinctly, at one time, having reported him; he made use of the term, "And in his hand a diamond sceptre." Laughingly I corrected him and said: "Of course there is no such thing as a diamond sceptre, Mr. Beecher." "What," said he, "I guess I know what I saw." No better illustration than that could be asked of his habit of thought.

12

CHAPTER XIV.

DISTRESSING EPISODE.

It was wnen his fame and influence were at their zenith, and at the very height of the usefulness of his church, that the most distressing episode in Mr. Beecher's life, both for him and his friends, occurred. At a time when men of character, intelligence, and piety hung upon his words, when the most cultured classes of the country accepted him as their guide, when the first place as a preacher and an orator was accorded to him on all hands, and when his writings were eagerly read from one end of the land to the other, a formidable assault was made upon his reputation. At first, vague hints were circulated reflecting upon him, then a direct charge appeared in print, but not in a quarter to which the people looked for reliable information. Finally, in an action at law, brought by Theodore Tilton against Mr. Beecher, with a claim for $100,000 damages, the whole case was disclosed, and for six months the malice of scoffers at Christianity was gratified by the details of the terrible accusation against the pastor of Plymouth Church. Three times did Mr. Beecher meet his accusers, and three times the charge was investigated. First it was heard by a committee of the church, appointed at Mr. Beecher's request, and the committee pronounced the pastor innocent.

Afterward it was tried in court, when the jury disagreed, and thirdly by a council of Congregational ministers.

Undoubtedly this clouded experience of his life was a cause of reproach not only to Mr. Beecher but to religion. That it would be so if it was made public, whatever the issue might be, Mr. Beecher and his friends had forseen from the first, and unhappily, in attempting to prevent its coming to trial, they actually prejudiced the case, and their efforts to keep it from the public were regarded as an admission of guilt. It was a noteworthy fact that Theodore Tilton, who brought the charge, was a protege of Mr. Beecher's, a man possessing undoubted talent, a sphere for the exercise of which had been provided by Mr. Beecher.

Its most disastrous effect was upon Mr. Beecher himself. It aged him, and, to some extent, it broke his spirit. His sensitive nature was not proof against the feeling that some suspected him.

The fidelity of Plymouth Church to its pastor during this fierce ordeal, the love and sympathy of his wife, and the unfaltering allegiance of a host of friends in this country and in Europe encouraged and supported him to continue his pastorate and public work.   His gospel cheered and instructed, it built up and made strong; and whatever were his mistakes, whatever his possible errors, the charity he had sent abroad returned upon him to comfort him, and the tolerance he had shown was in turn shown unto him. He passed through trial and came forth purified for better service than before.   He learned in personal anguish how to enlarge compassion, and, conscious of frailties in himself, he extended a vast pity to the infirmities of others.

Dr. Armitage, one of Mr. Beecher's life long friends, asked him shortly after the trial: "Beecher, how have you managed to live through it?"   His eyes filled with tears, and, with half-choked utterance, he said, "Armitage, I could not have lived through it if the Lord had not strengthened the back for the burden.   Sometimes I thought I must sink, but I said, 'Lord, here is my heart; whatever others may say, I know I am thine.'"

The great friendship that has always existed between Mr. Beecher and the Rev. Dr. Charles N. Hall, of Holy Trinity, has been a favorite theme of discussion among Brooklyn pastors, and the following incident shows the depth of that feeling: During the trial a celebration of some kind was being held in Dr. Hall's church.   To the surprise of the strict Episco-

BETHEL SUNDAY SCHOOL.

palians, Mr. Beecher attended, and to their horror was admitted behind the chancel rail. This provoked an expression of indignation from some of the members, who carried their grievances to Dr. Hall. That gentleman drew himself up to his full height and inquired, "What have you to say about it? Mr. Beecher is not convicted; he is only on trial; and I reserve the right to extend the right hand of fellowship to any man who needs it or deserves it. He is my friend, and what kind of a man is he who will not in time of trouble help his friend? What have you to say against it?"

"But the Bishop; what will he say?" asked the indignant members.

Dr. Hall's face grew blacker than ever. "The Bishop," he said; "what business is it of his? What right has the Bishop to interfere with my private affairs?"

Mr. Beecher remained, and the only comment of the indignant members was, "Well, Dr. Hall is the only man who could do that, and Mr. Beecher is the only one who could make him do it."

The country has not forgotten, and never can forget, how like a heroine Mrs. Beecher behaved during her husband's supreme trouble. Throughout the whole prolonged and humiliating trial, everybody knew she was constantly present in the court room, attentive but undismayed, pained to the last point of endurance, but still erect, steadfast and confident. It was not merely her husband's reputation, we must remember, but her own honor as well, and the highest interests of her children, living and dead, that were threatened with disaster. The tales to which she had to listen were of a kind which few women could have heard and yet stood firm and self-reliant, as she did—a picture of a wife and mother at her best, of womanhood at its proudest and noblest. If she had wavered for an instant, the scales might have turned to the swift and absolute ruin of the man for whom her remarkable devotion pleaded with such persistent and pathetic emphasis. Though she said never a word, she was Mr. Beecher's most valuable witness. He might, perhaps, have survived the terrible ordeal if she had been absent; but certainly the task would have been a much harder one, and there is reason to believe that he was himself convinced that the aid she rendered him was exceedingly fortunate, if not indispensable.

It is our custom, in these days of much dwelling upon the practical side of things, to speak lightly of the sentiment of love as the ruling force of a life; but every now and then we are brought face to face with a woman like Mrs. Beecher, whose fidelity to her husband shames our flippancy and compels us to recognize the fact that there is such a virtue as complete

devotion for devotion's sake, regardless of all hin-
drances. That there are many such women in the
world, we are bound to believe; and they contribute
far more to the success of the men whose fortunes
engage their thoughts and efforts than we are apt to
acknowledge or understand. They do not advertise
their faithfulness or ask to be commended or rewarded
for their ceaseless care, courage and fortitude. It is
enough for them to know that the objects of their
affection are enabled, by their help, to overcome the
obstacles which fate puts in their way, and to achieve
a degree of prosperity which vindicates their ability
and satisfies their ambition. For themselves they
claim nothing. It is in others that they seek and find
triumph and happiness. To do their utmost for those
whom they love and trust is their philosophy of existence; and they live their lives with a royal and beautiful perseverance which, as in the case of Mrs.
Beecher, deserves the highest praise that language
can be made to express.

In letters written in 1882, Mrs. Beecher speaks of the
trying times growing out of this trouble, their own
poverty, and Mr. Beecher's arduous duties. These
letters prove her sublime self-abnegation.

On Feb. 8, 1881, she wrote:

"You should see the immense pile of unopened letters before me, the punishment for a two days' absence

from the city. Nearly nine-tenths are addressed to Mr. Beecher, but he never reads letters unless there is some matter that he alone can decide. Such is not often the case. Thousands come to us that he never sees. Consequently they do not trouble his brain or, what would be more serious, grieve his tender heart. All correspondence is left to me, one of the cheerfully-accepted but onerous duties of being the wife of such a man."

June 7, 1882, she wrote:

"The pitiless blackmail persecution to which my husband was subjected a few years ago turned our heads white before our time, and nearly broken my heart at least. That trial cost us $160,000. We were not worth $60,000. The impression seems to be general that he is a wealthy man. He never was, but when comfortably well off his overflowing generosity enabled him to lay by nothing of any amount. Sometimes, now, if I do not discreetly purloin the contents of his too liberal pockets, the household expense would remain unpaid. He can not help returning moneyless because of the tales of woe that seem to lie in wait for him upon every street. Since that terrible trial he has worked incessantly to the detriment of his health, preaching, lecturing, writing, hoping to lift the heavy mortgage from our home here (Columbia Heights, Brooklyn), but it had to be sold in the spring."

In a letter written in December, 1882, she speaks once more of that "infamous blackmail scheme," and adds: "I am confident that history will refer to it as the most cruel and conscienceless of this or any other century."

With quaint humor, which was always characteristic of the man, he compared the unceasing efforts of his friends on his behalf as "the humane attempt of good men *to drag an ass out of a pit.*"

CHAPTER XV.

Mr. Beecher had passed through the ordeal of his life, and thereafter for twelve years he has been watched as no man before or since has been held up to public gaze. At first his public appearances were limited to his own pulpit, and he seemed to seek relief in activity, physical and mental. He went on a long tour through the South, speaking at many points, and generally acting as a bearer of peace tokens from the North and an observer of the progress of the South.

Though the authenticity of the following story has been questioned, we will venture to give it. If true, it is one of the most dramatic events in the oratorical career of Mr. Beecher. While in Richmond, the announcement that he was to lecture at Mozart Hall on " The North and the South " filled the old building. It was his first appearance in Richmond since the war, and he was rather doubtful about the kind of reception he would get. When he walked out on the stage he saw before him a distinguished audience of Southerners, including several of the leading generals on the losing side. In the fourth row of the orchestra sat

General Fitzhugh Lee and, just behind him, General Rosser, while near by were ex-Governor " Extra Billy " Smith and Governor Cameron. No applause greeted the great preacher as he stepped before the footlights. The ladies levelled their opera glasses at him with cold curiosity and the men looked coolly expectant. Some hisses from a few rowdies in the gallery did not tend to dispel the chilliness of the reception.

Mr. Beecher surveyed the audience calmly for a moment and then stepping directly in front of General Lee he said, " I have seen pictures of General Fitzhugh Lee, and I judge that you are the man; am I right?"

The general, slightly taken aback by this direct address, nodded stiffly, while the audience bent forward breathless with curiosity as to what was going to follow.

" Then," said Mr. Beecher, his face lighting up, " I want to offer you this right hand, which, in its own way, fought against you and yours twenty-five years ago, but which I would now willingly sacrifice to make the sunny South prosperous and happy. Will you take it, General?"

There was a moment's hesitation, a moment of death-like stillness in the hall, and then Fitzhugh Lee was on his feet, his hand was extended across the footlights and was quickly met by the warm grasp of the preacher's.

At first there was a murmur, half of surprise and half of doubtfulness from the audience, then there was a hesitating clapping of hands, and before Beecher had unloosed the hand of Robert E. Lee's nephew — now Governor of Virginia — there were cheers such as were never before heard in old Mozart, though it had been the scene of many a war and political meeting.

But that was only the beginning of the enthusiasm.

When the noise subsided Mr. Beecher continued:—"When I go back home I shall proudly tell that I have grasped the hand of the nephew of the great Southern chieftain; I shall tell my people that I went to the Confederate capital with a heart full of love for the people whom my principles once obliged me to oppose, and that I was met half way by the brave Southerners, who can forgive as well as they can fight."

Five minutes of applause followed, and then Mr. Beecher, having gained the hearts of his audience, began his lecture, and was applauded to the echo. That night he entered his carriage and drove to his hotel amid shouts such as had never greeted a Northern man in Richmond since the war.

He went into military matters in a quiet way, and

since 1878, as the Chaplain of the Thirteenth Regiment of Brooklyn, has had opportunity to say much to the young men of the country. He lectured in short courses through the country each year.

Mr. Mumford, who planned Mr. Beecher's great lecturing trip West, said:

"It was the most memorable lecture trip ever made. I was then one of the managers of the American Literary Bureau, at Cooper Institute, New York, and our correspondents in the large cities often besought us to secure Mr. Beecher for them, but to all overtures he turned a deaf ear. He had not been West for twelve or fourteen years. Some of the large cities in the West he had never seen at all. In the East he had lectured very seldom, and was not considered "in the lecture field." At last we concluded to make him an offer which would startle him into acceptance if anything could have that effect, so we sent him a written proposal to pay him $10,000 for two weeks of time. Still we hardly expected a reply, for it was his habit to take no notice of business letters making proposals which he could not accept, and acceptance was hardly looked for. When his reply came there was commotion in the office. It said that he had special use just then for a little more than $10,000, and if we would make it $12,000, and pay all his expenses, he would give us three weeks instead of two, simply stipulating that we should get him to Brooklyn on the morning of the third Saturday, so that he could rest and prepare for Sunday. To this we readily agreed, and the bargain was made. I started out to lay the route, and, having finished it, went over the ground a second time, to see that all instructions were carried out. Mr. Brelsford, who joined the silent majority some years ago, accompanied Mr. Beecher. The route was: Harrisburg, Pittsburg, Cleveland, Cincinnati, Louisville, Cincinnati again, Indianapolis, St. Louis two nights, Peoria, Milwaukee, Chicago two nights, Toledo, Detroit, Rochester. We treated Mr. Beecher the best we knew how, and the expense to us amounted to about $1,100 per night. But we had faith in it, and made no effort to sell the lectures. We did sell five—two in Chicago to Carpenter & Sheldon for $2,500, one to the Y. M. C. A. of Toledo for $1,200, one to the Excelsior Boat Club of Detroit for $1,250, and one to C. R. Gardner, then of Milwaukee, for $1,000. All to whom we sold made money, unless it may have been Mr. Gardner; I am not sure about him. Our net profit on the trip was $5,500. The losing nights were the first and the last—Harrisburg and Rochester."

Once, when Mr. Beecher was speaking on Communism, in Chicago, a rather dramatic and very characteristic thing happened. His lecture was half finished.

HENRY WARD BEECHER AT THE AGE OF SIXTY.

He was standing before an audience of 10,000 people in the old Tabernacle Building, a temporary structure on Franklin street, put up to accommodate the vast audiences which thronged in those days to hear Moody and Sankey, then in the heyday of their early work and enthusiasm. The great room was packed. Beecher rolled out sentence after sentence in his most telling manner. Word after word fell forcibly upon the vast crowd, which grew more and more silent as he went on. A reporter at the table down in front of the platform dropped a lead pencil, and one could almost feel the noise that it made, so breathlessly were all in that audience listening to the orator's voice. He was telling the story of the rise of the power of the people. Presently he ended a ringing period with these words, pronounced in a voice so deep and fervid and full of conviction that they seemed to have been uttered then for the first time: "The voice of the people is the voice of God."

Into the absolute and intense silence of the instant that followed fell the voice of a half-drunken man in the gallery: "The voice of the people is the voice of a fool."

Everybody fairly shivered. But Beecher was equal to the moment. He drew himself up, looked toward the place from whence the disturbing voice came, and "I said the voice of the people, not the voice of one man," he replied, with perfect simplicity and dignity.

It would be impossible to describe the responsive expression of the audience. It was not a laugh, it was not a cheer. It was a movement, a sound like one great sigh of relief and delight. The lecture went on; the air was full of electric sympathy, tingling toward an explosion of some sort. Beecher knew it, and seemed waiting for a chance to put his finger on the key of the pent-up personal enthusiasm which moved his audience. The drunken fellow suddenly gave him a chance. He staggered to his feet, feeling that the odds were against him, and mumbled out some unintelligible words. Beecher paused a second time in his lecture. Then he said with that smile of his, at once winning and condemning, which so many people know: "Will some kind person take our friend out and give him some cold water—plenty of it—within and without?" Two policemen had hold of the disturber by this time, and the audience had liberty to cheer—and such a cheer as it was! The tabernacle shook with it, and it is probable that at least nine-tenths of the people who clapped their hands supposed that they were cheering Mr. Beecher's wit, instead of that tremendous personal power which no one need try to analyze.

An incident, illustrative of Mr. Beecher's amiability, bonhomie and ready wit, is told by a Chicago reporter: "I had been sent to the Pacific to interview him. He had gone out, and a number of reporters were hanging around the office with the same object in view. Presently I saw him enter the Clark Street door, and I flew toward him, determined to engage him before any other reporter knew of his arrival. I understood his disposition very well, and knew how to take him. I said:

"Mr. Beecher, I am a reporter, and I—"

"Ah!" he said, "I thought you were a very good-looking young man."

"Now, Mr. Beecher," I said, in breathless haste, "I desire to roll the wheel of conversation around the axle-tree of your understanding for awhile."

"I see," he replied, earnestly. "You wish to unwind the thread of thought from the spool of my mind."

Having got started in this sort of fun, it was several minutes before I could switch him off on the track of business, and in the course of this agreeable prelude he said, with an expressive gesture, that he always thought "in pictures." During the interview he evinced the most childlike simplicity, humility and good-will. I remember that he had occasion to refer to some recent insulting references to him in the papers, and added, "But there is so much of that sort of thing that a little more or less does not matter."

A Southern friend gives the following reminiscence: "Mr. Beecher was lecturing at Lynchburg, Va., and came to the hotel where I was stopping. He seemed to have some difficulty with the committee which had invited him. He was to lecture on 'Evolution and Revolution,' but as I understood him the committee said the people of Lynchburg were so orthodox that they would listen to nothing respecting evolution or Darwinism. He changed the title to 'The Reign of the Common People,' but it was the same lecture.

"I offered to introduce him to the audience. He asked if I was popular in Lynchburg. I told him I was quite as popular there as he was before he voted for Cleveland. So he thought, he said, but I had not considered his topic. I suggested I could explain the physical evolution theory to a country audience by the tadpole turning to a frog, but that when I came to mental evolution I should take his case and show what terrible throes of nature were required to make so good a Republican into the imperfect Mugwump. He was fond of humor, declined my proffered services, but asked me to sit on the platform."

Mr. Beecher's writing was kept up at this time without intermission. Few persons know what an immense amount of literary work he accomplished. The following is a list of the published works: Sermons, ten volumes, of 475 pp. each; Sermons, four volumes, of 600 pp. each; "A Summer Parish," 240 pp.; "Yale Lectures on Preaching," first, second and third series; "Lectures to Young Men," 506 pp.; "Star Papers," 600 pp.; "Pleasant Talk About Fruits, Flowers and Farming," 498 pp.; "Lecture Room Talks," 384 pp.; "Norwood; or, Village Life in New England," 549 pp.; "The Overtures of Angels,"; "Eyes and Ears; or, Thoughts as they Occur;" "Freedom and War;" "Royal Truths;" "Views and Experiences of Religious Subjects;" and the unfinished "Life of Jesus Christ."

Of his literary tastes Mr. Beecher has himself given an idea: "I read for three things; first, to know what the world has done in the last twenty-four hours, and is about to do to-day; second, for the knowledge which I especially want to use in my work; and thirdly, for what will bring my mind into a proper mood. Amongst the authors which I frequently read are De Tocqueville, Matthew Arnold, Mme. Guyon, and Thomas à Kempis. I gather my knowledge of current thought from books and periodicals and from conversation with men, from whom I get much that can not be learned in any other way. I am a very slow reader. I never read for style. I should urge reading history.   My study of Milton has given me a conception of power and vigor which I otherwise should not have had.   I got fluency out of Burke very largely, and I obtained the sense of adjectives out of Barrow, besides the sense of exhaustiveness."

CHAPTER XVI.

In social life Mr. Beecher was always bright and cheery, and he appeared doubly happy in his own home.

Nothing pleased him better than to see the younger members of his congregation grow up, marry, and bring their children to the baptismal font. It delighted him to be called "Father Beecher" by the members of his church and congregation.

During the winter Mr. Beecher lived in Brooklyn with his eldest son, Henry Barton Beecher. All his children were married and settled in homes of their own. They are William Beecher, Mrs. Scoville, Herbert Beecher, and Henry Barton Beecher.

Mr. Beecher was for many years a sufferer from hay-fever, and spent his summers for a long time in the White Mountains. He was a noted figure at the Twin Mountain House, and one of the mountain pools near by, into which he fell one day, has been known in the guide-books as "Beecher's Pool." In the last few years the hay-fever seemed to leave him, and he had spent most of his summers since 1880 at his

Peekskill country house. From his fullness of habit and temperament apoplexy had long been feared by his physicians.

"Naturally enough," said a friend of Mr. Beecher, "he was frequently present at public dinners, and a singular feature of his conduct on such occasions was his total abstinence from the solid and liquid good cheer set before him. Just fancy the stoicism and self-denial involved in a man of Beecher's enthusiastic temperament, sitting through a long dinner, and waiting patiently for the time to come when he should share in the intellectual part of it. I have seen him occasionally drink a little water at a banquet, but beyond that indulgence he never went."

"He stopped here once in my house when he was in this city," said a Washington friend, "for a day or two. I remember that he sat at my desk and wrote an article for the Ledger. When he sat down he took an old shawl of mine and wrapped it about his feet and legs, saying that he could not write unless his legs were warm. Some physician speaks of his doing this lately, and noted it as a sign that he was breaking. It was twelve or fifteen years ago that he was at my house, and he was then in vigorous health. Years before that, before I knew him personally, I met him on a train between Portland and Boston, and he then had his feet thrust into a sealskin bag made for the purpose. That seemed to have been a habit of his."

Mr. Beecher's country home at Peekskill is said to have been built from the proceeds of lectures delivered by him in two years. He bought the farm on which it stands over twenty years ago, and for a time occupied a small cottage which stood on the place. The erection and interior decorations of the new house were personally supervised by him. It comprises a basement of granite, above which rise two stories of brick and a roof with many gables and dormer windows. Except in the vestibule there is no paint in the house from cellar to garret. Cherry is used on the first floor, ash on the second, and pine in the attic. The mantels are of wood decorated with tiles, and the walls and ceilings are papered. A broad veranda extends across the front and a portion of one side of the house. The site is a commanding one. The farm itself contains a remarkable variety of trees and shrubs. Not only many States in this country, but England, the Continent, China, and Japan were laid under contribution. The result is between two hundred and three hundred varieties of trees and shrubs, the number of maples and pines being over twenty of each.

"Norwood" was written mostly at Peekskill. As Mr. Beecher says in his preface: "There is not a single unpleasant memory connected with it. It was a summer-child, brought up among flowers and trees." When "Norwood" was ready for the press, he sent the following letter with it to the publisher:

MY DEAR MR. BONNER: You have herewith the last line of "Norwood." I began it reluctantly, as one who treads an unexplored path. But as I went on I took more kindly to my work, and now that it is ended I shall quite miss my weekly task.

My dear old father, after his day of labor had closed, used to fancy that in some way he was so connected with me that he was still at work; and on one occasion, after a Sabbath-morning service, some one in a congratulatory way, said to the venerable and meek old patriarch:

"Well, Doctor, how did you like your son's sermon?"

"It was good—good as I could do myself." And then, with an emphatic pointing of his forefinger, he added, "If it hadn't been for *me*, you'd never have had him!"

If anybody likes "Norwood," my dear and venerable Mr. Bonner, you can poke him with your finger and say, "If it hadn't been for *me*, you would never have had it."

"Five years ago," said an old friend, "I sat on the broad verandah of Mr. Beecher's house at Peekskill. It was a late summer afternoon. We had played a

MRS. HENRY WARD BEECHER,

See page 186.

game of billiards. He had taken his afternoon nap, and he came out and sat down by my side in a Shaker rocker. I shall never forget the dreamy luxury of that afternoon. The landscape, which is the most beautiful in the world and rich with legendary associations of André and Enoch Crosby, was blushing with the first sensuous dalliance of autumn. The air was heavy with odors and drowsy with the drone of insects. A sweet, steady draught from the Highlands brought with it occasionally the far-away roll of a drum—it may have been at West Point—and lifted the long, white locks of my companion gently. He seemed to take in the vitality and beauty of the hour without being conscious of it.

"A child does that. He doesn't stop and rhapsodize over the sunset. He lets it in and sings and dances. The charm of the moment made Mr. Beecher happy and he talked freely and pleasantly.

"At that time he was formulating in his mind the wholly unorthodox compromise with evolution which afterward took more definite shape in his lecture. He had been studying Spencer carefully and more lately Buchner, and he talked the best natured amalgam of rationalism and orthodoxy I ever heard.

"I thought then that he had lost his anchorage and I wondered if at his time of life he would get another.

I remember how surprised I was, when in close contact with him, to find the methods of the orator continually and unwittingly disabling the metaphysician.
He had struck back several fierce blows at New England Calvanism, but they were actuated by a growing
sensibility that shrank from the cruelty of eternal
punishment rather than by a conviction of its impossibility. I remember how he laughed when I told him
that I thought the rationalistic arguments against hell
were not so much the conviction of the reason as the
squeal of weak nerves. I did not think that a morbid
sensibility could weigh theistic truths — for as a rule
they hurt. It was about this time that Col. Robert G.
Ingersoll replied to Judge Black in the North American Review, and I asked Mr. Beecher what he thought
of Ingersoll.

"His reply was characteristic: 'Bob is a good
fellow,' he said, 'but he is trying to do in thought
what Nature has never been able to do in physics—
create a vacuum, and what is worse, he is trying to do
what Nature would be ashamed to do—make us believe that a vacuum is admirable.'

"I asked him why he did not reply to Ingersoll.
He said the best man to reply to him was John B.
Gough. It struck me at the time that that was as
severe a thing as could be said of Ingersoll. But I
don't think Mr. Beecher intended it to be severe. I

don't think he could be personally severe. It was not individuals that roused his combative spirit so much as general wrongs. The fact is I was not half as much charmed with the theologian as I was with the man. I soon enough found out that it was not easier to love Mr. Beecher than it was to disagree with him. But I never met a more delightful man to disagree with.

"He put on a broad-brimmed felt hat and we walked through the lanes on the domain where the afternoon sun came golden through the gaps. He knew every tree and bird and flower; the very weeds and stones wore a new air of companionship on account of him. I think the birds came nearer to me during that walk than ever before. I could not escape the consciousness of closely fluttering wings.

"For Nature, too, has her loves and her hates. Her timid songsters are closer to some than to others. Her little germs swell and grow with alacrity under certain eyes and the mute beauties of the field do wave their tasselled caps and blow their odorous kisses—only to their friends.

"An instinctive sense of the benignity of the great plan, and of the yearning of the whole creation upward, was an abiding and beautiful thing in Mr. Beecher. He believed in the primacy of love. He saw in it the seminal and conserving force of the uni-

14

verse. It was mentally impossible for him to conceive of purpose and design without love, because he
conceived of hate as a destructive force always.

"I am told that animals and children always came
to him, and that I can readily believe, for I have on
more than one occasion observed the sixth sense
which enables animals and children to instantly dis-
criminate. I have always believed in that beautiful
story of Francis of Assissi which the Catholic Church
cherishes and the Protestant Church regards as
a fable.

"A gentle masculinity pervaded Mr. Beecher's personality. His large, sensuous nature was a wholesome one, and never developed the sentimentalism
which is so often the penalty of acute sensibility.
He was essentially an outdoor man. He could not, it
is true, live in the luminiferous ether of the mystic,
but it is equally true that he demanded oxygen and
sunshine.

"Like all such natures, he had a keen natural
sense of the dramatic and demonstrative. Many
times as I had heard him on the platform and in the
pulpit sway the multitude from pole to pole of
emotion, I could never make up my mind whether he
arranged beforehand what the dramatist would call
his 'situations,' or only let the occasion and its
emotions supply them.

" Years ago, when I was quite a boy, there was a great disturbance in this city over the Five Points, which at that time was the most disgraceful cesspool of iniquity on the face of the earth. The authorities either would not or could not do anything for its regeneration. Under the lash of public agitation the women of New York came together and organized what was called the Ladies' Home Missionary Society, and called a series of mass-meetings in Tripler Hall, an enormous building on Broadway that had been erected in anticipation of the arrival of Jenny Lind. These mass-meetings were unique. I think they took place on Saturday nights. Never before had so many 'big guns' been brought together on the platform as the ladies gathered for these meetings. Half-hour addresses were made by all the most eloquent orators of the American pulpit, irrespective of denomination, and the great hall was regularly packed to the doorways. On one occasion I remember Cheever Cuyler, the lamented Dr. Foster, of the Methodist Church, and a score of others, including Henry Ward Beecher, were announced. And the Hutchinson family and the Alleghanians were to sing. The speakers were all on their mettle, for they were pitted against each other in a good cause. My recollection is that Dr. Foster fainted from excessive emotion, after one of the most startling appeals I ever heard. Somewhere in the

course of the evening Henry Ward Beecher was introduced.   He was then in the full flower of enthusiasm,
and far more clerical in cut than when in his maturity.
Instead of taking the centre of the platform, as all the
preceding speakers had done, he walked to the extreme
end and began an imaginary dialogue in which a politician took part.   He asked him all kinds of questions
as to the proper way to regenerate the Five Points, and
got all kinds of absurd and evasive replies.   When he
had exhausted the ignorance and indifference of this
functionary, he walked to the other end of the platform, and, with both hands extended and body bent
over, as if looking into a hole, he said: *'We lay you
down there for so much!'*

"Then back across the width of the platform to begin
another conversation with a physician.   The whole
character of the dialogue changed instantly.   The new
man spoke in a new vein.   He had gases and thera-
peutics at his finger ends.   He would regenerate the
Five Points with a six-foot sewer and chloride of lime.
He was visionary, technical and wholly inadequate,
and he was carried over and placed in the same hole
'for so much.'

"Then the same process was gone through with an
editor, and a philosopher, and an engineer, and by this
time the vast assemblage was worked up to a pitch of
intense expectation and suspense.

"The one dominant interrogative emotion was — 'Who will do this thing?'

"Never have I forgotten the effect produced when the speaker took the middle of the stage for his peroration and said, 'Now we'll take down the Christian women of New York.'

"And they seemed to us to sweep down like the Valkyrie, with flaming swords.

"Boy as I was, I knew, as soon as I got away from the magnetic influence of the speaker, that this was a trick of oratory, in which the method of the playwright had been employed. We had been listening to a little drama, with its well-defined dramatis personæ, its situations, its five acts, with a curtain, and its final dénouement.

"Years afterwards, standing there on his lawn under one of the trees he had himself planted, trying to recall in the ruddy, white-haired man at my side the eager, impassioned, somewhat gaunt and irresistibly earnest speaker who had made such an impression on my young mind, I reminded him of the scene in Tripler Hall and asked him if he had planned that effect beforehand or left it to the suggestion of the moment.

"His recollection was that it had occurred to him just before he appeared on the platform. He assured me that all his best results in oratory were due to the inspiration of the moment.

"And then he told me how on one occasion he was making an anti-slavery speech at the old Broadway Tabernacle, and there had been left there, by Arthur Tappan or somebody else, a chain that had been worn in the South by a slave. 'In my closing appeal,' said Mr. Beecher, 'I saw the chain for the first time, and going over I picked it up and throwing it down trampled upon it as I finished. The effect was electrical, but it was unpremeditated.'"

"There is one curious place," said another old friend, "at Mr. Beecher's country home in Peekskill, which I think very few people know anything about. I discovered it accidentally, one Summer, while making a journey on foot through the upper part of the State. It was late one afternoon that I found myself on a hill overlooking a country residence, which I afterward discovered was the great preacher's. On a level piece of ground between me and the house was a high mound of small stones which had evidently been carefully placed there, and in a few minutes I discovered by whom. A short, fat man, clad in a long duster and a sun hat, came out of the house and walked over to the pyramid. Then he looked around on the ground and presently started off on a brisk walk for a distance of fifty yards, when he stooped down and, picking up a stone, carried it back to the mound. Then he started off after another one, and kept that exercise up for fifteen minutes, when his journeys brought him up to the tree behind which I had placed myself, and I saw that it was Mr. Beecher. He recognized me at the same time, and started the laugh, in which, of course, I joined. Then he took me to his 'monument,' as he called it, and explained that he did all this work for exercise. There were numbers of stones in the ground near him, but he wouldn't touch those, preferring to get his exercise and his 'monument' at the same time. He made it a rule never to carry back more than one stone at a time, and, when he showed me other similar mounds on various portions of his property, I saw that he had collected enough of the small rocks to make a fence around his grounds."

CHAPTER XVII.

Mr. Beecher's energy and versatility seemed to increase with his years. He took the closest interest in politics, speaking at large gatherings not only in his own but in other cities.

In 1880, he once more came to the front in the Presidential campaign as an advocate of Garfield's election. The cheers of his fellow citizens when he made his appearance on the political platform, and the persistent cries for "Beecher, Beecher!" showed that his influence and popularity remained to him.

It was in the fall of 1880, that Mr. Beecher introduced Col. Robert Ingersoll to a great political gathering in the Brooklyn Academy of Music, saying that the Colonel was the most brilliant living orator in any tongue. A day or two afterward the Colonel was asked by a reporter what he thought of Mr. Beecher. He at once sat down and wrote as fast as his pencil could trot over paper thus:

"I regard him as the greatest man in any pulpit of the world. He treated me with a generosity that

216

nothing can exceed.   He rose grandly above the prejudices which are supposed to belong to his class, and
acted only as a man could act without a chain upon his
brain, and only kindness in his heart.

"I told him that night that I congratulated the
world that it had a minister with an intellectual horizon broad enough, and a mental sky studded with stars
of genius enough, to hold all creeds in scorn that
shocked the heart of man.   I think that Mr. Beecher
has liberalized the English-speaking people of the
world.   I do not think he agrees with me.   He holds
to many things that I most passionately deny.   But
in common we believe in liberty of thought

"My principal objections to orthodox religions are
two—slavery here and hell hereafter.   I do not believe
that Mr. Beecher on these two points can disagree
with me.   The real difference between us is, he says
God, I say nature.   The real agreement between us is,
we both say liberty."

"What is Mr. Beecher's forte?" the reporter
asked.

"He is of a wonderfully poetic temperament.   In
pursuing any course of thought his mind is like a
stream flowing through the scenery of fairyland.   The
stream murmurs and laughs, while the banks grow
green and the vines blossom.

"His brain is controlled by his heart.   He thinks

in pictures.   With him logic means mental melody.
The discordant is the absurd.

"For years he has endeavored to hide the dungeon
of orthodoxy with the ivy of imagination.   Now and
then he pulls for a moment the leafy curtain aside,
and is horrified to see the lizards, snakes, basilisks,
and abnormal monsters of the orthodox age, and then
he utters a great cry, the protest of a loving, throb-
bing heart.

"He is a great thinker, a marvelous orator, and,
in my judgment, greater and grander than any creed
or church.   Besides all this, he treated me like a king.
Manhood is his forte, and I expect to live and die his
friend."

The campaign of 1884 saw him take an entire change
of front.   He became the chief among the Mugwumps,
and went out as a vigorous stump orator in favor of
Cleveland.   He spoke everywhere, and always with
exceptional effect.   He was derided by the opposition
press, but he met all blows as an old campaigner, and
gave them back with interest.   It was a novel sight,
that of this ardent Republican appearing on Democratic platforms, and it caused him the loss of many
old friends, who urged him if he was unable on conscientious grounds and for personal reasons to support
the candidate of his party, at least to hold his peace
and content himself with a silent vote.   But he could

not be moved or restrained, and he continued his efforts until the day of election.

On the evening of October 22, in that year, he delivered a campaign speech at the Brooklyn Rink to an audience which for numbers and enthusiasm had rarely been equaled in this State, and followed this up by making a series of such addresses in this city, Brooklyn, and in New Jersey during the remainder of the campaign.

This action of Mr. Beecher was the subject of much severe criticism by certain members of his congregation, who thought that the pastor of Plymouth Church should not have allowed himself to express such extreme views as he had done. Sunday, December 28, Mr. Beecher, from his pulpit, delivered a long and most eloquent defense of his previous actions. He said that his motives were wholly pure, and he offered in the end to resign his pastorate should a majority request his resignation. No such request was ever made.

General Horatio C. King first met Mr. Beecher in 1865, during a leave of absence from the army. He was introduced to him by Miss Howard, who afterward became his wife, and was always accorded the same treatment that Mr. Beecher accorded the members of Mr. Howard's family.

"I sat on the platform," said Mr. King, "when

Mr. Beecher made his speech in favor of Cleveland. Mr. Cleveland owed much to Mr. Beecher. There were many other things that contributed to his election, but a great deal was due to Mr. Beecher's coming out in his support, and I think my son, General Horatio C. King, was mainly instrumental in bringing Mr. Beecher to that point.

"I suppose you have heard Mr. Beecher speak as often as I have. Every one has heard him. His Friday evening talks—informal talks—to the Plymouth Church people, on all sorts of topics, were especially interesting. Yes, it was wonderful the great amount of work he did, writing and speaking. Some people believed him inspired. I think Mr. Beecher believed it was inspiration. He should have stopped and taken rest. What has killed him, in my opinion, is 'The Life of Christ.' He should not have undertaken it; it was too great a task."

In Mr. King's collection of autographs is an interesting scrap from Mr. Beecher's pen, illustrating his manner of work. To it is attached a ticket to the platform at the Academy of Music, Brooklyn, on the occasion of the address of Mr. Beecher on "The Issues of the Canvass." The scrap of writing contains the headings made by Mr. Beecher for his address. They are written in a bold hand, apparently with a quill pen, and many of the words are underscored. The headings are as follows:

ISABELLA BEECHER HOOKER.

" First—Origin of party—historic logic of our history
and principles. Second—What has it done to deserve
well of the people? Third—What charges are brought
against it? (1) Not restoring the Union; delaying
for party reasons. (2) Oppressive taxes. (3) It is
refreshing to hear Mayor Hoffman express his conscience on extravagance in public moneys. Fourth—
By whom are they accused? Who is it that proposes
to take their place and finish the work of liberty?
(1) Their relation to every event and step gained by
war. (2) Their proposed remedy. Overturn all that

Congress has done. Reverse legislation. Throw down State enactments. Send back Senators and Representatives. Remand Southern States to turmoil and confusion."

Upon the platform Mr. Beecher, with these few notes, under the inspiration of the moment, delivered a splendid address, occupying two hours or more.

Speaking of their political differences of opinion, Gen. King said a few days ago: "In my long intercourse with Mr. Beecher, differing as we always did politically until the campaign in which Mr. Cleveland was a candidate for the Governorship, Mr. Beecher never uttered a word of censure or attempted to influence my opinion, except by argument or playful badinage, which he sometimes plentifully bestowed. In all this time, though I have seen him angry, I never heard him give vent to his anger. His self-control was wonderful."

CHAPTER XVIII.

In his church he was always ready for his pulpit duties, saying all manner of startling things. In 1882 he withdrew from the New York and Brooklyn Congregational Association. He made the occasion one for the utterance of his belief and a reaffirmation of his theology, and then declared that he was no longer a member, while he would continue to work with them.

When Mr. Beecher was most severely criticised by his Congregational brethren for what they were pleased to term his heterodoxy, he preached a series of sermons, and at the close of the anniversary sermon made this explanation: "This month completes the thirty-fifth year in which I have been the preacher in this church—since the third day of October, 1847. I have not changed the line of my preaching from that day. I have adopted no new thing that I had not at least some conception of in my mind when I came here. I think I could say of one-half my sermons of thirty-five years ago, 'I believe them still,' and of the other half, poor as they are and imperfect, yet I believe always that I was attempting to preach the truth of the power of God for the salvation of men. Nobody can put a lower estimate upon his ministry than I do. It is very little to me what men think about that. I am not to be judged by being compared with other men, but with God and by the work I have done. I have never preached what I did not believe; I have never asked myself whether to preach a truth that I did believe would be popular or unpopular. I have never been afraid of man, though I have been afraid of God as the child is afraid of the father it loves. The whole conception of life that I have had has been to serve my fellow men, and when, in the day that men despised the poor, oppressed negroes, that could not plead their own cause, I was more than will-ing, I was inexpressibly grateful to be permitted to stand for them, and not to forsake them until they were clothed in the majesty of equal rights by the great revolution. I attempted all my life long to take the part of those who had no defender; and I have done it. And in all matters in my own church I have steadily sought one thing,— to reproduce, so far as I was able to reproduce, the lineaments of the Lord Jesus Christ in your hearts. If the day should come when I could not avail myself of every revelation of God in nature — if the day should come in which you would not bear and forbear, I should depart. I should say, my work is done, the harvest is gathered, and my life is ended."

In January of this year he was protesting against the action of the Brooklyn Board of Education, and overstated some reports which had reached him, but promptly withdrew them when his attention was called to the error.

Jealousy had no place in Mr. Beecher's composition. Too candid to be always considered a man of tact, his nature never prompted him to speak ill of a rival. Certainly no one stood in that relation to him more than did Mr. Talmage. Their personal relations, however, were always most pleasant. The following note shows with what a kind spirit Mr. Beecher regarded the man whose congregations was the first to eclipse that of Plymouth Church:

MY DEAR DR. TALMAGE: I congratulate you most heartily on attaining to the ripe age of 53! From the summit of these years may you, like Moses, look over into fifty more, but unlike Moses be spared to go over and possess them. May labor sit light upon you! May your audiences grow larger and your cares grow less, until heaven calls you home, and there largest of all, may you find a great multitude whom you have helped on their heavenly way. Fraternally yours,

HENRY WARD BEECHER.

To Rev. T. DeWitt Talmage, D. D.

15

At this time Mr. Beecher was, in personal appearance, one of the most striking men about New York. He was of medium height, with broad shoulders, and a heavy girth; so stout and fleshy, in fact, that he looked short in inches. His head was large, though not bulging or irregular. His forehead was high, and his features were strong and full. His color was high, his cheeks and neck being always full-veined and ruddy. His hair was gray, turning to white in recent years, and hung in loose locks down on his black coat collar. His face was always smooth-shaven. His eyes were of a grayish blue, full of fire and expression in his moments of feeling, always humorous and inquisitive. He never paid great attention to dress, though far from being an unkempt or slovenly man. He wore dark clothes usually, and a black slouch hat habitually. He never could be brought to put on a silk hat or a " claw-hammer " coat, wearing a Prince Albert coat on formal occasions. Even in the pulpit he substituted a turn-down collar and black necktie for the more conventional clerical " choker " and white tie. He was in fact unconventional and indifferent in most of the smaller details of life.

An old time New York journalist, who had had intimate associations with Mr. Beecher for many years, said one day: " In all this time I have never found anything about Mr. Beecher more characteristic than his humor. He is filled with amusing anecdotes about public men, and loves to hear one at his own expense. I met him one night on the steps of Moulton's house, in Brooklyn, and he sat down on the cold stone to listen to a story about his first volume of the 'Life of Christ.' It came to me from Samuel Wilkinson, one of the firm of J. B. Ford & Co., the publishers of the book. Mr. Beecher laughed heartily over it, and admitted its entire truth. When the book was ready for the press a steel plate costing $400 was made for the title page. It read, as engraved, 'Life of Jesus Christ. By Henry Ward Beecher,' but Mr. Beecher had written on the margin for insertion after Jesus and before Christ the word 'the.' The idea had not come to him until after the plate was made, and the question of expense never occurred to him."

Beecher's friend, Major Pond, tells this story: A short time ago he visited Brattleboro, Vt., in company with Mr. Beecher, and the latter told him that fifty years before that date he had delivered a Fourth of July oration in that town. He lived ten miles away, and the committee gave him the choice between $10 in cash, and his expenses. He took the cash and walked to and from Brattleboro. That was so much like Beecher that no one can doubt the genuineness of the story.

Some time ago Mr. Beecher addressed a telegram

to "Mr. S——, Syracuse, N. Y." The message was sent as directed, but the person to whom it was directed could not be found. The telegraph company notified the great preacher of the failure to deliver and this was his reply:

"Mr. S—— lives in Utica, N. Y., and if anybody told you Syracuse, he did not know what he was about.

"There are just such folks in the world, always making blunders, and if you could lay your hands on them and abate them as a nuisance it would be well.

"Please put a double battery on this delayed message, so as to get it to S—— speedily, lest he be too late for to-night's train, and my money be spent in vain.   HENRY WARD BEECHER."

The original message, in his own handwriting, addressed to Syracuse, was sent back to Mr. Beecher with his letter. The letter came back to the operator with this written on it in Mr. Beecher's writing:

"I'm glad you nabbed him."

Another story is told that Mr. Beecher and U. S. Grant were, at one time, together at a public dinner given in Brooklyn, when Mr. Beecher suddenly looked at his watch and remarked that as the time was rapidly nearing a certain hour, he would have to ask the company to pardon his early departure as he had a marriage ceremony to perform. Saying this, Mr. Beecher arose from the table, and as he did so General Grant, who had been sitting next to him, removed a rosebud from the lapel of his coat, and handing the flower to Mr. Beecher, said:

"Will you kindly hand this to the bride, and give to her and her future husband my best wishes?"

Mr. Beecher accepted and fulfilled the trust, and the bride of that time still has the faded flower, and treasures it as a precious souvenir.

Mr. Beecher began in May, 1885, a series of sermons on Evolution, which drew unusually large audiences to Plymouth Church. The series was continued until the summer vacation of that year. The object of the sermons was to show the moral evolution of man rather than to give a scientific discussion of the theory. Mr. Beecher's idea was that man began on a very low basis, and that there was a long period when he was developing so as to understand the existence and nature of God—a period of incubation as he described it. In closing his first sermon on the subject, clasping his hands, he said:

"There shall come a day when life and all its troubles have passed away. There shall come a day when I shall know even as I am known, and as God the all-knowing looks through and through me and knows me altogether, I shall behold Him as He is, and shadows, figments, and partialities will have passed away forever, and I shall know Him as I am known."

Mr. Beecher touched lightly on the Darwin theory, but went so far as to say:

"I am inclined to believe that man is, in the order of nature, in analogy with the rest of God's work, and that there was a time when he stepped ahead of his fellow-animals."

In the series, Mr. Beecher spoke of evolution in connection with inspiration of the Bible, inherited sin, regeneration of man, design and evolution in the church.

While he was engaged in delivering these sermons he described his religious faith fully and concisely in the following letter to the Rev. George Morrison of Baltimore:

BROOKLYN, N. Y., June 13, 1885.

DEAR SIR: I thank you for your friendly solicitude. I am sure that in the end you will not be disappointed, though on some points you may not agree with me. The foundation doctrines, as I hold them, are a personal God, Creator, and ruler over all things; the human family universally sinful; the need and possibility and facts of conversion; the Divine agency in such a work; Jesus Christ the manifestation of God in human condition; His office in redemption supreme. I do not believe in the Calvinistic form of stating the atonement. I do not believe in the fall of the human race in Adam, and, of course, I do not hold that Christ's work was to satisfy the law broken by Adam for all his posterity. The race was not lost, but has been ascending steadily from creation. I am in hearty accord with revivals and revival preaching, with the educating forces of the church, and in sympathy with all ministers who in their several ways seek to build up men into the image of Jesus Christ, by whose faithfulness, generosity and love I hope to be saved and brought home to Heaven. With cordial regards, I am truly yours,

HENRY WARD BEECHER.

CHAPTER XIX.

ONCE MORE IN ENGLAND.

Mr. Beecher's seventieth birthday was celebrated by the church and the whole city with general enthusiasm. An ovation was accorded to him such as no minister has received in this generation. That it pleased him and cheered him was evident, and when it was repeated on the occasion of his setting out on an European tour, Mr. Beecher could not find words to express his grateful appreciation of this confidence and love.

Mr. Beecher had not been in England since 1863, and he much desired to note for himself the changes which had occurred during that long time. Accompanied by Mrs. Beecher and Major Pond, his manager, he sailed for England on the Etruria, June 20. For almost four months Mr. Beecher traveled all over England, Scotland, and Wales. His lectures delivered in London, Leeds, Cardiff, Liverpool, Manchester, and other cities and towns in the kingdom, were in every sense successful.

Mr. Beecher intended his journey to be in

large measure a rest from the labors that he had
been incessantly performing here, year after year,
in Brooklyn. But he went at an unfortunate
time. At that time all England was ablaze with the
national elections. It was a question whether Gladstone and Parnell should control, or whether home
rule should go to the wall. The period was a critical
one. Everybody knew in what direction Mr. Beecher's
sympathies tended, and there was a universal expectation that when he reached the other side there would
be something in the nature of a repetition of his war-
time triumphs over English prejudice. There was
some disappointment on this side, therefore, when he
failed to realize the expectations of some of the folks
who were hopeful that he would work toward the good
of Ireland.

But Mr. Beecher had gone over on no such mission.
There was nothing partaking of the war-like or the national in the manner of his departure. At his regular
Friday evening prayer-meeting he told a larger congregation than usual of his intention to take ship on
the following morning, and bade them an affectionate
farewell. Running through this regular Friday evening talk was one of those melancholy yet pleasing
veins of speech in which Mr. Beecher frequently indulged in late years. He told his assembled parishioners that he felt that he had but a short time to re-

main with them. There was a possibility that he might never return to them. There were plenty of moist eyes when he had concluded.

The next morning all Plymouth Church was astir. The steamship Grand Republic had been chartered to accompany the great preacher down the bay, and fully four thousand people got up early to see him off. Side by side down the bay, and outside of Sandy Hook, the ocean steamship and the smooth water steamer proceeded, hundreds of handkerchiefs waving continuously from the latter, while Mr. Beecher and his wife stood on the forward deck of the Etruria and returned the parting salutations. His trip over was one of those agonizing experiences of the flesh that fell to the lot of Mr. Beecher whenever he left the land. He was not thoroughly well until, just a week after his departure, he stepped aboard the little tender in the River Mersey, and, escaping the Custom House officials who were looking only for spirits and cigars, got into the Northwestern Hotel at Liverpool.

There he found, however, that his troubles had only begun. He found lots of telegrams and letters awaiting him, asking his attendance at the home-rule meetings that were then being held throughout the land. He was compelled to ignore them all. Delegation after delegation waited upon him to urge his presence at this, that, or the other place throughout the

United Kingdom where Gladstone's policy was to be upheld, but to all of them Mr. Beecher returned, in substance, this answer:

"I am here simply as an American citizen. Whatever may be my personal feeling in this matter, I am debarred just now from thrusting my views upon the voters of the country. From an international standpoint it would not be courteous, and from my standpoint it would be impertinent."

At the same time he could not restrain himself entirely. His sympathies were so thoroughly aroused in the cause of the Irish people, which was to him broader than the mere question of sectionalism, that he was, perforce, embroiled to some extent in the contest. His meeting with Gladstone in Liverpool at that time is noteworthy.

Mr. Beecher delayed his departure to London, where he had engagements, for three days in order to be present at Gladstone's closing address in the campaign at Henglar's Circus, Liverpool. The "two grand old men" met in the ante-room at that meeting, and when they went upon the platform there were almost as many and as enthusiastic cheers for Beecher as there were for the latter-day industrial liberator. Despite the urgent calls for some utterance from the man who a quarter of a century before had quelled the pro-Southern Liverpool mobs and brought them to reason, Mr. Beecher would say no word, adhering to his belief that at that time it was not fitting that there should be any American interference.

For a month he stopped in London. On Tuesday, Sept. 28, 1886, the Board of London Congregational Ministers, with their wives or other lady friends and a few invited guests, entertained Mr. and Mrs. Beecher at a social meeting in the Memorial Hall. On that occasion Mr. Beecher made an address in which he said:

"I say in regard to all church worship, that is the best form of church economy, which, in the long run, helps men to be the best Christians. In regard to ordinances I stand very nearly where the Quakers do, except that they think that because they are not divinely commanded they are not necessary. I think they are most useful. Common schools are not divinely ordered, Sunday schools are not divinely ordered; but would you dispense with them? Is there no law and reason except that of the letter? Whatever thing is found when applied to human nature to do good, that is God's ordinance. If there are any men that worship God through the Roman Catholic Church—and there are—I say this in regard to them: 'I can not, but you can; God bless you!' In that great, venerable church there is gospel enough to save any man; no man need perish for want of

CATHERINE BEECHER.

light and truth in that system; and yet, what an economy it is; what an organization, what burdens, and
how many lurking mischiefs that temptations will
bring out!   I could never be a Roman Catholic, but I
could be a Christian in a Roman Catholic church; I
could serve God there.   I believe in the Episcopacy—
for those who want it.   Let my tongue forget its cunning if I ever speak a word adverse to the church that
brooded my mother, and now broods some of the nearest blood kindred I have on earth.   It is a man's own
fault if he do not find salvation in the teaching and

worship of the great Episcopal body of the world.
Well, I can find no charm in the Presbyterian government. I was for ten years a member of the Presbyterian Church, for I swore to the confession of faith;
but at that time my beard had not grown. The rest
of the Book of Worship has great wisdom in it, and
rather than not have any brotherhood, I would be a
Presbyterian again if they would not oblige me to
swear to the confession of faith. On the other hand,
my birthright is in the Congregational Church. I
was born in it, it exactly agreed with my temperament and with my ideas; and it does yet, for although
it is in many respects slow-molded, although in many
respects it has not the fascinations in its worship that
belong to the high ecclesiastical organizations;
though it makes less for the eye and less for the ear,
and more for the reason and the emotions; though it
has, therefore, slenderer advantages, it has this: that it
does not take men because they are weak and crutch
them up upon its worship, and then just leave them as
weak after forty years as they were when it found
them. A part of its very idea is so to meet the weakness of men as that they shall grow stronger; to
preach the truth, and then wait till they are able to
seize that truth and live by it. It works slowly, but I
tell you that when it has finished its work it makes
men in the community; and I speak both of the Con-

gregationalists that are called Baptists and those that are called Congregationalists; they are one and the same, and ought to be hand in hand with each other, in perfect sympathy."

His social reception there was of the most emphatic and flattering description. But he was too humorous. Alas! he said funny things in the pulpit, and some of the sombre newspapers there published, had lugubrious editorials upon "Humor in the Pulpit." Mr. Beecher could no more refrain from painting a moral lesson there, with some animated and possibly jocular allusion, than he could help breathing, and before he left he convinced the Britishers that a spice of humor was not absolutely incompatible with the most thorough-going and straight-laced religion.

CHAPTER XX.

After a four months' absence, during which he met most distinguished Liberals in England, Mr. Beecher returned home and was received with open arms by a people who cherished him as a man of large heart, great brain, and large manhood.

He resumed his labors, ardently looking forward to years of activity and usefulness. To his brother he wrote:

BROOKLYN, N. Y., Jan. 25.

MY DEAR BROTHER: You are ahead of us all in years. But we are all hard after you, Edward, Mary, Charles and myself. To think that this coming summer I shall be seventy-four years old. It is high time that I should leave off all boyish ways and study grave and dignified manners. But as I have no rheumatism, no neuralgia, no baldheadedness, no need of spectacles, no deafness — how could it be expected that I should behave properly? No, Providence meant me for a squirrel, but suddenly changed its mind and made a man of me, and so I must, squirrel-like, frolic on to the end.

Charles and Edward are well, Edward preaching

twice on Sunday and walking six miles to do it. I suppose that some one sent you a paper account of the celebration of his sixtieth anniversary of ordination. Next summer I shall have been ordained fifty years, married fifty years, and settled in Brooklyn forty years. There's figures for you.

My wife has been quite sick for six weeks. She had a compound made up of rheumatism and neuralgia, with a substratum of dyspepsia and a touch of heart trouble. Poor thing, she did suffer! But she is better and getting about again. With love to all your household and yourself, I am, your affectionate brother,

HENRY WARD BEECHER.

To the Rev. William H. Beecher.

When Oscar S. Straus, now Minister to Turkey, was being urged for that office by his friends, Mr. Beecher, a warm friend of Mr. Straus, wrote the following letter. It is a peculiar letter. It tells more definitely than any words describe, the broad statesmanship and advanced position of Brooklyn's famous pastor:

BROOKLYN, N. Y., Feb. 12, 1887.

Grover Cleveland — DEAR MR. PRESIDENT: Some of our best citizens are solicitous for the appointment of Oscar Straus as Minister to Turkey. Of his fitness there is a general consent that he is personally, and in attainments, eminently excellent. But I am interested in another quality — the fact that he is a Hebrew. The bitter prejudice against Jews, which

16

obtains in many parts of Europe, ought not to receive any countenance in America. It is because he is a Jew, that I would urge his appointment as a fit recognition of this remarkable people, who are becoming large contributors to American prosperity, and whose intelligence, morality, and large liberality in all public measures for the welfare of society deserve and should receive from the hands of our Government some such recognition. Is it not also a duty to set forth in this quiet but effectual method the genius of American Government, which has under its fostering care people of all civilized nations, and which treats them without regard to civil, religious, or race peculiarities as common citizens. We send Danes to Denmark, Germans to Germany; we reject no man because he is a Frenchman; why should we not make a crowning testimony to the genius of our people by sending a Hebrew to Turkey? The ignorance and superstition of medieval Europe may account for the prejudice of that dark age. But how a Christian in our day can turn from a Jew I can not imagine. Christianity itself ˉsuckled at the bosom of Judaism; our roots are in the Old Testament. We are Jews ourselves gone to blossom and fruit. Christianity is Judaism in evolution, and it would seem strange for the seed to turn against the stock on which it was grown.

HENRY WARD BEECHER.

Always indefatigable and unremitting in his literary labors, Mr. Beecher had been — ever since his return from Europe — even more assiduous at the toil of the desk than before. He contributed several articles a week to newspapers, and worked day and night upon his great task, the preparation of his long delayed "Life of Christ." That work is now about two-thirds finished, and as the written pages accumulated under his pen he never wearied. So it seemed to Mrs. Beecher, his devoted wife, and to his sons, Colonel Henry B. Beecher and Mr. William C. Beecher, with whom he lived in the old fashioned, commodious four story brick building on the corner of Hicks and Clark streets.

It was with difficulty that his family could prevail upon him to leave off work at the desk in his study, on the second floor, to go down stairs to his meals.

Mr. Beecher's health did not appear to suffer from the confinement, but there is now no doubt that it did. It was a complete change in his habits. He had always been accustomed to take a great deal of outdoor exercise. Full blooded and inclined to gain flesh rapidly, he always said that the more he lived out of doors the better he felt. He was not a hearty eater. Always accustomed to take good care of himself, he adapted his eating to his physical needs rather than to his appetite, and often ate less than a child. He was in the habit of taking long walks every day, and there was no figure so well known on the streets of New York or Brooklyn as his.

The sudden changes in his way of life, which followed when he came home from England, and secluded himself to complete his "Life of Christ," undoubtedly had a more serious effect upon his health than any one knew at the time. He was not in the best of health when he returned from abroad. The ocean voyage never did agree with him, and he had not recovered from its fatigues when he renewed his labors upon his great literary work.

Mr. Beecher, with his enthusiastic nature, never did things by halves, and when he set himself the task of completing his book, he went at it vigorously, and denied himself the outdoor exercise and the recreation he needed.

Some fifteen years ago, when he stood above the coffin that held the lifeless form of Horace Greeley, Mr. Beecher, saddened by the burden of a personal sorrow, uttered these words:

"Death is always hidden, no matter how long it may have been expected. Death is always impressive, no matter where it strikes. But when it comes no man looks for it; when it strikes down men whose words have been treasured in every household and whose teachings have inspired the nation, then, indeed, it becomes impressive and momentous."

In the Brooklyn Magazine for last March he wrote:

"We are going home. Men shiver at the idea

that we are going to die; but this world is only a nest. We are scarcely hatched out of it here. We do not know ourselves. We have strange feelings that do not interpret themselves. The mortal in us is crying for the immortal. As in the night the child, waking with some vague and nameless terror, cries out to express its fear and dread, and its cry is interpreted in the mother's heart, who runs to the child and lays her hand upon it and quiets it to sleep again, so God hears our disturbances, trials and tribulations in life. Do you not suppose that He who is goodness itself cares for you? Do you suppose that He whose royal name is Love has less sympathy for you than the mother has for her babe? Let the world rock. If the foot of God is on the cradle, fear not. Look up, take courage, hope, and hope unto the end."

Said an old acquaintance: "The day ex-President Arthur was buried I passed down the side aisle of the Church of the Heavenly Rest, and paused when near the altar to look about in the gloom for a seat. I felt a hand laid gently on my arm, which drew me into the pew.

"As we went out of the church, following the funeral cortége, all were impressed with the solemn rendering of 'I Would Not Live Alway.' As the last note died away I turned to Mr. Beecher, who had so kindly made place for me, and said: 'I would not live alway, would you?'

" 'No,' said he firmly. 'I have lived almost as long as I want to.'

" At that moment a friend greeted us near the door. 'Mr. Beecher and I have decided,' I said, 'that we do not wish to live to be a hundred.'

" 'I do,' replied the gentleman.

"I remarked that the Rev. Dr. Tyng once said 'that he did not want to die from the top first.'

" 'That indeed would be dreadful,' were Mr. Beecher's last words, as he grasped my hand with a vigorous 'good-bye,' stepping off like a man of twenty-five."

One of Mr. Beecher's Sunday letters, published the first of the year, seems to have been tinged with the sadness that might come from a premonition that he was entering upon a year that was to be his last. His thoughts turn to the harvest of death reaped by the year that was closing as he wrote. The following is its opening paragraph:

"As one who saunters through the fields in autumn gathering flowers, leaves and fruits, so Time comes to this new year with arms full gathered from among men of the gentle, the forward, the strong and wise and of those who die as 'the fool dieth.' But, besides the men of name known and talked about, what numberless hosts have gone into the shadow-land silently, unannounced, unknown, except to the half dozen who lived under the same roof!"

At another time:

"Life insurance is not only not wrong, but is a duty. No one has any right to leave those who are dependent upon his love and care to the chances of industrial paralysis and poverty."

Again, Beecher said years ago:

"I never had any sympathy with the Episcopal prayer, 'From sudden death deliver us.' When I go I pray that I may go swiftly, like a falling star; go in the midst of my usefulness, and not be chained in some living death, a burden to myself and the friends I love."

CHAPTER XXI.

In the midst of work, and "with his harness still on" Mr. Beecher was suddenly stricken down.

J. T. Howard was one of the first to welcome Mr. Beecher to Brooklyn, and a close friendship at once sprang up between them, and was only broken by death. The last evening spent from home by Mr. Beecher was passed at the residence of Mr. Howard. This was Wednesday evening of the week. Mr. Beecher was as buoyant in manner and as full of life as at any time in the last dozen years.

Mr. Beecher's last charitable work of a public character was his effort to provide the nucleus of a library for the Western branch of the Old Soldiers' Home at Leavenworth, Kan. Gov. Smith was at the head of this institution, and in his anxiety to provide mental food for his veterans he never forgot to depict their wants in the way of a library, not only to personal friends, but to any one whom he thought would give the project helping hand. It is supposed that he asked Mr. Beecher's assistance and Mr. Beecher promptly responded. A concert was to be given by members of Plymouth Church, and he promised Gen. King to give the Soldiers' Home library scheme a " good notice." He urged his congregation to send what books they could spare to Leavenworth, and, saying that he intended to practice what he preached, contributed books which filled two wheelbarrows. None who ever approached him to ask for proper assistance ever expected to meet with refusal.

" On Thursday morning, before his last illness," writes a friend, " I received a note from Mr. Beecher asking me to call and see him that evening. I did so and found him in his accustomed good health and the very best of good humor. After supper he asked to examine the catalogue of a Western publishing house, which he had requested me to bring. Turning over the leaves he made running comments upon the appearance of certain authors whose portraits were on the pages ; I remember his humorous allusion to George Eliot's portrait. The picture was a small head of the famous novelist, and by some accident the face had become very much darkened by a surplus of ink, which made her strongly resemble an Indian squaw, and her features hardly distinguishable. 'Now why,' said Mr. Beecher to me, 'will men print such pictures as that one? The Lord knows George Eliot was homely enough, and the devil knows it by this time. Do you know what that picture suggested to me?' he continued. I said it looked very much like an Indian woman. 'No,' said Mr. Beecher, 'it looks to me as if George Eliot had been in purgatory and there had been some terrible explosion with her in the center of it.'"

Sunday, February 27, morning and evening, Mr. Beecher preached two remarkably vigorous sermons. The evening sermon, which was his last, was reported by Mr. Wiman, as follows:

"And He said unto His disciples, There was a certain rich man which had a servant, and the same was accused unto him. * * * No servant can serve two masters; for either he will hate the one and love the other, or else he will hold to the one and despise the other. You can not serve God and Mammon."

Text—Luke, xvi. chap., 4th verse, the first clause: "I am resolved what to do."

"I read in your hearing this narrative, this parable of our Lord. The unjust steward had been accused, and rightfully, of betraying his trust and wasting that committed to him. His master called him to an account, and he was satisfied that the end had come; and he communed with himself, and as the result of that, and looking over all the circumstances, he said: 'I am resolved what to do.'

"What he resolved to do was not very honest, but

it was very shrewd.   He resolved to make friends of
all the debtors of his lord.   He called them up and
settled with them in such a way as to lay them under
obligations—gratitude to him   And so, although he
and they cheated the master, he made his own nest
warm and the master praised him—not Jesus, but the
man that owned the property is the one.   When he
heard of it he said to himself: 'Well, that is shrewd;
that is cunning; that is wise,' and the comment on it
is: Children of this world are wiser than the children
of light; that is to say, men who are acting in worldly
reasons, for worldly reasons, are very much wiser than
the men becoming good from the highest moral considerations.   But that, that they have selected, is simply this: 'I am resolved what to do.'

"What, then, is the nature of a resolution—what
is the scope of it, the potency?   And what are the
drawbacks?   The self-consideration of these questions
may throw light upon the path of many of us.   Now,
our long effort of making up our mind is equivalent to
forming a purpose.   When a man resolves, he means,
or should mean, to do something; and all resolutions
carry, or should carry, not simply the end sought, but
also the capable and necessary means by which the
end is sought.   I am resolved to cross that river, by
the bridge, by boat, or by swimming.   To stand on
one side and to resolve to be on the other, without any

intermediate means of doing it, would be folly indeed. I am resolved to-morrow to go to market. All the intermediate and implied steps by which that resolution could be carried out are included in the resolution itself. A resolution is a purpose in so far as simple things, uncompounded, incomplex, are concerned. A resolution may be executed immediately, without loss of time; indeed, the greatest number of resolutions are those which, like the stroke of the hammer· or the explosion of the gun, are almost without any appreciable interlapse of time. 'I am resolved what to do.' Natural resolutions: At the cry of fire the man instantly looks out to see what to do; at the call of a man to step to the door and see a stranger or a friend; he resolves to do it; although the resolution is latent in such a sense by repetition, that he is not conscious of making up his mind.

" In regard to a great many of the acts of a man's life, cerebration — that is to say, the action of the brain — has become so common that it takes place without any appreciable appearance of taking place. A multitude of things — if one gets in a crowd, and a man would strike him, his defense is not the result of reflection, and yet it was in him as a result of experience to protect himself; and, if it be a shadow, it is just the same, for a shadow seems like a substance, and he puts himself in a ludicrous attitude of defense;

he smiles, and he goes on, but the action of the mind,
the unconscious cerebration, is there. As, for instance,
in things that apply to the now, that are uncompounded and simple, a man resolves and executes
almost at the same moment. The child calls from
above, 'Father,' and incidentally there is no thought
whether he shall or shall not answer, yet the train
goes on within him, and he replies, 'My son what?'
Or the call has come to him for help, and instantly,
before the last echo of the sound dies out of his ear,
he is on his feet, on his way. But these are very
simple things; they are the primary forms, which
afterwards, becoming more and more complicated, running through longer periods of time, imply a great
many intermediate steps. For a man can resolve that
he will go to bed — it doesn't take long, either — he
resolves that to-morrow morning he will get up and
go 'cruising,' but to-morrow is dark and stormy, and
the resolution is not half so strong when he wakes up
as it was when he went to bed. There are a great
many considerations that come. Or the man resolves
that to-morrow he will go to market; neighbors come
in; he waits; it is noon, and then time is too little to
go. 'And come again.' And he puts it off until the
next morning. So between the resolution and the
night — for one takes hold upon the other — there is
a delay and the intermediate history

"Now, as you go on in life, as society itself becomes more complex—civilization is growth in complexity — as the things that you resolve to do or not to do, are largely in their times, and are clustered together by cause and effect, resolutions, spreading over so long spaces and so much intermediatism, are somewhat different from the first resolve.

"Resolution, then, means a purpose, the will itself; and it includes in it, also, all indispensable intermediate steps; and some resolutions execute themselves immediately; some with some delay; some with long delay; some, through many subordinate resolutions, that carry out the primary one. And a man may resolve at a critical moment, that which will determine the whole career of his life; yea, he may determine in any one single, final moment, that which will take the whole of his life to carry into effect. This is the case of ten thousand men. When my father was young, a lad (he was brought up by, substantially, an uncle), he had in him all that was necessary to make him what he was in his professional life. But he did not do it; he was careless; he was heedless; he was forgetful of things external; and so Uncle Lot Benton one morning, going out, found that being out late with the horses the night before, visiting some young company, the bridle was placed over the water-trough and the saddle was thrown down behind the stable door, aud the horses turned in without a halter, and he said, 'Oh, well, Lyman will never make a farmer; he is not fitted for it.' And so, talking in the orchard with him one day, he says: 'Lyman, how would you like to go to college?' No answer. They went on working all day. Next day, about the same hour, as they were working together in the orchard, Lyman says: 'I would like to go, sir.' That settled it. In that beginning was a purpose that shaped differently his whole life; it never gave out; it branched in every direction; he made what he was; that was owing to the parting; by not, he would have been a miserable farmer; he made a tolerably good minister and a tolerably good father.

'So, then, a man may form a resolution without noise, without parade, but that holds infinite sequences in its development. It may include in itself a short process and an intermediate; it may include in itself a longer process; it may include in itself the whole scope of a man's life, and thrice ten thousand resolutions will be formed successively to carry out the great primary resolution which a man makes. Thus, if a man is to be a lawyer he is not going to be a blacksmith, nor a sailor, nor a soldier, so that there is the resolution of exclusion; it turns him away from those things inconsistent with the first element. If he is to be a lawyer there must be the question of education, and a professional education, and all the conditions which are prerequisite to the presenting himself to the court and his license to plead and the beginnings of practice. All of those are wrapped up in the first determination, 'I will be a lawyer;' but that determination don't make him one; it starts him on a long train of events that are necessary to make him a lawyer. And so in regard to morality, a young man may stand on the threshold of life; he may resolve that he will see the world; and the man that means to see everything in the world will probably see a good deal under the world, by and by, that he won't care about seeing. A man who resolves, on the other hand, 'I believe in honesty; it is the best principle' (but it is better than nothing to say); that is the best policy; it is good policy; all good policy is a principle; all good principles carry with them a policy. And a young man, he says, 'I am determined to be an honest and upright man;' that at once spreads to other men; he won't associate with certain ones, he will associate with certain others; he won't follow certain things; he will seek other paths; the resolution sifts life for him out of its discipline, and another resolution is a growing, crude thing. Now, there are a good many people who don't seem ever to have a resolution ; they are like sieves, all their thoughts run through and are wasted; there is a great

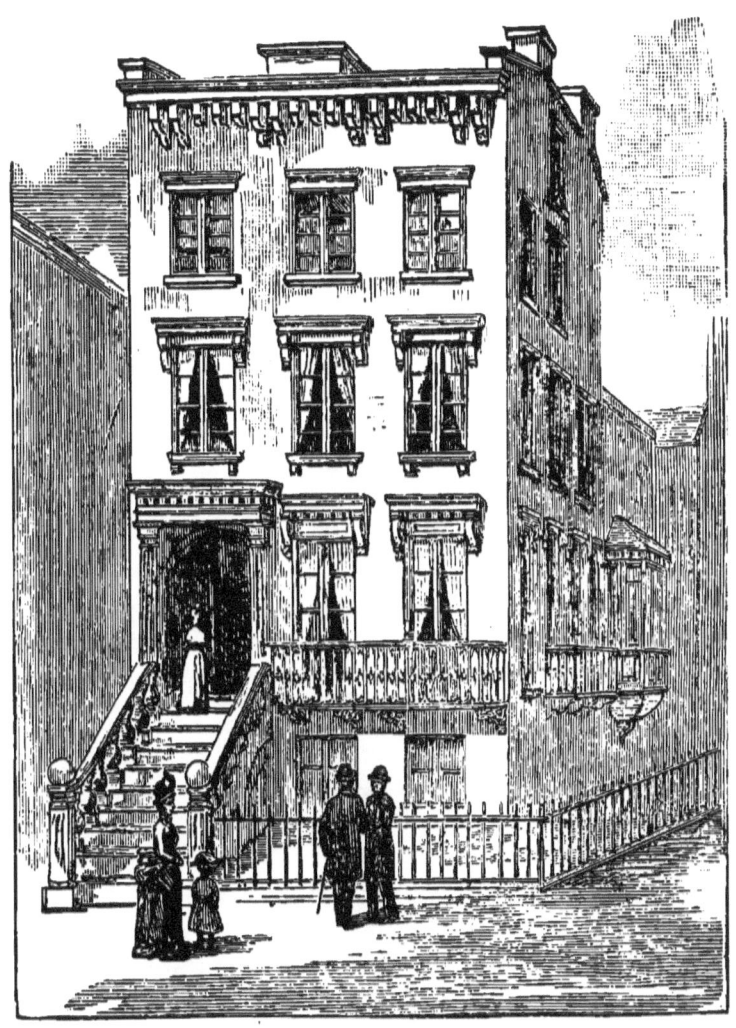

BEECHER'S BROOKLYN HOME.

See page 165.

257

deal of diffidence about them; there are some men whose thoughts are like the ratchet-wheel, the wheel that has, notch by notch, to hold what it has got; and there are a great many whose thoughts are like thistle downs that are going everywhere, and don't know that they are going anywhere, and are subject to the mutations of the wind. There is a great deal of difference—need be—to win men to form resolutions, sometimes, of a strong nature and a sterling strong purpose; when once they have resolved never to flinch, they never know in any hour a downsliding; they may be less active at one time than another, but they don't turn back. Once having put their hand to the plough they don't look back again. But then there are those that have the same policy resolution, but they are made of different stuff; it slides away; they forget it; they are not stiff enough to stand up against the wind, it may be, that shall come upon them.

"The general qualities of the resolutions which men make are of every grade; even a frail woman, walking in the boisterous March wind, may find that with all the sail she carries she can not make headway against it, and supports herself by a fence that is stiff enough to hold her until the wind lulls. And as it is in the community so it is in regard to individuals—there are many persons who, left to themselves, waver;

they do so sometimes from good reasons, sometimes from those not so good, sometimes because the purposes were formed in a moment of excitement and have nothing left of them when the excitement cools. There is instability also arising from disability of organization; that is to say, a man may be susceptible while one class of effects is being produced, and in that mood he may form a resolution, but to-morrow some other blessed, beautiful thing may come up, and he is just as susceptible of that, and the secondary state of mind obliterates the first. A man is under the influence of music, and all his purposes run under that power or influence, but, by and by, the outbreak of politics brings up patriotism, as it is called, and his moods change, and those early sensations at first are no longer operative upon him; another powerful influence causes digression. There are many men who have such ancillary elements brought to bear upon their wills and upon their temperaments that they are almost persuaded to be Christians, and think they will be, but, going home in a hurry, fall in with company, and the day following business instincts and interests. It is like another scene that day. So that there is this changeableness in men. Then the decrease of the power came from the nature of the mind. There is, this idea however, not to be neglected—the distinction between the man's willing and his wishing. A

great many people think that a wish is a resolution.
Oh, it has gone into a proverb. 'If wishes were
horses, then beggars might ride.' A man wishes he
were rich, but he is too lazy, and he never will be;
a man wishes that he knew more; probably never
will; he is lazy; a man wishes that he could have
entrance into certain circles in society, but the steps
requisite he never will have patience or wisdom to
take. You might just as well carry a candle around
the field and think it is agriculture, because it is
light shining on the crops. Thousands of people
think they wish to be Christians; they don't. That
is the interpretation given much of the instruction
of Jesus. Men came to Him and said: 'Lord, we
will follow Thee whithersoever Thou goest.' 'No,
you won't; you don't know that I am destined to suffering, poverty, persecution, death; you think that I
am going to be a royal personage and shower honors
and gold.' 'Ah,' says one, 'I will follow thee, but
suffer me first.' Ah, there is that 'if' and 'but' in life.
Ten thousand people say, 'I would like to be a Christian if,' and that settles it. 'I want to be a Christian,
but'—yes, that settles it again. And so Christ was
surrounded by swarms of persons, following him
around, wishing and wishing, with various degrees of
excitability in them, and he put them all off; he would
have nothing to do with them. 'Let him take up his

cross and follow me, whosoever would be my disciple.'
There is something to do, something to prove, and to
wish.   There is a great distinction between wishing,
then, and willing; for when a man wills the purpose
carries with it the instrument to effect itself.   You
wish to be a Christian; do you will to be one?   Your
wishing is tantalization if *will* be accomplishment.

"Now, Christian life is the only reasonable one,
whether you regard it as a duty or as a means of the
greatest satisfaction; that is to say, we were made to
be Christians, and being a Christian is simply putting
yourself in those relations to yourself, to your fellow-
men and to your God for which you were created.
Did you ever undertake to take apart a watch?   That
is very easy.   Did you ever undertake to put it
together again?   That is not so easy.   You don't
know which screw goes into which hole; you don't
know exactly which wheel goes in first; but one thing
is perfectly certain, and that is that nothing else will
fit together but that of which the watch was made,
and each wheel was destined to one place and to one
avocation, and if you can bring them together, according to the intent of the maker, it will perform, and
otherwise it will not.   Now, a man was built with a
great deal more care than ever a watch was.   He has
definite relations to himself.   A man was made to live
with men, and there is only one way and one principle

on which men can live together—kindness, love. Justice means love; justice is not something else; and we have a test, an example, a revelation in Jesus, in the Old Testament as well as in the New, but in the New with clearer emphasis and larger light, seeing there how we have got to live toward our fellow men, what are the interlacing relations and what is the predominant spirit in which we are to treat them. 'Thou shalt love thy neighbor as thyself.' Self-love is made to be the very model and type of that affection which you are to give to all people. Then we know perfectly well that we are affianced to yet higher beings than man, and to the invisible cosmos as well as to the visible; and we can not live when we are out of joint with any of these relations in ourselves and to our neighbors and to our God. Now, I say it is reasonable that we should endeavor to live after this type upon which we were created. This is reasonable. A great many men can; but, to the weak, Christianity is nothing but priestcraft, and it is not reasonable for a man to be damned because he could not believe, and, especially, because he could not gulp and swallow all the dogmas and all the forms. But that is wide of the mark. True Christianity means living in those relations for which we were created—harmonization of ourselves, harmonization of our relations to our fellow men, harmonization of our relation to the invisible future. And I say that is reasonable; I say more than that, that it has in it the inherent, the greatest amount of happiness. For although, for temporary reasons, a man may defer to his passions, taking the average and the whole life, he loses rather than gains; he is loser now, but suffers then. A man may think, because he runs through a dissipated period and then reforms, that the dissipation is all over. No, no, no; the causes sink under and run subterraneously, as it were; and there is many a man that has grumbled at forty-five years of age from the misconduct of twenty years. You know that there are the seventeen-year locusts; they lay their eggs, and those eggs lie incubating in the ground for seventeen years; then they hatch and come forth. A man may by evil deeds lay the eggs that will hatch twenty years after that, and as a general truth I think it is demonstrable by actual observation and experience that the true happiness of a man lies in that self-control, in that virtue, in that integrity, in that love-power, which is the substance of religion itself. It is not learning your catechism, it is not learning your verses of faith, it is not going through ecclesiastical achievements. 'Thou shalt love the Lord thy God, and thy neighbor as thyself.' Therefore, you must lift yourself, and he that lifts himself shows, not by partiality toward the lower and worst features in himself, but towards his whole self

— the regent understanding, the moral power and elements and spiritual in him. Now, when a man has this presented to him, and he is urged to enter upon a Christian life as the only honorable one, the only one that has the greatest satisfaction in it, the only one that carries in it the idea of duty and gratitude towards God, how thoughtlessly men heed that. To-night how many are there of you that say in thus looking over the sphere of life — life to come: 'I am resolved what to do.' Bearing in mind what a resolution means and what it includes, how many men can say to-night, 'Yes, I am resolved what to do.' There are very few of you that would say, 'I am resolved not to be a Christian.' That is a very hazardous thing, which very few men care to resolve. Men may say, on the other hand, 'I hope some time to be a Christian; I feel sometimes as if I would like to be one; I wish I was one;' just as a lazy man wishes he had the products of industry. But how many men are there here to-night that can say, 'I am resolved what to do,' 'I am resolved what to do.'

"Are you then resolved at once to become a Christian? Can I be a Christian at once? In one sense, no; in another sense, yes. Nobody ever learned a trade at a blow, but he can begin this day; no man ever became a scholar by a resolution, but he never can become one without a resolution; it is a complex one and a constantly repeating one, ancillary resolutions upholding the main one. Are you resolved to be a Christian to this extent — I will begin to-night? 'I am resolved as far as I have light and as far as I know my way, I am determined, God knows I am determined to square my life hereafter on Christian principles. I am resolved to be a Christian man.' Now, this may include churches. I may be a Roman Catholic and resolve it, or a Protestant and stay out of that church, and stay out of any other church. This resolution doesn't mean I will be a Christian like to this scheme or that scheme, according to this church or that church; it simply means in its simplest form, its primary condition, 'I will regulate my 'life, both inside and out, according to the principles laid down for me by the Lord Jesus Christ.' Is not that a very simple thing? But what does it carry with it? It carries, in the first place, this: 'I will therefore begin by excluding everything that I know will hinder this resolution; from a consciously wicked way, I will begin as a part of the fulfilment of this resolution, I will stop.' That is the meaning of the repentence John began and Christ took up. Repent, for the kingdom of heaven is at hand, that is to say, I will get over every known wrong that is inconsistent with this purpose that I have formed; I am going to live as a Christian man, as a Christian woman; and if there be that which I know to be fundamentally wrong I shall carry out my resolution by repenting or turning away from that. And then, in the next place, a resolution to be a Christian applies immediately; it is not that I will be a Christian next year, or by and by, or a long time — death, but it is going on, beginning at once to live, as far as I know how, righteous. Do you mean, then, to take the steps that are necessary? Are you ready to begin your attempt to live a Christian life by saying in sincerity, ' God show me the way; give me thy help?' Are you willing? Not to say your prayers; there are a great many prayers said; a great many, too few prayers that are felt and not true. Is there sincerity in you? I would to God that you have spiritual refilling and the sustaining power of the whole spirit, that you have the certainty that he was working in me to will and to do his good pleasure. Are you ready to begin your Christian life then by opening the word of God and reading, not a chapter, nor a verse or two every day, but to make it the line of your counsel? When any great combination scheme is being formed in New York — any syndicate — there is always the lawyer, and they will never take a single step until they consult him, and he is about all the while; he is the man of their counsel; it is a complicated thing and a great deal depends upon it, and they can not afford to go wrong. Are you willing to take the New Testament as the line of your counsel? See what it says about lusts, about appetites, what it says about crime and envy and jealousy and all ill will and evil speaking and all selfishness in its grasping moods. Are you willing to look through the New Testament to see what the law of the Lord is? Not by discussion. God will take care of his own defense and doesn't thank you for any help; nor has he any occasion to thank anybody. Are you willing to take the Bible just as a shipmaster takes the chart? When he leaves the last shore light and takes his direction he never says, ' Read me a direction or two of the sailing directions, and then read me the draughtings inside again and then again.' They have no relation at all to his course, to his actual sailing; but he is not going to read so many parts of his chart and of his sailing directions. Why, no; he lays out his voyage from the beginning and every day he takes observations, and then he checks down on the chart just where he is. At noon to-morrow he takes another observation; not because there is any need of reading his chart, in reading any book on navigation; not because he is studying astronomy for the sake of anything that is in astronomy. He has got a definite purpose in life; after which he sells his astronomy, and after which he sells his books, or those which lay his course. Are you willing to begin a Christian course and voyage by going to the word of God to ascertain exactly what is expected of you, both what you are to reject and what you are to adopt? That is sensible, that is right resolving, according to a practical basis and resolution. Or, on the other hand, are you, while you are weighing, that is, in yourself, are you saying to yourself: ' My other people of God got on the best way. There is my father and mother. If there were ever any Christians they were such. I believe they were real Christians?' Now, a man's mother is infinitely more to him than the Virgin Mary is to any devout Catholic.

" You come into the church because you find sympathy there and kindly help there. Are you willing to take advantage of all these kindly helps, so that you may be able to keep your purpose and your will? Are you willing to begin it now? You don't need any more knowledge. You have been brought up in Christian knowledge from the very cradle; you have no bad associations; you have necessarily none by the average, but what Christian life was and Christian duty, is — there is not a man here that needs to have additional instruction; he knows that he is bound to live obediently to God and in love with Jesus Christ. But can a man come into a state of emotion? Can a man by simply saying I will, feel? No; no; but by saying I will feel he can take the steps to feel. A man shivers and says, 'Chills and fever are not agreeable; I am determined to get over them.' Well, you can not get over them by determining it, but if you will take quinine enough you can. Now, let your purpose be not simply this, 'I am resolved to be a Christian,' but 'I am resolved so unostentatiously. I am going to feel myself for all the help I can and all the Christian institutions that are necessary for my weal.' Now, that is practical, and that is common sense as well as moral sense. Or are you going to say, 'Well, I will see about it.' No, you won't; you know it. And that thing we have in our times, when a loath debtor, he has given a note for the sake of paying a debt—but for the sake of getting rid of paying it they put it off for four months, and then they give another note. It is the greenback business, in which they pay one note by giving another. There are multitudes of people that form a resolution for the sake of not fulfilling a duty, and a man says, 'Well, I have made up my mind I am going to be a Christian as soon as I get ready.' When are you going to get ready? It has clouded your conscience and clouded your reason now by promising to do that, by and by, when the convenient time comes; and the devil will see to it that it never comes. It is a resolution that simply means the feeling of having done your duty. And I think the most scandalous meannesses and dishonorable-ness that can very well be imagined, when the parties concerned are regarded, is that resolution that people form to be a Christian, when they have wasted themselves in the service of selfishness, and when they have come into old age and lie on their death-bed. I should think myself very mean if, in the summer time, I should gather a peck of peas and shell out the peas, and send the pods over to my neighbor as a present. That is what men mean to do with God; they mean to live in youth after their passions; they mean to live in middle age after their ambition; they mean to live in old age after ease, and before they die they hope to whip on the right side and get into heaven. When you come to examine such conduct in its relations to men, there is not a savage that would not feel that was infamous — to repay protection, divine benediction, the ministration of God through all the channels of nature and the kindness of God through Jesus Christ for the ministration of the gospel; and the man deliberately says, we will seek all the money out of these things and all the rest that is in life, and when we are no longer of use to ourselves we will repent so as to get into heaven. Two Dutch elders had been warm friends, and yet one day they fell out with each other and the fire grew fiercer until they came positively to hate each other, and one Sunday morning the dominie going behind one of the elders heard him mutter to himself, 'Van Alstyne is a hypocrite; he will go to hell, he will go to hell.' The old dominie spoke up to him and said: 'Oh, oh, my brother, he won't go to hell.' 'Yes, he will go to hell.' 'Well, but, my dear fellow, he may repent.' 'No—well, he is just mean enough to do it.' But this is—it is, candidly—the condition in which some of you are. You mean to live hatefully, disobediently, dishonorably, and yet in the last estate you mean to whip up and get into heaven—you are 'just mean enough to do it.'

"Now, on the other hand, blessed be God, he is long suffering, and he is patient, and as we would pay a debt, by instalments, little by little, showing all the time that we endeavor to do it, he respects your endeavor to live, to repent and to live a Christian life, by instalments.

"If you make up your mind honestly to do it, he will bear with your incompetence and your ignorance and your endearments; he will bear patiently with you, and help you from day to day, and from month to month, and from year to year, 'growing brighter and brighter unto the perfect day.' Is there any man here that can say in regard to the past, I am resolved that I will cut loose from everything that has been a detriment to me, dishonorable to God? Is there any man that will say in regard to the future, 'I am resolved what to do? I am resolved to take a higher life, the nobler ideal; I am determined, by the help of God, that I will live in such a way that I should live.' And if there is, don't wait until to-morrow morning; readjust your life to-night; go home and tell God of it; go home and tell your wife of it. That is the very thing you don't dare to do, because when a man has once committed himself he is ashamed to go back; and if you are ashamed to tell anybody 'I have made up my mind to live like a Christian man,' it is because you have not made up your mind. When a man has determined that he will live a Christian life he will be willing to show to all that are around about him. 'I am going to try. I have made up my mind to try.' If you have, mind you will enter upon your journey. 'The time is past in which I have served the will of the flesh, and now, to-night, I have determined that I will begin, with the help of God, to live a Christian life.' Are there any of you that are willing to make that resolve? God help you. For a little while it will be a troublesome thing, for a little while, but then easier and easier, with remuneration and exhilaration and joy and final victory."

At the end Mr. Beecher offered this prayer:

"We thank Thee for the day, for the light that has shone, for that brighter light that we have felt. We thank Thee for the consciousness that has been in us

18

that we have been accepted of Thee, and that our souls are endeavoring to walk in Thy way. We thank Thee for the quiet of our home, and that Thou hast among any of us brought the twilight hour within the midnight, as it were. We thank Thee for the sustaining grace and for the kindling up before us of a brighter future interpreted by hope; and we thank Thee that Thou hast taught us that all things shall work together for good to them that love Thee. We have learned largely and yet are poor scholars. We believe that in looking back upon life we have discerned the fulfilment of Thy declarations. The things that once wet us with tears we now see to have been mercy; the things that we sought for and mourned because we had them not we rejoice that they were denied us. Our children are perpetually getting from us refusals; we rejoice that Thou art not less tender of us than we are of our children. And so we submit ourselves to Thy province and rejoice in it, and not alone because Thou hast declared but because Thou hast fulfilled in our experience Thy words. We praise Thee and rejoice in Thy will made known to us in the unfolding processes of our lives. Now, we beseech of Thee that Thou wilt in love chastise us; arouse us from stupor; suffer us not to lose ground as a slumberous man; we pray Thee that we may be spared by Thy truth and by Thy providence and have cast Thine

EXTERIOR OF MR. BEECHER'S HOUSE AT PEEKSKILL.

own soul on ours by the Holy Ghost. We beseech of Thee that Thou wouldst grant unto every one of us, day by day, the consciousness that we are walking under the guide of Thyself. Sanctify to us the dealings of Thy providence, whether they are painful or joyful; make them all joyful, and grant unto us that power by which we can forego temptations; grant unto us that will by which we can hold our own will in subjection; and grant unto us the power to hold our will in union with all that is right and good and work in us to will and to do for Thy good pleasure. We beseech of Thee that Thou wouldst grant Thy blessing according to the several necessities of life. To all that are gathered here—are we not all yet acknowledging ourselves to be Christ's in purpose or in disposition? But yet Thou makest Thy sun to rise upon the good and the evil; Thou sendest rain upon the just and upon the unjust, and so are we not the children of Thy benefaction? Grant Thy blessing upon us all; make our hearts tender to Thy truth; cleanse our lives; help us to search what things are individually for advantage; accept our thanks for so many mercies and bounties and grant that Thou may not make us vain; take not away from us the hunger and the thirst after righteousness. Let Thy kingdom come in us, and Thy will be done as it is in Heaven. We ask it in the Redeemer's name. Amen."

CHAPTER XXII.

HIS WORK IS DONE.

Mr. Beecher's last public appearance was made at Chickering hall, at the mass meeting to advocate the passage of the Crosby High-License Bill, and in favor of which he spoke. He said:

"I plead for high license as mitigating our great peril and in behalf of every day laborer in the city where I am. Thousands of men there are who drink because they have a sorrow, or because they inherit a love for it, or from social bias, or social influences. I speak against this traffic, not because I am a minister, but because I am a humane man, because I love my neighbor. These liquor dealers not only make the laws, but they break them. [Laughter.] All movements to-day are converging toward the limitation of the saloon. I think we should have to-day restrictions in the form of high license, if it were not for the unwillingness of Prohibitionists to join with us. I think that if in a few years we can demonstrate that high license has been of great benefit to the people we shall have the Prohibitionists with us."

On Tuesday he went to Peekskill and returned on Wednesday morning. He was troubled with a dull headache, but did not think much of it. He worked all day at his book and went out with Mrs. Beecher in the evening. Thursday morning, in company with his wife, Mr. Beecher went to New York for the purpose of buying new furniture for the church parlors, which have lately been painted and altered. After driving around the city all day they returned to his home in the evening. The next day he was prostrated by apoplexy.

On Saturday night the news that Henry Ward Beecher lay dying at his home in Brooklyn, flashed over the wires reaching to every part of the civilized world, and was the one topic of conversation and subject of universal sympathy on Sunday.

Not since the assassination of Garfield has there been so general an expression of honest and deep feeling as over Mr. Beecher's bed. Not alone in the sorrowing meetings of his own people on Sunday and on Monday evening, but in the demeanor of the groups who have quietly and sadly lingered about the house, waiting for the latest bulletins; groups made up from every grade of life, poor as well as rich, famous and unknown, mingled together; and in the general tone of conversation and press comment, was seen the warmth and extent of that wonderful personal influence that extended from Mr. Beecher, not only to those who knew him, but to those who had merely heard him speak.

But Fortune — or, as he would have put it, Providence—was kind to Mr. Beecher to the end. The lifelong worker was stopped at his work. The warrior fell with his armor on his back. The orator's voice was hushed between the delivery of one sermon and the preparation of another. It was thus that Henry Ward Beecher wished to die.

How much better that he should fall thus under a single swift stroke, rather than fall into an old age that would deny to him the activities of mind and body which were an inherent and inseparable part of himself, none knew so well as he. And it was no doubt the picture of himself in imagination as in "the lean and slipper'd pantaloon," with "big, manly voice turning again toward childish treble," or the "last scene of all," "second childishness and mere oblivion," that caused the still robust man of three-score and ten to pray often for the kind of death which he died. The spectacle of his remarkable sire, Dr. Lyman Beecher, graphically said to have been "the father of more brains than any other man in America," wandering aimlessly about, alive only from the head down, was familiar to the great preacher, and no doubt contributed to his desire to be spared such a fate. It would have been indeed a hard experience for

Henry Ward Beecher to become consciously superannuated, and a sad sight for those who remembered his superb virility, his intellectual pugnacity, his diffusive humor and genial wit, to see him in a feeble old age waiting and longing for the summons to go. Referring to his father's experience he once said to a friend: "I know there is a purgatory, for I have seen it." Only last week he met on the street a member of Plymouth Church whose father, a strong, well-preserved man over eighty, had recently been stricken of paralysis of which he died in a few days. Mr. Beecher said to the son: "When my time comes I desire two things that were granted to your father. I want that it should be said of me, 'a good man has gone,' and I want to go in the same way."

After the first few hours of restlessness on Thursday night (March 3) he sank into a condition of unconsciousness, in which, as his physicians were able to assure his family, he suffered little, if at all.

The doctor met Mrs. Beecher by the bedside, and she asked him in a voice 'subdued but clear' if there was any hope. The physician answered in deeper tones that appearances were disheartening, and after an interchange of further remarks, Mrs. Beecher suddenly whispered:

"I believe that he understands what we are saying."

"Ask him if he does," suggested the doctor.

With a strong effort at composure Mrs. Beecher raised her voice and said directly to the silent, motionless figure before her:

"Henry, do you understand what we are talking about?"

A moment of profound suspense ensued and then the grandly shaped head moved forward and backward twice, and with extreme difficulty; but there was no mistaking the affirmation it signified. But the eyes remained closed. There was not even a quiver of the lids.

"Perhaps he can speak," whispered Dr. Hammond; "tell him to say what we were talking about."

"Henry, Henry," pleaded Mrs. Beecher, bending over her husband and speaking more loudly, "do you know what we said about you?"

Mr. Beecher seemed to make a supreme effort. His lips unclosed and his breathing came more quickly. His right hand opened and closed convulsively, and at last a murmur of words came forth that fell upon ears strained to the utmost. But the eyes never opened.

"You — were — saying — that — I —could—not—recover," was the disjointed sentence so painfully uttered.

Then a strange thing happened. The words

seemed as if spoken in a dream, but the shadow of a
smile fluttered across the mobile mouth, only to van-
ish into an expression almost of indifference. The
intonation of Mr. Beecher's voice expressed absolute
indifference, as if he spoke of the chance of life or
death for an entire stranger. There was neither hope
nor hopelessness, neither gladness nor sorrow, neither
confidence nor despair. These were the only words
he uttered.

The Beecher house was full of birds and flowers.
Canaries hung everywhere, keeping each other melodious company. Flowers bloomed everywhere in pots,
and here and there roses and scattered bunches, for no
man ever lived who loved the living ornaments sup-
plied by nature better than he who lay upstairs. And
oh! how blithely sang the golden-plumaged birds!
The house was filled with their melodious chatter.
But the ears that had loved their song so dearly
had grown deaf. Wasted and worn, the master of
the house lay in his second-story room, his left side
paralyzed, his right hand now and then waving in the
air in eloquent gesture, and his lips silently moving,
as if, perchance, in his dreams he was preaching the
sermon which he had failed to preach on the Sunday
just past. Who could wonder that his children and
grandchildren, who looked on him as a demi-god, were
convulsed with grief in their different apartments!

Who could wonder that the members of his flock who •
were permitted to look upon this spectacle came down
the steps with tottering gait, and blushed not that
they wept in the open street!

On the following Tuesday, he died, so peace-
fully that his weeping wife and the relatives who
surrounded his bed could not be sure when the final
change had occurred. Dr. Searle stood by the bedside holding one of Mr. Beecher's hands, and at 9: 30
he said, "Mr. Beecher is no more; he is dead."

A ray of sunlight, full and strong, flashed into the
bed-chamber through the window just as his last
breath was drawn. Calmly, and with no struggle,
the regular breathing had ceased and the great
preacher was gone. Mr. Beecher's long gray hair
lay on the pillow, brushed back in its customary
fashion from the broad brow. The face, though worn
by the terrible illness and lack of nourishment, looked
peaceful and noble. The blue eyes which had looked
for the last time on earthly scenes were closed, and
the eloquent tongue was silent forever.

It is difficult to describe the scene at this moment.
Nothwithstanding the fact that his death was looked
for — that it had been expected hourly — it seemed to
come with such crushing force that the family were
perfectly prostrated with grief. They could not bring
themselves to the sad realization that the kindly,

musical voice of the husband, father, and grandfather was forever hushed in death, and that they had only the remembrance of his kind admonitions. Mrs. Beecher, who had borne up so bravely from the first, and who had watched so constantly at the bedside of her dying husband, was utterly broken down, and when supported by her son Harry as she tottered from the room looked as if it would not be long before she would follow her beloved husband.

No crape was hung on the door, Mr. Beecher having always objected to the use of this and the gloom associated with it in the presence of death. Instead, a magnificent wreath of flowers hung from the left side of the doorway, at the top of the stoop, composed of white and red roses and lilies of the valley, and tied up with white satin.

In the street outside the house the drama was but a repetition of that of the day before. Respectful crowds hung about the corner of Hicks and Clark streets waiting for news, eager to learn the latest developments.

One of the three policemen on duty at the house was very deeply affected when he read the bulletin. He told a reporter that on Washington's Birthday he had called on Mr. Beecher.

"How do you do, officer?" said the great preacher.

"I am always glad to see a policeman, I like to look at them. Is there anything I can do for you?"

The policeman told him that the members of the Brooklyn department were trying to get their pay equalized with that of their New York brethren, and asked Mr. Beecher if he would sign a petition in that interest.

"With pleasure," was the response, and the signature was affixed.

The Rev. William Beecher an elder brother of Henry Ward Beecher, has been a resident of Chicago for a good many years. A few years ago there was no more striking figure on the streets than his, but of late years he has been confined to the house. Four or five years ago he celebrated his 80th birthday by preaching a remarkable sermon at the First Congregational Church. At that time he bore his four-score years lightly, but since then he has, with every added year, aged rapidly, and is now very feeble.

A few days before his brother was stricken down Mr. Beecher had a dream which he interpreted to his daughter as an intimation that he was soon to be called home. When the family received the news of Henry Ward Beecher's fatal illness his daughters were in doubt as to what course to pursue fearing the effect of the shock. They sent for the family physician, who advised that Mr. Beecher be informed at once as to the contents of the message. One of his daughters went to his room and said: "Father, you were mistaken as to the meaning of your dreams. It was not you who was to be called, but Uncle Henry." After asking if Henry was dead, and after listening to the particulars, he said quietly: "His work is done. I would like to go in the same way."

Mr. Beecher always manifested the greatest interest in his younger brother, Henry, and while not in sympathy with him in some things, was always ready to say a good word for him. Whenever Henry Ward Beecher appeared in the pulpit or on the platform in Chicago some member of his brother's family has been present, and it will be remembered that when some years ago Henry Ward Beecher was taken suddenly ill in the midst of his lecture at Central Music Hall, one of the first persons to reach his side was his niece, Mrs. Preussner.

Within a few minutes after Mr. Beecher's death was announced the bells on Plymouth Church and the City Hall were tolled, and half an hour later flags were at half mast on all the public and many private buildings. The shipping along the river front and all the Union Ferry boats carried their flags at half mast; the work of draping the City Hall in black was begun, and the entrance to the St. George's Hotel was in mourning before noon.

A special meeting of the Brooklyn Common Council was held at evening in the City Hall to take action in regard to the death of Mr. Beecher. A long letter from Mayor Whitney, eulogizing the dead Pastor, was read. Resolutions which were adopted by the board spoke of the great loss which had been sustained by the people of Brooklyn, and dwelt upon the noble works of the dead Pastor, whose "memory ought to be held in lasting honor by the American people." It was resolved to place emblems of mourning on the City Hall, to close the public offices of the city on the day of the funeral, and that the Common Council attend in a body, and present the condolences of the board to the family of the deceased.

The news of the death of Mr. Beecher was received at Peekskill, his summer residence, with profound and genuine sorrow, for he was well known and much beloved there.

From all quarters messages of condolence and sympathy began to accumulate at the Beecher house. The following are some of them, the first being from the daughter of Mr. William Beecher.

CHICAGO, March 8.

Col. H. B. Beecher.

Father sends sympathy. Would gladly go in his brother's stead.

MARY WARD BEECHER.

EXECUTIVE MANSION, WASHINGTON, D. C.,
March 8, 1887.

Mrs Henry Ward Beecher:

Accept my heartfelt sympathy in this hour of your bereavement, with the hope that comfort may be vouchsafed from the heavenly source you know so well.

GROVER CLEVELAND.

WEST NEW BRIGHTON, March 7.

Mrs Henry Ward Beecher:

Be sure of our deepest sympathy and sorrow.

GEORGE WILLIAM CURTIS.

LONDON, MARCH 8, 1887.

My deepest sympathy, dear Mrs. Beecher, with you all. HENRY IRVING.

CINCINNATI, March 8.

Mrs. Henry Ward Beecher:

The Lane Seminary Club in session this day sends you and your family their sympathy in your affliction. We are entered into the fruits of the labor of your husband's father in the field where your husband was graduated for a seminary course fifty years ago, when he began his great life work. We join you in the suffering God has laid on you and all who love our Savior. May the Christ your husband loved fill all your hearts with His grace and love and comfort in the Holy Ghost. H. A. ROSSITER, President.

H. P. SMITH, Secretary.

The following letter to the press about the arrangements for the funeral, was issued:

19

1. Strictly private funeral services will be held in the presence of his family at his late residence on Thursday, March 10, at 9:30 A. M., Rev. Dr. Charles H. Hall officiating.

2. At the close of these services the body will be removed, under escort of the Thirteenth Regiment, from his late residence to Plymouth Church, where it will remain until Saturday morning.

3. Upon the arrival at the church the remains will be placed in front of the pulpit. Company G will be detailed to furnish from its numbers a guard of honor to guard the remains until their removal to Greenwood. The regiment will then pass through the church and review the remains, after which they will be dismissed.

4. The body will lie in state at the church during the remainder of the day, and any civic organizations desiring to view the remains in a body may do so. But to insure this such organizations should send notice of their intention to do so to the undersigned as early as 9 A. M., Thursday, and should form either on Hicks or Henry street, as may be assigned to them, as early as 11 A. M. of that day.

5. After such civic organizations have viewed the remains the public will be admitted, entering Orange street by the way of Hicks street.

6. When the church is closed Thursday night it will not be opened until 9:30 Friday morning, when it will be opened for the funeral services. At that time Orange street, from Hicks to Henry, will be closed to

HALLWAY AT THE PEEKSKILL HOUSE.

all persons except those holding tickets to the ceremonies in the church.

7. Admission to the church at that time will positively be by ticket only. Tickets have been sent to pewholders and the members of the church and to some invited guests.

8. At the close of the funeral services, conducted in the church by Rev. Dr. Hall, the congregation will view the remains and after them the public will again have an opportunity until 4 P. M. of Friday.

9. At that hour the children of the three Sunday schools connected with the church, in charge of their superintendents and teachers, will view the remains.

10. Upon closing the church Friday the public services will be closed and the removal to the cemetery will be private on Saturday morning.

11. Notice of the action of a citizens' committee who have desired to take part in the funeral services elsewhere in the city will be given in the morning papers. By order of the Executive Committee.

S. V. WHITE, Chairman.

"Inspector Reilly will have 100 men along the line of march from the house to the church as well as a corps of detectives. Although no request has been made for the services of any mounted men, a squad in command of Sergt. John H. Johnson, who was in charge of the body guard from Grant Post at the funeral of Gen. Grant, will keep the streets clear. Capt. Eason will have a force of fifty men at the church."

CHAPTER XXIII.

LYING IN STATE.

On Friday the body of Henry Ward Beecher lay in state and five churches of Brooklyn were crowded in his honor.

Writes a member of his church:

"He loved the people well and wrought for their good, and in the day of his passing they remembered. There were tears that his great heart was stilled and because they should behold him no more, but for the triumph of his days there was thanksgiving and all that was mortal of him lay among blossoms, for there could be no mourning that this great sentinel, after his long vigil and patient endurance, had found the reward of his valor and toil and was at peace. Death had sought him in the hour of rest and awakened him not; his eyes had closed without knowing pain, and with the smile of his quiet sleep still upon his lips he came once more to the scene of his labor, among those who had known him and loved him.

"The great die not, and although all that was mortal of him was given back to unoffended nature, the spirit was living and the spell of its power was yet felt in the temple. He loved the multitude, and the multitude came; he loved the flowers, and a thousand thousand buds breathed their fragrance and clad his resting-place in their beauty; he loved music, and the holy voice of the organ was lifted, and the anthems which had delighted him again rolled their harmonies to the rafters; he loved the sunshine, and it streamed through the windows and was a halo around him. No emblem of sorrow or parting was there, but the symbols of love and faith and hope, the glad tokens of resurrection, immortality and eternal reward, such as befitted his life, his death, and his fame, which shall endure, for many generations shall approve him and bless him.

"There was a hush in the city he had chosen for his toil, and people thronged to do him reverence. The flag his great eloquence had helped to defend rippled its glories in the sun; the doors of the public buildings were closed; the busy hum of commerce was stilled; bell answered bell from the solemn spires; there was the throb of drums in the street, the flaunting of his regiment's colors and the flash of arms, and through the thoroughfare streamed the rich and the poor, men of all creeds and nationalities, the aged, bowed with many years and troubles, and children with curls tossing and cheeks aflame, mothers and maidens, the strong and the feeble, all pouring in one common stream to cast a last look on the tranquil face of him whose greatness was of deeds wrought for love of them. Orator, teacher and statesman, philosopher and poet, diplomat, journalist—he was these as well as minister of God; he was the comforter of those in sorrow; he was. the helper of those who needed; he enlightened the ignorant; he fought for the slave and the oppressed; he defended those who were in danger; he lifted those who were trodden upon; he guided those who had wandered from the right, and his strength became the strength of the weak—he was all men's friend, and all men's thoughts now turned to him.

"There was nothing of gloom in this last public tribute of Brooklyn to her greatest son and to the nation's foremost citizen, whose life, full of worthiness and honors, had fallen ripe from the branch of mortality to become immortal. All day long, through the aisles which led to his coffin, passed the ceaseless stream, never pausing; yet night fell and found tens of thousands still ungratified. Churches were thronged to hear his praises and thank God for such a man, yet not a tithe of those eager to do him reverence could find a foothold; the streets about his resting-place teemed all day with patient hundreds awaiting their turn; no building in the world could have contained the myriads gathered in his name.

"And this was the victory of death. Flowers, sunlight, music, the pageant of arms, the dip of the nation's colors, the recital of his glorious life and achievements, the voice of ten thousand in thanksgiving and prayer, the gathering of friends and .lovers, the clanging of great bells whose tongues tell only of the passing of the great, the stopping of the wheels of busy life, the hush upon the city—these were answers to the boast of the Destroyer, and upon the lips of the mighty dead was a smile of love and of peace to tell all who beheld him that his last slumber had been blessed and was welcome.

"There were flowers—flowers everywhere—in Plymouth Church. The casket looked only a mound of blossoms, for its sides and supports were hidden in a swathing band of roses and its top was lost under a white coverlid of lilies of the valley, with just enough green to break the glare of the white mass. The platform was out of sight, and all that could be seen as a background for the coffin were great masses of buds, of bloom, of blossoms—white roses and pink, and lilies by the hundred. Climbing up to the gallery rail, the rich profusion of the florist's art extended, and then seizing the organ front, the greenery ran up, with great callas and tiger lilies flecking the green ground until the ornamentation lost itself in an outburst of mingled white and green close under the ceiling at the top of the organ case. Extending away along the sides of the church ran the surplusage of love-sent blossoms. Green festoons were on the walls, while at certain points on the balcony front, the rich gems of the world of flowers were effectively concentrated. At one other point, too, there were flowers, rich in color and odor, lovingly laid by hands which for forty years had sustained the Plymouth pastor in his church work. Those pieces were in the third pew to the right of the central line of the church—in the pew where the great pulpiteer and leader of the people so often looked to gather inspiration from the motherly face of the wife who had helped so much to make him what he was.

"This was the interior to which millions would have gone and in which thousands did gather. The weather could not have been better—clear sunlight, crisp, bracing air—on just such a morning Pastor Beecher would have filled his lungs for joy and shouted in the exuberance of the youthful spirits which were always his. It seemed as if many thought they could not be too early at the side of the bier, and fully two hours before the time announced for the opening of the doors there was a throng in Orange street gathered before the plain old barn-like edifice which Mr. Beecher thought so beautiful.

" The doors were opened at 9 o'clock. An hour previous a coach took the chief mourner of all the thousands to the place. This was Mrs. Beecher. She
came, supported by her son, and, throwing her arms
around the flower-laden casket, wept long and deeply.
It had been her desire to attend the main services, but
the effect of the surroundings, when she was compara-
tively alone in the church, was so great that the family
physician dissuaded her from any further effort, and
when Colonel Beecher led his mother from the casket
side, it was to take her to the seclusion of her bereaved
home, there to weep in unison with the thousands
gathered in so many churches.

" When the doors were opened it required something
of a battle on the part of the police to prevent a great
crush. At either end of the street block a line of police stopped all passers-by save such as were provided
with tickets. Then at the one door another squad of
police somewhat awkwardly got the gathering filtered
down into something like a line, and the great edifice
began to fill. There were seats reserved for the special guests on the main floor, and in the galleries a
section was set apart for the press and there forty reporters were massed.

" It was an odd gathering in one sense. Not a trace
of mourning garb anywhere, not one of the customary
habiliments of woe. It was an assemblage appropri-

ately dressed, but no long black pall caught the eye, no crape, no heavy fringing of sombre hangings. The illogical insignia of grief were absent. Beecher had preached for fifty years that death to the Christian was the opening gateway to a better life; that it was a time of joy in a spiritual view, and that this view should be made prominent after death. The expression of this idea was the keynote to the whole proceeding. There was a sense of bereavement hanging over the whole and weighing down every heart, but the occasion was ridden, as far as could be, of every suggestion of desolation and misery. Such strangers as were present, and there were many, looked with something of wonder at it all. The regular attendants at the gospel of love and joy, of which Mr. Beecher has been so long a zealous apostle, were not surprised. To them the whole arrangement seemed one of Mr. Beecher's own ordering.

"There were members' tickets issued to the number of 2,500. These brought many faces well known in public life and added to the list of those present many names known far and wide in connection with big events, great schemes and prominent position. They were scattered all over the church and the number of gray-haired men, men who have won fame and renown, was commented on as showing what a close hold he had upon the best thought of the time.

"In a dozen pews near the front were members of the Brooklyn Clerical Union, to which Mr. Beecher belonged. They were of all denominations, and among them were Presbyterians, Congregationalists, Lutherans, Baptists, and Methodists. Further in the rear was a group of sable mourners. They came in a body and were seated with quiet respect and attention. They were a company of representative colored clergymen who had sent as a floral token a large plaque with the inscription, "The Friend and Champion of the Slave," and then had come to hear the spoken words of praise and respect over the remains of one who had done so much for their race.

"There was scant room left for those who were to conduct the services, after the thousands of roses had been heaped up about the platform. Two chairs had been crowded in among the natural ornaments. One other chair was there, but its broad proportions were lost under protecting blossoms, lest any should profane his chair by sitting in it at such a time. In the narrow space, such as it was, was Rev. Dr. Charles H. Hall, clad in the white surplice and black scarf of the Episcopal Church vestments. It was the only bit of black seen in any official way in connection with the ceremony. He began directly and simply with the grand words of the Anglican Church ritual, "I am the resurrection and the life," and read a few passages, when the choir took up the strain in the burial chant, "Lord, let me know mine end," rendered as an antiphonal chant."

The lesson of the day was read from the fifteenth chapter of the First Epistle of Paul to the Corinthians, beginning with the twentieth verse. The minister read from a small copy of the ritual, which he had carried to the platform with him. There were no graces of elocution about his effort. He seemed at times as though about to break down through the feeling which was almost too strong to master. He seemed relieved when he could turn again to the bank of flowers behind him as to an altar, and stood with bowed head in a prayerful attitude while the choir above rose up and gave Spohr's anthem, "Blessed are the Departed," with Mrs. Shelley, Mrs. Rosan, and Messrs. Graff and Levinson as members of the quartette and a full chorus. It was a worthy effort. Dr. Hall turned and from a manuscript read the funeral oration.

As by a common agreement, a thousand eyes welled out tears, and all over the house, among the invited guests on the main floor, among the members of the church and the ladies in the galleries, handkerchiefs were applied to wipe away the drop from eyelid and cheek. They saw the scene which the word-picture of the orator brought before them. They saw their

beloved preacher as he was, and then the silent mound
of flowers reminded them that he was not, and the
tears started despite all efforts at repression. The
oration was not long, but it was not too short for
the speaker, who more than once found it necessary
to readjust his spectacles.

Dr. Hall said: "The hand that rests so still yonder laid aside the pen over a page of the unfinished
'Life of Christ.' Possibly the last flash of thought,
as the conviction grew upon him of the probable end
of life, was that his work was to be left unfinished—
that he had not told men all that he would have them
know of that precious revelation. Possibly, as the
spirit fled away to be with Christ, whom he had been
serving, the full knowledge came to him of that shore-
less ocean of eternal life, which is to know God and
Jesus Christ, whom he hath sent—that is, the beatific
vision, the love of Christ which passeth knowledge.

"We dwell on one tiny bay of it here and dream
about it. The departed saints of God have already
put out on its immeasurable spaces, and learned that the
life of Christ is never finished. It is the one word of
God which is ever being spoken — echoing again and
again, on and on with ceaseless reverberations, down
the centuries. If there was one thing that stirred the
heart that now rests from its labors more than any
other, that has marked his life and makes his memory

precious to us now, it was his many-sided utterances of a Christ living, as going about among men, a master who first and last asks us to believe in him rather than to believe what others say about him. The radical question of this age has been: 'Is there a faculty of illuminated reason to recognize a living Christ, who can talk to us, and by the great communication of his Mind and Spirit directly lead us to all truths?' As monarchies and hereditary institutions and at last African slavery have fallen to the dust, the question gathers voice and insists upon an answer—it will not be put off by any compromises with past orders and institutions — but renews itself at every turn, echoes in every advance in science or art, comes up in every development of literature ' and social progress. 'Is there a faith in a Christ behind the consciousness of the individual that can be to him the very word of God, the illuminated mandatory conscience?' In a country that dreams as yet of a government of the people by the people and for the people that question is inevitable, and even if it should send the sword among us for a while in the effort for peace, it must be answered. It is not an accident then, altogether, that the man whose life has been moulded by that question and its possible answers should have paused on the unfinished volume of 'The Life of Christ.'

"He has been a man of the people, Christwards. We remind you that though the English-speaking race to-day mourns his call and recognizes his loss, the Americans feel that he has been a great leader or adviser in the guidance of all manner of substantial interests, though the Legislature of the State has paid him an unusual honor—of adjourning — as his right, though the presses and divines and orators of all degrees are trying to compass the mighty theme in glowing words, in words of exulting grief that we have had him with us so long — and have lost him — yet that as he lies there so quiet, we may look at him as one who has been, through all and in all things, an apostle of one supreme thought, a preacher of the everlasting Gospel of the ever living Christ. You who knew him best — you who have listened to him here in this church, know well, that first, last and always, in no barren or dreaming sense, his life has been absorbed in this work and hid with Christ in God. In the prayers which he breathed out here for forty years so simply, you have been hearing an inner echo as if it had come out of the heart of Jesus. In his ordinary teaching, in lectures and sermons, the one thought in them has been to lead you to believe— not something about Christ, but to believe himself. In his intellect — his heart, his common life — wher-ever we, his neighbors, have felt him — he has been

20

a witness to the presence of a Word of God, the ideal man, the light that lightens every man that cometh into this American world, that cometh into this Brooklyn life — that cometh within reach of the testimonies of this platform. Perhaps some would have wished him to have shown tender care of the withes that bound him as with nine-fold strand, but God sent on him the fire that burned them and it was not for him to stay its power. Men talk occasionally of his lack of a theological system, of quotations and learned references and courtesies to the authoritative erudition of past ages. But the living Christ is always greater than divinities or creeds. The cry is as old as Christianity. 'If we let this man thus alone, the Romans will come and destroy our city.' Jesus, to the Pharisees, had never learned letters, and yet the common people heard him gladly. As in his war on slavery, there were few persuasive authorities, individual or ecclesiastical, to go back to and set in among, and he could only fall back on a living Christ, as Seward did on a 'higher law.' So the undertone of his life here has been a faith in Christ, a faith filled with New England sap and silicates, a faith freed by the tonic airs of wild prairies and vigorously set to work here on every department of human life in which the Creator may be imagined to take an interest. Please note that we are here 'to bury him, not to praise him.' My opinion may be indulged that the one fact about him, which endures in that life into which he has now gone, was his fidelity to the great law of faith, which, in its last analysis, means that he has taken his part in making the life of Christ a reality. He would be the first to allow that in this work there is a law that reverses to the eye all worldly modes of comparison. 'The last shall be first and the first last.' The poorest serving girl that has caught the meaning of his preaching and hid her hard life in Christ's wondrous love, and now meets her spiritual teacher in Paradise, finds him gladly confessing his wonder at their surroundings — as being, like her, 'a sinner saved by grace.'

"If the life of Christ is never finished then we may consent to go to all manner of teachers for instruction about it, and wade through all manner of learned wisdom, and accept for trial all manner of hereditary experiments so as to know all that we may about him, but then to cast them all aside in his presence when that light that shone on Saul of Tarsus comes blinding down on us, and to ask, 'Lord, what wilt thou have me to do?' This is my thought of him to-day. This single chaplet I would put upon his coffin. He lived, moved and had his being in the Word of God, on its cisatlantic side and spoken in its American accent. The children of the poor, the oppressed and the afflicted, the slaves, the publicans, sinners, have had a gospel preached unto them here by a preacher who had little apparent anxiety about the serried files of systematic divinities, in imitation of One who somehow seemed to value more a voice that came to him at times out of a blue sky, 'This is my beloved Son,' or again saying when his soul was troubled, 'I have glorified and will glorify again.' The poor, weary souls who have accepted this gospel at his hands have rejoiced with the peace which the world does not give — and, thank God! can not take away.

"Is the Life of Christ ever finished? Is not always the last volume lying in sheets wanting the last touch — always receiving the newest revelation of its oldest meanings? Give a glance at his history. St. Luke, the most scholarly of the Evangelists, supposed that he had finished it once — but now we hear from him, 'The former treatise, O Theophilus! of all that Jesus began (*erxato*) both to do and to teach '— began, not finished. There was a new power in the world coming to the surface. There was a mystical Christ, entering into the weary heart of humanity and continuing both to do and to teach. St. Luke tells us of an Hellenistic youth who pleaded with radiant face against the blindness of hereditary traditions, and saw 'the glory of God and Jesus standing at the right hand of God.'

At his word the scholar of Gamaliel rides forth to
crush the new heresy that threatens to break down the
old traditions and is smitten to the earth with the
splendors of the new Shekinah in the temple of the
individual heart and starts on a new career. Or again,
Paul goes back to the old temple of his fathers and
Jesus confronts him there, and bids him depart and
go far hence to the Gentiles. Men became possessed
with an inspiration that changed all things with a
royal regeneration, and it is Jesus always who continues to do and to teach. Miracle passes into law and
the Evangelist has only begun again the story of the
unending life and left its final volume unwritten.

"St John the Divine once thought that a gospel of
his had told the wondrous story of that sacred life—
but again, on a holy evening as he mused, lo! the
high priest stood before him in the great temple of
the universe, and gathered the splendors of the sunset
clouds as his garments and took on the sound of many
'waters' as his voice, and royally served the little
churches of Asia, in what men now call the 'progress
of events.' His message was, 'I am he that liveth
and was dead; and, behold I am alive for evermore,
Amen! and have the keys of death and hades.' So
John tried to give utterance to the grander sides of
Jesus. Before, in his gospel he had posed him as
meek and lowly, sitting languid with the summer heat

and dusty with the way; as he wrote it, 'sitting thus on the well.' Now he shows him as still on the earth, the high priest making intercession — the knightly Rider—the throned Lamb of God—the King of Kings and Lord of Lords. Did his life end with the Apocalypse? Let the sufferings and triumphs of the Christ that remained answer.

"So again, when Northern barbarians crushed the fair and seemly defenses of Roman civilization in which the Church was tempted to rest — then the great Bishop of Hippo revealed to his age the city of God—the spiritual organization of the mystical Christ and his kingly reign began.

"So again, when the brutal age ensued, of fierce contests with iron-mailed kings and savage lords, the great Hildebrand roused the faithful to a new obedience to organized spiritual forces as supreme, and founded the papal throne as the visible sacrament of an invisible monarch. The crosier testified again to a higher conception of the great high priest, who went forth with every poor missionary, monk or hermit, and thrilled all Europe with new life. When that rule became in time corrupt and tyrannical, other men of renown arose to recall their ages to the Christ who bade every soul find its justification in faith and accept from him directly its election to the everlasting decree of the ageless Creator.

"But to come at once to our American soil, every advance that the world has made has been towards the rights of all men, to a free conscience, to equality of privilege, man with man, and to the solemn duty of faith in a Christ, who comes to all directly in the might of the spirit and mind of Jesus. Forty years ago that question of a living Christ, in whom to live and believe, was knocking at the doors of men's consciences, on the side of orthodox traditions. On its intellectual side it was bound to disturb the whole Christian life of this country.

"That question was predestined to produce some man or some men who would be driven to reinvestigate the platforms, which had sufficed for a humbler past. Whether this man has done it well or ill we leave to the verdict of the future. He has certainly compelled all men to think of it and recognize it. He has left a broad mark upon the Christian life of his age—rather a stimulus in its heart to earnest and devout effort to make the Christ a true presence, to honor daily life as capable of a genuine transubstantiation, so that a plain man may say now as an earnest man once said, 'I am crucified with Christ—nevertheless I live; yet not I, but Christ liveth in me; and the life which I now live in the flesh I live by the faith of the Son of God, who loved me and gave Himself for me.' Making no pretense to being a theologian or a scholar, my faith rests

in the possibility of an illuminated conscience. My
gratitude goes forth to him who lies here, that he has
enunciated that creed with body, soul and spirit. He
loved all things, and his eloquence has adorned and
beautified all in subservience to that belief. If the
Christ indeed now feeds the oil to the golden lamps of
special churches and lives on as truly God-with-us as
ever he was, our brother comprehends that his last
symbol of earthly work was properly the unfinished
volume of his ' Life of Christ.' Let us follow him as
he followed Christ. Let us turn away to another
thought. Abraham was to the Israelite, in some
things, what Jesus is to us—the type of a covenant
system. We now refer to him in a single point. The
Lord came to the old Hebrew of His own 'divine will,
as He saw him somewhat resting in earthly happiness,
and tried him to the quick—deliberately shocked him
into those days of awful agony—with his very faith on
the totter. Then, as the angelic vision held back his
hand the patriarch found in his trial the ideal of the
cross. He 'saw the day of Christ and was glad.'
Paul, in the same line, tells us of a desire in his heart
' to know the power of the resurrection and the fellowship of his sufferings, being made conformable to his
death; if by any means he might attain unto the resurrection of the dead.' Jesus also means much the same
when He bids us take up our crosses and follow Him.

Whenever He sees us too full of earthly wishes or cares or success, and in danger from prosperity, He does for us what He did for Abraham and Job and Paul, and what He did for our brother. He sends a cloud over prosperity to win us by wholesome discipline, 'if by any means we can attain unto the mysteries of the resurrection.' A brave and weary heart is here at rest—brave of old to dare brutal force and to defy the violence of mobs and ruffians in speaking for the slave; brave to accept the murmurs and doubts of his political friends, when conscience prompted him to part from them; bravest to wrestle alone with a great sorrow, when he could find no earthly help. We honor him for the courage of his former acts—we love him and wonder at him for the calm, sweet, gentle resignation of these last years. God, I believe, has led him step by step to spend his last days among us with a wisdom gained from the cross; a tender, gentle, soberer wisdom which helped him to see 'the Captain of our Salvation, who was made perfect through suffering, that we may all be as one, and the great sufferer not ashamed to call us brethren.'

"On Sunday evening in this place, two weeks ago, after the congregation had retired from it, the organist and one or two others were practising the hymn

I heard the voice of Jesus say,
Come unto me and rest.

"Mr. Beecher, doubtless with that tire that follows
a pastor's Sunday work, remained and listened. Two
street urchins were prompted to wander into the building, and one of them was standing, perhaps, in the
position of the boy whom Raphael has immortalized,
gazing up at the organ. The old man, laying his
hands on the boy's head, turned his face upward and
kissed him, and with his arms about the two left the
scene of his triumphs, his trials and his successes
forever.

"It was a fitting close to a grand life, the old man
of genius and fame shielding the little wanderers,
great in breasting traditional ways and prejudices,
great also in the gesture, so like him, that recognized,
as did the Master, that the humblest and the poorest
were his brethren, the great preacher led out into the
night by the little nameless waifs.

"The great 'Life of Christ' is left unfinished for
us to do our little part, and weave our humble deeds
and teachings into the story. Men will praise our
brother for genius, patriotism, victories and intel
lectual labors. My love for him had its origin in his
broad humanity, his utter lack of sham, his transpar-
ent love of the 'unction from above' that dwells in
and teaches and beautifies the lines of duty. He said

of his father, 'The two things which he desired most were the glory of God and the good of men.' So was it with him, as the hearts of grateful myriads attest. But we bid him here farewell, and to me oftenest will come the vision of him, passing out of yonder door with his arm about the boys, passing on to the city of God, where he hears again the familiar voice of the Master saying, 'Of such is the Kingdom of Heaven.'

"And now, brethren of Plymouth Church, I have fulfilled the promise made to my friends, I have offered my whole heart to the public simply to show that I loved him and loved him dearly enough to pay his memory the little honor that I have. The bond that has bound us together, though often unknown to many and not very often expressed, I believe can word itself in two voices of a Quaker poet of America. Our dear brother and I, although he was a Congregationalist and I an old hereditary Episcopalian, both like the Quaker, believing in the Spirit's presence, alike held these words as true:

> "'I sit beside the silent sea,
>   And await the muffled oar;
> No harm from him can come
>   To me on ocean or on shore.
> I know not where his islands lift
>   Their frondent palms in air;
> I only know I can not drift
>   Beyond his love and care.'"

As he closed he turned to Rev. Mr. Halliday and

invited him to pray. The associated pastor had been
sitting in the shadow of a great spreading palm. his
eyes red with weeping, and his face as thorough a picture of woe as one could wish to see. He rose,
caught the familiar reading-stand for support, and
then, amid his sobs, in a voice lost often as he gulped
down some rising sigh, he said: "Oh, God, we come
to thee, but our hearts are very sore and heavy with
care and sorrow as we look up to thee this morning,
for thou hast called one welcome and dearly beloved
from our midst.   O Lord, help us and draw near to us
and make us realize even in this sore hour of trial,
as we come to thee this morning, that thou art
our God, that thou art a living and good God.   We
thank thee that we may come thus to thee.   We look
to thee as though thou art in the flesh; we remember
thy work of mercy; we remember thy tender sympathy. 'Our hearts are so sore when thou dost not
visit us and our souls so depressed when thou dost not
extend thy solace and comfort to them.   As little children run to their mothers when their hearts are sore
or weary for comfort, so here in the child spirit we
come to thee this morning.   We bring our hearts to
thee, sore, for thee to heal them.   (Sobs.)   We have
many, many things to be thankful for, even in this
hour of sorrow.   Oh, how mercifully we rejoice and
give thee thanks.   We do bless thee, O God, our

Silver Wedding at Plymouth Church.

317

Heavenly Father, that thou didst spare our dear pastor to us so long; that he was with us so many years, and that thou hast given the thought to us to-day that we have not lost him. He is not dead. There comes back to us from the other eternal shore the voice of him we so dearly loved, 'I still live.' O God, we feel that we have not lost him, but we know that thou hast called him on high and that he is only awaiting our coming to him. Then, O Lord, may we not rejoice that it is but a very brief separation, and that we are not so far separated by space as it seems to us? O Lord, come thyself this morning to us and help us to realize this. We have loved him; we shall love him none the less that he is where he is this morning. O God and Father, although he is away from us, yet is he not with us? Do not the poor ones that have gone from us, and are with him now, look down upon us? Have our fathers and mothers forgotten us? How he loved us while he was here! Will he love us less now that he is with thee? Oh, will it not be with an affection transcendently beyond that which he had for us here? He knew our faults. He sees them now in another light. Blessed Lord, come to us this morning and imbue us with comfort; touch us with the soft hand that thou didst lay on the heads of the little children and blessed. O God, we would be as little children before thee to-day.

Now, our Heavenly Father, we ask thee that thou wouldst endow us with strength and help us to make such use of this occasion that thou mayest be glorified and that souls may be redeemed. O Lord, thou seest how wide this sorrow is; it is not shut up in this house; it is not shut up in the bosom of this bereaved family; it is universal. O Lord, we feel very grateful that thou hast given to us the sympathy of thy people. We thank thee that though we have had so much sorrow thou hast given us the sympathy of so many. God bless all who have pitied us and who have loved us, and, O Lord, grant that we may reward them in the time when trouble comes to them. Give to them a thousand-fold of what they have granted unto us. We pray it not for our city alone, but for all lands where the words of our beloved pastor have gone. O Lord, although he is dead as our pastor, his words are alive to us. We pray thee, our Father, accept our thanks that we may come so near to thee that we can open wide the portals of our hearts to thee. Thou knowest our wants better than we. Come, then, our Father, and supply all that we need — all the wants of this great people. And we pray thee, our Heavenly Father, now to help us to be moulded by the teachings that he who is gone from us gave us so long, and that the world so largely enjoys. Remember, our Father, those, if there are any, who are not in with us. Oh, God, we pray thee to bless them the same as those who have sympathy with us. Oh, may the spirit of Christ come to them and dwell amongst us all. We thank thee for sending our dear friend to us; we thank thee for his kindness in speaking to us to-day. Bless him for his labor of love; bless him in his love and bless him in his ministry. May his life be full of peace and joy. Now we commend to thee, Our Father, this morning the dear family from out of the midst of whom our beloved pastor has gone, whose fond form they will see no more, whose sweet voice is to be heard by them never more. O Lord, come very near to that family, who will sink under this blow if thou dost not uphold them by thy grace, which is sufficient. We pray thee to speak gracious words unto us out of thine abundant store of comfort. Oh, mayest thou be so near to us that while the form is yet here with us we may know of thy presence with us and be comforted by thy voice saying, ˙It is I, be not afraid.' O Lord, be with us, not alone in this day, but, in the days that are to come, remember that as dear children who have parted with their beloved father, we need thy constant strength and comfort. We commend to thee not only the family but all the relatives. God bless and comfort them. May their hearts be glad and may they take courage

21

in thee.   Hear our prayer, poor and broken as we offer it, for Jesus's sake.   Amen."

The ritual was taken up at this point, and the hymn, " Jesus, lover of my soul," after Zundel's arrangement, was given in magnificent voice by the chorus, while the whole congregation glad of a chance to sing, lost some of its grief, and chased away many a rising crying spell as the whole soul was poured out in the familiar strains.   The burial service followed, with its assuring sentences.   As the words, " Dust to dust, ashes to ashes!" were uttered, undertaker Hopper dropped some earth upon the soft layer of flowers.

Then with the giving of the hymn, " Love Divine," to the tune " Beecher," by Zundel, the service formally closed by Dr. Hall asking that the 'congregation resolve itself into a procession and pass by the coffin. The undertaker removed the cover and pushed back the flowers from over the face.   One rose dropped to to the carpet and 3,000 envious eyes watched a lady pick it from the floor and pin it at her throat.   Mr. Halliday stood with his hands clasped resting on the stand above, looking down on the familiar face. From the front pews the brothers of Mr. Beecher who were present first led their families past the casket and then all went in reverent tread to look for the last time upon the face of the dead.   The organ played and Mrs. Lasar-Studwell, who had so long · been a favorite singer of the dead pastor, poured out her soul in feeling strains as the long line moved by the casket. The choir sang the one hymn which Mr. Beecher loved above all others, reading:

> "My days are gliding swiftly by,
> And I, a pilgrim stranger,
> Would not detain them, as they fly,
> Those hours of toil and danger."

Everybody sang and many went singing their way from the church. The line of mourners embraced all the prominent persons named and none passed in more reverent step than did the humble Dr. McGlynn. An hour, and the last had looked and left, and then for hour after hour the long line from without came in. Men, women and children who had filled a line in the sharp morning air, six broad, up Orange Street and down Henry, nearly to the bridge, moved slowly up, willing to wait, if only it were possible to look once again upon the pinched face, with its smile, below the heavy parapet of flowers.

By actual count, between seventy and seventy-five persons a minute got a chance to look at the life-like face of the dead preacher. Strong men wept and hurried by as if afraid that their emotions would overcome them. Along about 2 o'clock in the afternoon the crowd became so large that word was sent along the line to hurry the people. Lieut. Brown was at the organ playing a slow funeral march, but he quickly increased the tune, and for about an hour 110 persons a minute saw the remains.

At 4:30 o'clock the outside doors were closed, and then the little children of the Bethel and Mayflower missions, attended by their teachers, entered the church through the east rear door and passed up the aisle to the vestibule and down the center aisle. A platform about a foot high was put alongside the casket, and on this the little ones stood. Some of them were so small that the sentries had to lift them up and hold them over the glass cover.

The most touching incident of the day occurred about 5 o'clock, when the scholars of Plymouth Sunday-school came to pay their last respects to the illustrious preacher whom they knew so well. They carried roses in their hands, and as they walked past the casket they tenderly laid their flowers upon it till the mound of loosely-strewn roses grew to a height of almost three feet. Meanwhile the crowd outside waited patiently in the biting wind that raced down Orange Street and made it very unpleasant to stand still. At 5:15 o'clock the doors were opened again, and from then until nearly 9 o'clock the line continued its march. Even then the good deacons of the church were loath to leave, and they allowed all those who came to see the remains up to 10 o'clock. Then the doors were closed and the lights were turned lown. A number of ladies, members of the church, gathered around the casket and bade their pastor a ong farewell. Deacon Shearman distributed a hand- ul of roses which he took from the casket among the adies as souvenirs of the occasion. Then the police- nen and soldiers of company G looked into the casket, .nd the organ stopped playing, and the church was losed.

CHAPTER XXIV.

The same day, Dr. Talmage, in his own church service, drew three lessons from the life of the departed clergyman.

" As our departed friend can gain nothing from all the utterances of to-day, I ask myself what can be learned for the living? Three lessons: One for the ministers of religion; one for all toilers with the brain; one for everybody.

" Lessons for the ministers of religion: The power of similitude. Of all the metaphysical discourses you ever heard Mr. Beecher make you remember nothing, but his illustrations live and will live with you as long as your memory continues. His audiences waited for them. They rose up with flashing eye when they saw he was approaching a similitude. That was what most impressed you at the time. That was what you carried away with you. Much of his discourse was employed in telling what things were like. And so Christ moved his hearers. His Sermon on the Mount and all his sermons were filled with similitudes. Like

326

a man who built his house on the rock.   Like a candle
on a candlestick.   Like a hen gathering her chickens
under her wing.   Like a net.   Like a grain of salt.
Like a city on a hill.   Like treasures that moth and
rust can not corrupt.   Like pearls before swine.   Like
wolves in sheep's clothing.   And you hear the song of
birds as he says: ' Behold the fowls of the air,' and
you smell the flowers as he says: ' Consider the lilies
of the field.'   The grandest effects produced by Mr.
Beecher were wrought by his illustrations and he ran-
sacked the universe for them and he poured them
forth in floods and timbered sermonic literature from
dry and dull didactics into a marvelous resiliency.
He began the war which I hope will be carried on
until everything like humdrum shall be driven from
all the pulpits of Christendom.   It is complained that
the Sunday newspapers keep people away from church.
Then we must make our church services more interesting and more helpful than anything the people can
get outside the church.   We all need in our pulpits a
holy vivacity, a consecrated alertness and illustrative
facilities that shall be irresistible.   From the day that
Mr. Beecher came from Indianapolis until his last
sermon in Plymouth pulpit it was a victory of similitude.   Let all ministers of religion, especially all
young ministers, learn the lesson.

   " The second lesson is for all toilers with the brain,

and that is the danger of overwork. After Mr.
Beecher's brain, like a swift courser, had dashed along
for nearly seventy-four miles, lo! it is hitched to half
a dozen new loads, any one of which might be enough
to break down a fresh brain. After fifty years of incessant and exciting work, cisatlantic and transatlantic,
he allows himself to be harnessed to a syndicate of letters, to a life of Christ, to an autobiography, and to a
half dozen other enterprises. At a time when he had a
right to slow up, as the engineers say, the throttle-
valve is pulled for new velocities. With health and
strength enough to have kept him in active pastorate
for at least ten years more, crash! goes the whole
mental and physical machinery. But that is the way
the most of the toilers of the brain go. Somehow we
get under the delusion that we must enter all the
doors of usefulness opened. Well, if a man has been
industrious with his brain, by the time he reaches his
fiftieth year there are a hundred doors of usefulness
open all around, ninety-nine of which he ought to decline to enter. But of overwork Horace Greeley went,
Henry J. Raymond went, and one-half of the ministers
and attorneys and doctors and journalists are going.
Oh, that some one would invent an ometer which,
hung over the heart and lungs, might decide when a
man ought to stop brain work. The man who invented
such an ometer would make a fortune for himself and

prolong life to thousands of the overtaxed literary men and women of America.

"The third lesson is for everybody: The importance of perpetual readiness for quick transit from world to world—a lesson we learn every day and forget as soon as we learn it. The most powerful sermon Mr. Beecher ever preached he is preaching to-day from the text: 'Be ye also ready, for in such a day and in such an hour as ye think not the Son of Man cometh.' So often, as in Mr. Beecher's case, the last sickness is a time of unconsciousness. It behooves us while in health and strength to get ready for the next world, which may at any moment swing around and strike us out of this existence. 'Except a man be born again he can not see the kingdom of God.' By repentance of sin and faith in Christ all go safely. Would to God that the suddenness of this stroke might result in the immediate preparation of millions of souls for the eternal world upon which we must all soon be ushered. Do not wait until you see the flambeau of the Bridegroom coming through the darkness before you begin to trim your lamps. You may wait for your last moment, but when your last moment comes it will not wait for you. And now, farewell, illustrious brother departed. Carry him gently out along the streets with which he has so long been familiar. For the first time he passes without smile or cheerful recognition. Take him out to the silent city where sleep so many to whom he once ministered. They will not greet him now, but on resurrection morn will rise near him. Toll long and loud the bell at the gate. Put him to rest under the early crocus of the spring, for he loved flowers; his right hand closed, for there are no more genial words for him to write; his lips shut, for there are no more encouraging words for him to speak; his brow cool, for his head has stopped aching now; his heart quiet, for it will never break again. I would put upon his grave not a single wreath, not a single blossom; but I would put upon his casket and his grave a scroll plain and white, a scroll half open that you may read it from both sides: 'I am the resurrection and the life; he that believeth in Me, though he were dead, yet shall he live.'

> " 'On Christ, the solid Rock, I stand,
> All other ground is shifting sand.'

All the day the long line of people passing through Plymouth church to view the remains continued to increase, and the rush was so great to gain admission, that it was found necessary to increase the force of officers around the church-door. The throng was made up of almost all nationalities. As the day advanced the line of people extended until it reached Fulton street, then down one side of the next block and up the other,

with a wing across Henry street. It was estimated that nearly 20,000 people passed before the catafalque during the day.

There were so many wreaths and bouquets left on the bier that a special place had to be made near the platform at the foot of the pulpit to receive them.

The church until 11 o'clock was more crowded than during the afternoon. The line of people waiting to view the remains extended from the church to Fulton street, nearly three blocks, and one block down Fulton.

The will of Mr. Beecher was read that afternoon in the presence of the family. It read as follows:

In the Name of God, Amen:—

I, Henry Ward Beecher, of the city of Brooklyn and State of New York, hereby revoking all other and former wills by me heretofore made, do make, publish and declare this to be my last will and testament.

1. I hereby authorize and direct my executors, or such of them as shall qualify, upon my death to collect and receive the amount of my life insurance, to invest the same and to pay the proceeds of such investment to my wife during her life in equal quarterly yearly payments.

2. I hereby give, bequeath and devise unto my executors, or such of them as shall qualify, the rest, residue and remainder of my estate, both real and personal, in trust, for the benefit of my children.

And I hereby direct that my said executors distribute and apportion my said estate among my said children and in such manner or form and at such time or times as shall in their judgment be for the best interest of my said children, giving unto my executors full power to sell and mortgage such and so much of my real and personal property as they shall deem best and to invest or distribute the proceeds of such sale or sales as herein provided.

3. It is my will that if any of my said children should die before the complete distribution of my estate, as above provided, leaving issue them surviving, that such issue shall stand and take in the place and stead of their parent, taking per stirpes and per capita.

4. I hereby nominate, constitute and appoint my sons, Henry B. Beecher, William C. Beecher and Herbert F. Beecher, all of Brooklyn, N. Y., and my son-in-law, the Rev. Samuel Scoville, of Norwich, New York, the executors and trustees of this my will, and it is my will that no bonds shall be required of them, or either of them.

HENRY WARD BEECHER [L. S.]

JULY 11, 1878.

Signed, sealed and declared by the said testator to be his last will and testament, in the presence of us, who, at his request and in his presence, and in the presence of each other, have hereunto subscribed our names as witnesses.

Henry Ward Beecher left some things the mere glimpse of which would make people's eyes sparkle.

He had about a pint of precious stones of many kinds, though neither he nor Mrs. Beecher ever wore any of them, and few were set into jewelry.   Beecher also had a rare collection of silken scarfs.   They came from Eastern countries, principally, and were gifts, in most instances, from friends who knew of his singular fad, and who picked them up while traveling in the Orient. The great preacher had many feminine tastes and fancies, and was notably urbane and polite in his treatment of women.   Few pastors have ever commanded a nicer balance between dignity and urbanity in social intercourse with the adulatory sisters of their congregations.   One of the last occasions of especial lionizing of Plymouth's pet was a charity fair.   Beecher was there every evening, as in duty bound, and his adroit courtesy in receiving homage, repelling sickish demonstrations of admiration, and getting through the ordeal in comfort to himself and the spectators was worth a study.

Estimates of Mr. Beecher's earnings during his lifetime place them at $1,000,000, of which $500,000 was as pastor, $300,000 as a lecturer, and $200,000 as an author.   One of his leading parishioners estimated his estate at $100,000—his farm at Peekskill, worth $50,000, an insurance of $25,000 on his life, and his house in Brooklyn.

That night the Beecher residence was brilliantly

lighted, and everything around the house was made as bright as possible. Mrs. Beecher had been in her late husband's room a great portion of the afternoon looking over his papers. It seemed a delight to her to be near where her husband spent much of his time. The members of the family were dressed in bright clothing as though going to church Sunday, and everything around was made as bright and cheerful as possible, in accordance with the often expressed wish of Mr. Beecher in case of his death.

"I would not have a semblance of mourning about my grave," Mr. Beecher had said in one of his most eloquent sermons.

"Death is coronation."

"Life and death are equal kings, and death, even at its worst, is but perfect rest."

And so, while the hearts of those nearest and dearest to him were overwhelmed with grief, they endeavored to feel as he would have had them feel, and all the outward and visible trappings of woe customary when death visits a household were carefully avoided, in deference to Mr. Beecher's wish.

Hundreds of people called during the day and left cards.

CHAPTER XXV.

On Sabbath, it is estimated that 10,000 people made a pilgrimage to the vault in Greenwood where lay the remains of Mr. Beecher. The concourse of persons that came to pay their tribute of respect was composed of the plain people with whom the dead preacher's name was a household world. Their occupations had denied them the opportunity to be present at the formal obsequies during the past week. From early morning until sunset a wide stream of people passed through the massive cemetery gates and with unobtrusive and respectful mien gathered about the vault. Old white-haired men and women and toddling children were there. Hats were raised from heads and many an eye was moist with loving recollection. The tribute of flowers twined about the gates had begun to droop.

Mr. Beecher is quoted as once having said: " Oh, may the sun pierce through the trees, dear to many birds, to fall in checkered light upon my grave! I ask no stone or word of inscription. May flowers be the

22   337

only memorials on my grave, renewed every spring and maintained through the long summer."

In nearly all the churches in New York and Brooklyn the clergymen made some reference to the death of Mr. Beecher. In the Church of the Divine Paternity, where, six years ago, Mr. Beecher preached the funeral sermon over the remains of Rev. Dr. Chapin, the Rev. Charles H. Eaton spoke at some length upon Mr. Beecher and his work. "The two mighty friends of truth, Beecher and Chapin," he said, "walk together in glory. In the days that are gone Henry Ward Beecher was so associated with the nation that we all feel the sense of personal loss." The Rev. J. S. Wheedon, of the Thirty-seventh Street Methodist Episcopal Church, in speaking of the dead pastor, said: "When on his trial — and it may appear out of place to speak on such a subject — I did not know what to think of him until I heard him say, in reply to the question, 'Are you guilty?' 'By my mother's God, no.' Then I knew that he was innocent."

Said another clergyman: "Mr. Beecher lived a friend of the poor, a friend of the slave and a friend to his country in its darkest days, and when his days of trouble came there were thousands who did not ask if he were right or wrong, but flocked to his side and gave him the support he needed."

Still another: "No one man since Washington did

more to develop and enrich the history of this country than he did. We are all his debtors."

Rabbi Mendies, in his opinion of Mr. Beecher, praised him very highly. "Mr. Beecher," he said, "was a central figure in the history of this country, and it will be some time before the place that he has left vacant will be filled."

Another said: "Henry Ward Beecher I never knew, but from what I have read, heard and seen of him, I certainly consider him to have been a remarkable man—the most remarkable, in fact, of his age. His position in public affairs was a prominent one. As a theologian I could not and did not admire him, but as a man I certainly did. In late years I was not in sympathy with him on account of his teachings. Our spheres were widely apart and we did not have anything in common. I always looked upon him as a great man intellectually, and he doubtless used his intellect for good."

Again: "I look upon Henry Ward Beecher as having the biggest heart and the biggest brain that this generation has seen. Beecher I never considered a theologian, and I never could agree with his vagaries. His mind was an intuitive one—more like that of a seer or a poet. He arrived at his conclusions like a woman—by perception, and not by logical deduction. When he went into an exposition of

theology he was like a bull in a china-shop. His design was to do right. His mind was many-sided, but
in practical religion he was without a peer. The
heart makes the truly great preacher, and his heart
was an emotional one. He broadened men's views of
religious truths and freed them from old shackles.
Still, he was not a safe leader, as he kept so far in advance that his people lost sight of him. His influence, nevertheless, has been beneficent, and I look
upon the gap his death has made as a very great
one."

Still another said: "I can give no better estimate
of Henry Ward Beecher than by saying he suited me
in all respects. Some years ago I was requested to
write a chapter of his biography. I refused to do so,
as I did not consider myself equal to the task. His
work in the religious life of this country was very
great. What Tasso said of his instructor may be said
of Mr. Beecher, he was like a whetstone, for all that
came in contact with it were able to put a fine edge to
their tools. We are all brighter from contact with
pure souls, and so we were when brought in contact
with Beecher. To my mind he was the greatest
preacher on this planet, and had been since he arrived
at the fullness of his life. His thought will not die
with him, though it may become absorbed in other
minds, but never in books. His mind was like fine

wheat sown to spring in new harvests. His living
spirit can not die. Men will be his debtors for ages
to come, as he did so much in these plastic times,
when all things are so fluent. One great thing in his
character was that, with all the advance he made as a
pioneer of new truth and new life, he never lost sight
of the settlement in which his brethren lived. Then
he had such an inexhaustible fund of things to say,
illustrations pouring out of his mind as rivers pour
their tides down to the ocean, and never running dry.
A great many sermons are like a glass of Missouri
water. You must let it stand and settle before you
can drink; very often you will have to throw half
away. But his sermons were translucent, fresh and
pure as spring water."

"Our parishes were widely apart, and therefore I
never had an opportunity of knowing or speaking with
him. But I learned to know him from afar, and I
considered him a most extraordinary man, a peerless
man, a man of great, powerful intellectual force. He
was a Titan among men. His treatment of Scriptural
and doctrinal subjects was very free, though some expressions he made within recent years had the effect
of clearing him of the charge of heresy. The influence he exerted during his life will be wholesome
to mankind long after his death."

Rev. Roderick Terry, pastor of the South Dutch

Reformed Church, said: "In theology we did not agree, but in spite of that I could not fail to admire the greatness of his heart and character. Henry Ward Beecher came at a needy time in the history of our country—the period of slavery. Few could compare with him, and to know him was to admire him for his heart and sympathy and his great intellect. I do not think that his death will influence religious thought much. People are coming more and more together, and that union will not be influenced very much by his death."

In Elmira, the church of Mr. Beecher's brother, the Rev. Thomas K. Beecher, was crowded by people of all denominations, anxious to hear his narrative of the boyhood and later life of Henry Ward Beecher. It was not a sermon, but a familiar talk as to friends upon a subject very dear to his heart. He lifted the veil from a picture of family life as beautiful as it was instructive. "You that are here assembled," he said, "probably know more of Henry Ward Beecher than I do, but I know more of 'Brother Henry' than you do." The sketch was from the standpoint of a younger brother. Henry and Charles were to Thomas the heroes of the family. He touched upon the boyhood at home, the departure for college, the course in theology and the associations of the two as brothers until thirty-four years ago, when Thomas came to

Elmira, and established the church of which he is now the head. The congregation were several times moved to tears by the touching incidents recalled.

In the house of Thomas A. Edison, at Llewellyn Park, is a remarkable memento of Beecher. The inventor's phonograph for impressing on a soft metal sheet the utterances of the human voice, and then emitting it again by the turning of a crank, has never been put to any very valuable use, and Edison has only gained from it a few thousand dollars in royalties from exhibitors. But he utilized it to make a collection of famous voices. Since he became famous his visitors have included hundreds of celebrities. Instead of asking them for their autographs or photographs, he has, in two or three hundred instances requested them to speak a few sentences into a phonograph. He has kept the plates in a cabinet, and occasionally he runs some of them through the machine, which sends out the words exactly as uttered. Edison is probably the only man who can revive the silenced voice of the great preacher.

To Mr. Beecher books were only a means to an end; he did not stop at them, as some men do at the cobwebs on the window, and so men called him unbelieving. There was not a phenomenon of nature that he did not study, in the hope of finding a trace of God in it, and he has left that faith to you as a legacy.

He flung his doors wide open to every form of serious thinking. He has been called a mystic. He was not a mystic, for he never hesitated to put his witnesses of thought on the stand and submit them to every questioning. He had no fear of what any philosophy could say of him. He could not think that God was a dead God, in a sealed and musty book, but looked upon Him as a living and loving being. To him Christ was God, not a messenger from God.

The press and the pulpit have vied with each other in expressions of praise and honor.

From the many eulogies in the editorial columns of the religious press the following have been selected as representing many different denominations:.

Christian Leader (Universalist): Beecher will live in history as one of the oratorical wonders of the century. No other man has had such magnetic power on the platform and in the pulpit. No other man has in the same length of time done so much to make over and make almost new the theology he inherited. No other man has so dared to confront the prepossessions and prejudices of his co-laborers, or has had a tithe of his power in compelling a new generation to accept his lead. The saddest chapter in his history is the most remarkable of all. What other man could have stood so firm with such an awful weight resting upon him? What other man could have passed through the fear-

THE FAITHFUL WIFE'S VIGIL.

345

ful ordeal and have held intact so large a proportion of the prestige put in peril? Single-handed, save in the important regard that he has had a vast and enthusiastic following, Beecher has been to his age a fourth estate. In some regards he has not wrought wisely and consistently, but in the judicial average he must be set down as a reformer to whom the age is profoundly indebted.

Christian Intelligencer (Reformed): A great man has fallen—a man great in intellect, great in heart, great in personality, great in influence—fallen as he desired, in the midst of his work and suddenly. All his lecture engagements were cancelled for two years to enable him to devote his time to the completion of " The Life of Christ" and to writing his autobiography. Truly he was cut off in the midst of his purposes.

The Christian at Work (Congregational): His people, afflicted by his loss, will cherish his memory, and his name will survive in history and will be a household word on the lips of many of the present generation for years to come. His bereaved congregation will have a hard task before them to supply that pulpit; the vacancy they will not expect to fill.

Christian Advocate (Methodist): The name of Henry Ward Beecher is more widely known than that of any other minister which the American continent has produced. His personality has been more vividly suggested by his name than that of most public men, whether in church or state. Accordingly, the impression caused by the stroke to which he has succumbed is profound.

Brooklyn Examiner (Catholic): He was an intense lover of his country and of humanity. Whenever danger from any source threatened the great Republic, his voice always sounded with clarion clearness and wonderful eloquence. Human misery, wherever seen or heard of, ever appealed to his practical help. He was not a churchman; he was a humanitarian. He was an apologist for human weakness and sinfulness, and would advocate the cause of humanity against revelation itself. He was a free lance in religious matters, who could not be held by the restraints of doctrines. The virtues he practiced emanated rather from natural than supernatural motives. While almost without location in the religious world, yet he possessed many of those qualities that go to make greatness in a secular sense. Brooklyn will place his memory in a niche of distinction, and many a year will roll around ere his name shall be forgotten.

Hebrew Standard: Whenever great questions or principles awaited the decision of the people the voice of Henry Ward Beecher was heard pleading for justice, right and humanity, and the people looked up to him as a safe and trusted counsellor. His was an originality of conception unsurpassed by any other living mind, and in the presentation of public questions he had no peer. As a theologian he had the courage of his conviction, and he always dared to match his own liberal views against the preconceived and traditional creed of the Church. He combined sincerity in the faith of which he was an exponent with the broad liberality and tolerance which recognizes the equality and justice of other creeds, proceeding from the consciousness that absolute truth is withheld from mortal man. As an orator he occupied the highest rank; he held his audience captive with magic spell; they hung upon his lips as upon the oracle of wisdom and truth. Many of his utterances will live in the future as "winged words."

Boston Pilot (Catholic): The death of Henry Ward Beecher leaves a wide gap in the leading rank of eminent Americans. Mr. Beecher was notably a large figure, by his warm sympathies, his eloquence, his manliness, his patriotism. These were stronger than his clericalism. He was a great preacher, it is true; but he preached these very things—he preached Beecher. His theology was unstable and personal, and had more of sentiment than principle. His divine "Yes" was a coin with a human "No" on the back of it, and when he tossed it up before an assembly it seemed haphazard which side showed at the end of the speech.   It was so also with his patriotism and his politics.   A lesser man might have been a stronger, but the deep human kindness of his nature rolled over difficulties and dangers and won for him love and respect.   He will be profoundly mourned by the American people.

Baptist Weekly: Never has the removal of a minister of the Gospel produced a wider and deeper impression on the public mind.   Endowed with unrivalled powers, his public utterances on all the great questions of the day commanded more attention than any other living man; and at a period of life when other men are forced to remit their labors and retire from the toils and conflicts of the world he was girded with strength and fired with an energy equal to anything that he had shown in the meridian of his years. In the removal of such a man all Christendom mourns the loss of a great leader, a man endowed with a mind second to no living mortal, and who, while leaving his impress on living generations, has projected his marvellous influence for charity and righteousness into coming centuries.

Jewish Messenger: The loss of Mr. Beecher is national.   He was the sturdiest of our pulpit orators, and ever the most popular on any platform.   As in early life he braved success among his own circle by talking and working against slavery with all the powers at his command, and won enthusiastic attention by the courage with which he defended opinions that were unpopular, so his later years were devoted to exposing evils in the party at whose birth he had assisted, and his independent bearing in the last general election, while it provoked much criticism, was in keeping with the frankness of his whole public career. He was a manly preacher, ardent in his love for his form of Christianity, but respecting his neighbor's creed, and earnestly looking for good in all phases of religion. His place can not be filled in his church and in the community. That is the verdict of all who knew him.

CHAPTER XXVI.

LOST AMONG THE HILLS.

Judge Tourgee, in writing of Mr. Beecher, says: There is no more grateful duty than the acknowledgement of obligations to the dead. The great Plymouth pastor is already embalmed in eulogy. Thousands of pulpits have given utterance to critical expositions of his merits. All will find much to applaud in the remarkable life that is just ended; some will be constrained to utter words of blame, while in many voices will lurk some tone of apology. It is a curiously mixed tribute that will be offered to this man of singular genius, this restless worker, this bold almost defiant nature, with its wonderful tints of sunshine and softness, its tenderness, cheerfulness and unfailing love of the beautiful.

It seems to me that the tendency at present is to consider him too much in the light of a religious teacher, rather than as an intellectual force. It is no doubt true that he was the most distinguished pulpit orator the world has ever seen. For forty years he ministered to the most notable congregation that ever gathered to listen to a Christian preacher, and in all that time probably saw fewer vacant seats before him than ever met the eye of any other occupant of a pulpit. Old and young, stranger and familiar, friend

and foe, learned and unlearned, high and low, all felt
alike the charm of his wonderful personality. His
words seemed to have the pentecostal power of universal comprehensibility. It might mean one thing
to one heart and something different to another, but
it was meaningless to none. Everybody understood
and everybody felt the charm. To one his words
brought smiles and to another tears. One blamed,
perhaps, and another commended, but no one was
apathetic. To measure his power is quite impossible
because of its unique character.

Perhaps less than any other religious thinker did
his influence depend on what he taught. Indeed,
hardly two of his habitual listeners could be found
agreeing as to what his teachings were, yet there was
no conflict between them. Whether he were right or
wrong, whether he taught one doctrine or inclined to
another, mattered little.

He touched somewhere the thought, feeling, aspir-
ation of every one who listened — so that the mere
delight of listening rendered secondary all other considerations. His speech was a sort of intellectual
hasheesh which expanded and exhilarated every nature. The dullest listener dreamed wonderful dreams
while under the intoxicating influence of his words.
The bitterest enemy forgot his hate and followed with
delight the footsteps of his fancy.

He had in a perfection, unrivalled by any man of
his time, the faculty of obliterating himself to his
hearers. What seemed ofttimes most striking and
characteristic to his readers, to those who listened

23

seemed most natural and matter of course. Men applauded what they heard and questioned what they read. He charmed and startled with his pen, and charmed and captivated with his tongue. He followed his own thought with such apparent pleasure that his hearers unconsciously engaged in a like pursuit. They forgot the man in watching the operation of his mind. The listener seemed to have the power of forecasting his utterances, which, if they startled by their boldness, seemed always to be the only thing he could naturally and reasonably have said. Thus those who heard became in a singular degree partners in what was uttered. Each felt it to have been his own thought. He gave him credit for clothing it in new and attractive garb, but each one claimed the thought himself as a familiar child of his own consciousness. So men followed where he led them with a supreme delight, never anxious as to the end or apprehensive as to the correctness of his conclusions, but knowing that he led in the direction which their hearts and hopes pointed —along a way their feet delighted to pursue.

With the utmost positiveness, he had the least possible dogmatism. He cared little for method, but had the utmost confidence in good intentions. In a religious sense he was a gardener who did not believe in pinching and pruning—or, rather, they were methods it never occurred to him to use. Air and sunshine, a fresh soil, stimulating influence, and a free growth were the instrumentalities he relied on for good effects. Frames and borders, conventional forms and an enforced symmetry were as irksome to his mind as his eye. He sought to trample out the weeds, clear away the overshadowing branches, and let each soul grow in its own way. He did not seek to make the vine an oak, nor compel the oak to put forth tendrils. Each heart was to give him a flower to which he sought not to give uniformity of growth and hue, but to enable each to seek its own peculiar development— its especial characteristic excellence.

Because of this his influence is especially difficult to trace. Even those whose lives he has done very much to shape are often unconscious of specific influence. He seldom gave advice, and when he did its quality was not remarkable. With all his wonderful fertility of mind he was not given to suggesting new fields of action or methods of operation to others, but he had a wonderful faculty of judging the suggestions of others.

Said one who had rare opportunity to observe him in this respect: "If a man goes to him and asks, 'What shall I do?' I would not give a fig for his answer. If he lays before him three courses and asks which he shall pursue, his instinct is unerring." It is not as a religious teacher, nor even as a religious trainer, therefore, that he was greatest or most distinctively great, but as an intellectual impulse—a psychic influence. He was not so much a guide or a leader as a stimulator of mental activity and moral sensibility.

It is for this reason that his influence was harmful to some natures and weakening to others. Some people need to be led, others to be restrained. He could do neither. He encouraged—nay, he compelled, growth, expansion, enlargement. He thought it better to be deformed than dwarfed. Some natures he stimulated until efflorescence brought decay. Others ran riot under his influence and produced an abundant but imperfectly developed fruitage. Still others were weakened by premature luxuriance, while others, like clinging vines, were distraught by vain searching for something to which their tendrils might cling.

For myself, and I am sure my experience is not exceptional, while I found his occasional touch most helpful and inspiring, constant or continuous following of his thought, while it did not produce satiety yet became depressing and in a sense weakening. This is no doubt due to a mental habit that can not endure over stimulation. While a page now and then, a sermon once in awhile, brought always to my mind a most healthful glow indicative of renewed vigor, its frequent recurrence weakened and relapsed. For this reason I both sought and avoided him, and while regarding him with the utmost admiration, it was perhaps not the unquestioning reverence with which those standing nearer to him were almost sure to be affected. Not that he seemed to me less admirable on near approach, but I seemed always to desire rest after having my imagination fired by the strange luxuriance of his thought. He always started in my mind trains of speculation which I desired to pursue to the end, while his influence was constantly leading me off into some new path. I felt something like one hurried through the main avenue of a park of wonderful beauty, with a constant desire, despite its ever varying brilliancy of scene, to stop and loiter in the bosky glades which stretch away half seen on either hand.

Among the merits that will be universally accorded him there is one that seems to me pre-eminent. As an æsthetic force his influence has been singularly marked, universal, and intense. The generation to which he belonged had three high priests of the æsthetic—three great apostles of the beautiful—Carlyle, Ruskin, and Beecher. The one was concerned wholly with moral loveliness in man. He was a terrible frothing iconoclast, who tore down and trampled in the dust all that did not seem to him fitting and noble in individual manhood. He raved and cursed and scourged, but he raved always of moral grandeur, intellectual strength, and the essential harmony of human attributes. For externals he cared nothing. To all that appealed to senses he was absolutely dead. He saw no beauty in form and was deaf to the harmony of sweet sound. No woman's loveliness enchained his eye nor any siren song delighted his ear. Apollo was to him only a type of senseless vanity; Venus only a flimsy cloak of vileness. The moral quality to him was everything. He did not see the toad, being blinded by the glitter of the jewel in its head. He scourged our natures to an appreciation of intellectual beauty, and a hatred of moral ugliness which the world never knew before. He was the great apostle of fitness and force — moral grandeur and intellectual uprightness. To him all beauty was human and the divine was only a grander humanity.

Alas! we did not know pitiably he illustrated his own ideals.

Ruskin's idea was the mystic unity of nature, art, and intellect. To him humanity was an harmonious compound of brain and sense. Nature was a mass of types of human passion, and art the reflection, combination, and etherealization of both. To his mind nature existed only for art's sake, art only for man's enjoyment, and man only for the development of the artistic sense and the perfection of artistic types. As Carlyle might be termed an Anglo-Roman, Ruskin might be fitly styled a nineteenth century Greek. Both hated shams and pretense — the one in thought, the other in expression — the one in substance, the other in form. Both were pagans. Neither saw any God in nature, nor any superhuman motive in man nor art. Both thought themselves moral teachers! because they hated moral ugliness. The one cared nothing for the outward expression; the other believed it inspired by essential harmony. To the one moral obliquity hid all external harmony; to the other external loveliness was an essential concomitant of inward purity. While the one saw the jewel despite the toad; the other could never believe in the jewel's existence because of the toad. Ruskin was sweet, Carlyle fierce, and both all the more intolerant because each thought himself the especial apostle of a new and exclusive liberalism. They were both worshipers of the beautiful, but each in his own pragmatic and exclusive way. There was a certain harmony between them, and yet their teachings were mutually subversive.

THIRTEENTH REGIMENT SALUTING THE REMAINS.

Whosoever would go all the way with Carlyle must some time part company with Ruskin. Yet they were the greatest expounders of the beautiful the world had ever known. Merged into one they would constitute the perfect type of human ideality. Together they stamped ineffaceably upon the intellectual life of their generation the essential harmony between the ideal and the concrete — between nature and art — between essence and expression — between form and passion — between the beautiful and the true.

To this was added a third idea, of which Mr. Beecher was almost unconsciously the chief exponent. Sympathizing alike with the moral grandeur of Carlyle's ideal of humanity and the subtle sensuousness of Ruskin's interpretation of nature, he exalted and glorified them both by introducing another element —a perfect solvent of their essential differences— the thought of God. Nature, humanity, and art he saw only in their relations to the divine. Like the others he hated shams above all things, but he believed in the true and the real, because he saw God in everything and everything in its relation to God. With Carlyle he would tolerate the toad for the sake of the jewel, and like Ruskin he was inclined to the existence of the jewel because of the toad, but unlike both he felt that toad and jewel were both divine and that somewhere and somehow there was discoverable between them an essential harmony. He could not conceive of any toad without a jewel; of humanity unrelated to deity; of a nature that did not reveal the mind of a creator. He has been called a

Christian pantheist. Nothing could be wider of the truth. He did not worship nature, but saw in it the evidence of God. He did not worship God as a divine man, but looked upon man with a peculiar and universal reverence as the clearest exponent—the nearest analogy of the divine. This idea of the holiness and divinity of beauty, he impressed not only on our religious thought, but on our literature and even on our politics. The tender, exalted, and truthful religious, patriotic, and artistic ideals of the generations which have listened to his teachings owe to him the fusing, intensifying, and enlargement of the thought of his great contemporaries. He was pre-eminently the Christian interpreter of nature.

He has pointed out more of the pleasant by-ways "from nature up to nature's God" than any other man has ever noted. If Darwin saw in nature the evidence of an inflexible law of development operating through myriads of millions of years, Beecher saw in that law and in the all but illimitable period of existence it required new evidence of the beauty and grandeur, compassion and glory of the One Divine. He stamped upon the human consciousness as no one else had ever done before the divinity of beauty—the divinity of its origin and the divinity of its mission to humanity. As a Christian humanitarian he was not perhaps without his equals, but as a Christian lover and interpreter of nature he is without a peer. Of the pleasant facts of nature others have taught us even more than he; but of nature as an inspired oracle no one has given such wondrous expositions. He has traced better than any other the divine harmony between God and nature and humanity—the unity that pervades, assimilates, and exacts.

Notwithstanding the fact that every page he has written, every sermon he preached, and every lecture he delivered are living witnesses of the truth I have endeavored to elucidate, I may be pardoned for illustrating it by an incident within my own knowledge.

Something more than thirty years ago a homesick Western boy wandered about the Berkshire hills. Despite their picturesque beauty they seemed petty to one accustomed to the mighty forests and vast horizons of the West. It may seem a curious thing, but the very ruggedness and irregularity of the outlook oppressed him. He longed for the silence of the great woods; the sight of its familiar denizens; the blue lake in the distance, gilded by the sunshine or flecked with white-caps by the storm. In short, he was homesick — not for home, perhaps, but for the West — for his accustomed surroundings. Of course he did not know what ailed him. He had been accustomed to the woods and a gun almost from infancy, and with a gun he sought the dwarfed and scraggy thickets upon the mountain side as a cure for the nostalgia he did not understand. Though he could traverse miles of level woodland with an instinct as unerring as a homing pigeon, he was easily lost among the hills through which the Housatonic flows in and out with puzzling uncertainty.

One autumn day, when the blue haze hung over the hills; when the maples flamed out against the hemlocks here and there in gaudy rivalry; when the beeches were growing brown; the birches beginning to show their white limbs and the willows a yellow fringe between the green aftermath of the meadows and the dark blue of the waters, he had strayed beyond the limit of his knowledge.

Perched upon the outermost point of a cliff that marks the face of one of the most noted peaks that overlook the valley, he sought anxiously but vainly for some familiar landmark. Whether it was Lee or Lennox, Stockbridge or Great Barrington that lay at his feet he could not determine. Of course everything that ought to have been familiar was absolutely unrecognizable. He was utterly lost. The only way out of his predicament was to go to some of the houses in sight in the valley, inquire his way home, and sneak back ignobly and shamefacedly along the highway.

As he was about to take this course he heard some one clambering along the rough pathway at the foot of the ledge, nigh a hundred feet below him. Screened by the thick laurels he watched the new-comer's advance, himself undiscovered. He knew Mr. Beecher by sight, and knew where the country house, which was then his haven of rest, was situated. He recognized at a glance the flushed face and stalwart figure, then in the prime of manly strength. His brow was covered with perspiration, for besides the rough walk he had taken, he was burdened with an armful of trophies he had gathered on the way. Just at the point of the cliff a clear spring bubbled out from under a gray, mossy rock. He threw his variegated armful down, tossed off his soft hat, and, lying prone upon the ground, quenched his thirst. Then he stood up, threw back his long hair, wiped his brow, gazed at the prospect that lay outspread at his feet, sat down upon a spur of the rock, and picked up one by one the leaves and flowers he had gathered. Then he sat for a long time, silent and unmoving, looking down into the quiet valley and off at the hazy hills beyond. The boy had overcome his shyness, and was about to descend and inquire his way homeward when he heard the soft, full tones which stole with such insensible power into every ear. Looking down he saw his companion in the luminous solitude kneeling in the midst of the painted leaves he had scattered on the dun rock, the bright autumn sunshine lighting up the warm, brown hair and touching with unwonted radiance the soft lines of his placid face as he prayed — alone — upon the mountain, with no thought that any one but God could hear.

The boy listened in amazement. He had been accustomed to prayer. The family altar was an almost universal institution then. Prayer as an act of duty; prayer as a religious rite; prayer as a religious service — all these were familiar things to his consciousness. He even had his own ideas about prayer, and when he felt that he had been exceptionally bad or had a desire to be exceptionally good, he had sometimes tried praying on his own account over and above his share in the evening and morning devotions. He regarded it as a pretty serious business, however, a thing that

needed to be done and ought by no means to be neglected, and which, if persevered in, brought at length
a sort of fervid rapture which carried the worshiper
into a mystic realm of supernatural bliss. But such
a prayer as this he had never heard before — indeed,
he has never heard such another since. A calm, tender, quivering rhapsody of thankfulness that God
had made the earth so beautiful. A burst of gratitude
for mountain and valley, river and spring, rock and
brake, sunshine and shadow, tinted leaf and whirring
pheasant — everything that had gladdened the eye or
charmed the sense during the autumnal stroll.

I have no idea how long he prayed. For the first
time I thought a prayer too short. I wished he
might have kept on forever. I had some curious
fancies during its continuance. Perhaps, as I looked
at his glowing face and saw his dewy, luminous
eyes as it concluded, I may be pardoned if I thought
of the Mount of Transfiguration. I trust there was
no sacrilege in it. After a while I stole down and
timidly asked my way home. I felt ashamed of having been an eavesdropper on his devotions. He evidently noted it, and to put me at my ease asked me if
I did not think it was "a pretty cradle God had made
for His children." He walked nearly a mile with me
away from his house, which must have been three or
four miles from our starting point, to make sure that
I did not lose my way. I do not remember anything
he said, but I walked all the way home in a sort of
delicious dream, full of strange, vague aspirations and
sweet, tender recollections. Somehow, I came to see

more in nature afterward than I had ever done before, and I have never ceased to be grateful that I heard this prayer in the mountain oratory. My relations with him were not close enough to justify recalling the incident to his memory, and I suppose he died quite unconscious of the identity of the uncouth lad whom he that day initiated not so much into nature's mysteries, for I was no mean woodman even then, but into their mystical relation to God, the giver, and man the happy recipient. It is probable he had long since forgotten the trivial incident, but for this sweet lesson, in common with many thousands, I still remain his grateful debtor. ALBION W. TOURGEE.

Judge Tourgee, after bringing all his splendid powers to a discriminating analysis and a picturesque characterization of Mr. Beecher, turns with reverent tenderness to speak of his kindness to and his influence upon a boy. The Rev. Dr. Hall, after dwelling with rare and touching eloquence upon Mr. Beecher's personality and power, turns with the same tenderness to speak of Mr. Beecher's kindness to the children of the street. Nearly every one who has criticised Mr. Beecher, or who begins an address, or a letter, or a sermon upon his personality and character ends with a tender reference to his love of nature and of children. Many of the thousands who heard Mr. Beecher preach in his own church were wont to say as they went away: " I don't agree with him, but I feel more kindly toward all men for having heard him."

This element in Mr. Beecher's character, this surplusage of love for his fellow men, this quick sympathy for helpless or suffering humanity, this richness of heart supply, this emotional overflow that led him on one great occasion to kiss the Rev. Dr. Storrs on the cheek, this wonderful responsiveness to the longings of the average man and woman—all these things must be counted at their full value in any estimate of Mr. Beecher's life and work.

No man, at once so courageous and pugnacious, was ever so tender and considerate. There was no vindictiveness in his pugnacity and no timidity in his considerateness. In some way, without apparent effort on his part, he maintained the friendship of those who were classed as his opponents. Judge Neilson, before whom the great scandal case was tried, beginning with distrust of and hostility to Mr. Beecher, became his steadfast friend. Hating him as few men in the North were hated during the war, the South at the close of the war came to regard him with favor. Disliking him above most Republicans, the Democrats in the later years of his life came to speak of him with profound respect. Regarding him at first with a feeling akin to resentment, the old Abolitionists came in good time to give him their sympathy and to follow him

with enthusiasm. Beginning their public acquaintance with him when he went to England in 1864, with
sneers and scoffs and hisses, the English people ended
by respecting him and by following his advice.

In the darkest hour of the anti-slavery movement,
when the nation clamored for the blood of John Brown,
and when all doors were closed against those who
would defend or excuse the old man, Mr. Beecher
threw wide the doors of Plymouth Church that Wendell Phillips might, as Fred Douglass said, "Throw
the shining shield of his eloquence over the bleeding
head of the grand old hero and martyr." When Fred
Douglass was without friends and at the beginning of
his public career, Mr. Beecher made it a point to call on
him personally and help him with his sympathy and
influence. When Anna Dickinson first asked a hearing of the public it was Mr. Beecher who held out the
helping hand.

When it cost a man almost his reputation to be an
abolitionist Mr. Beecher was an abolitionist. When it
was regarded with disfavor in the North to speak ex-
cusingly of the South, Mr. Beecher was the friend of
the South. When Republicans were least inclined to
forgive luke-warmness or desertion in 1884, Mr.
Beecher strode out of the Republican camp into the
Democratic. When the theory of the evolutionists
was most unpopular, Mr. Beecher flung a series of
24

sermons on evolution in the face of the public. So it happened that nearly every individual, nearly every sect and class had something to forgive in Mr. Beecher, and more to be thankful for. He was so near to the people, he understood the people so well that he trusted them implicitly, and the public estimate was seen in the tender observance of his memory at Brooklyn on Thursday and Friday. That was the turning, not of his own people, not of his own church alone, but of all the people who knew him in reverent earnestness to testify their appreciation of his worth and to acknowledge their own sense of loss.

The people loved the man and they had never any need to ask why. Mr. Beecher's love for mankind was not ostentatious, but it was sincere and the people knew it. It was like his love for diamonds. He prized them, not that he might wear them for show but for themselves. It is said that his love of precious stones and jewels was a passion, and that he owned many of the rarest, and yet he wore none at all, but carried several in his vest pocket wrapped up in soft paper. This love of diamonds, of flowers, of trees, of nature was but one phase of his love for all that God has made, and he directed always the eyes of his fellow men "from nature up to nature's God."

CHAPTER XXVII.

Mr. Beecher is mourned most sincerely in England. Writes an English correspondent: "It seems but yesterday that Mr. Beecher was here, looking hale and active; and while his friends throughout England had no reason to hope they would see him on this side again, they were hardly prepared to hear so soon of his death. All the papers of yesterday contained special telegrams from New York giving particulars of his attack of Friday morning, and sympathetic words were heard everywhere. There could be no more convincing evidence of the esteem in which Mr. Beecher is held by the English public than the universal interest taken in the news of his illness. If the President himself had been stricken down, the impression made would not be more widely extended or keenly felt. On every hand I hear the opinion expressed that he was not only the greatest preacher in America, but the greatest man there, the greatest thinker, the greatest writer; that no one had done so much to give character and direction to both the religious and

371

political tendencies of his country during his time as he.

"I went out to Hampstead this morning to see the Rev. Dr. Joseph Parker, who has been called the Beecher of England, and certainly has many points in common with him. He is the leading Nonconformist preacher of Great Britain, and he and Mr. Beecher have been warm personal friends ever since the latter made his celebrated speech at Manchester in October, 1863. Dr. Parker lived at Manchester at that time, and was one of a party of prominent citizens on the platform. When Mr. and Mrs. Beecher arrived in London last summer Dr. Parker and his wife met them at Euston Station and drove them to their comfortable home in Hampstead, where they remained six weeks, all members of one happy family. Dr. Parker is a broad-faced man of thick-set frame, and with a warm-hearted cordiality like that of Mr. Beecher himself. He met me with a look of the deepest anxiety and suspense. He had the night before received a cablegram saying there was no reasonable prospect of Mr. Beecher's recovery. 'I am only waiting for the end,' said he. 'I know it must come. I am completely prostrated by this terrible news.' Dr. Parker held in his hand a manuscript which he had just brought up from his study. 'This,' he said, 'is a tribute to him which I have begun to write. I am

LYING IN STATE IN PLYMOUTH CHURCH.

trying in this to express something of my appreciation of that great and good man. Ah! this is a blow indeed to this household. Mr. Beecher lived with us all the time he was in England last summer. He came and went as one of us, and we loved him more every day—so simple, so childlike, so sympathetic, so full of the broadest and best sentiments, and indeed always cheerful. Supper over, he would sit at the table and talk with all the glee and ardor of a boy. I have heard him pass from some profound discussion of philosophy, religion and statesmanship to the story of a cat or dog. Well do I remember how he would laugh over something he told about a cat and a fire-cracker; the quick surprise and bewilderment of the cat as the fire-cracker burst close to its head. He said it reminded him of an old woman who suddenly remembered she had left her umbrella. When I would come home late in the afternoon, I would find him sitting on the doorstep just as he did no doubt when he was a boy. In fact, the boy in him never died. He had a perennial youth because he was nature's own child. He was not a man of masks and faces, subterfuges and secrets, but one whose life was lived before the whole world, and from whom the whole world would always be learning something. For he had in him a mine of thought and sympathy that embraced everything and that was inexhaustible. When he falls it will not be the falling of a splendid column, a Cleopatra's Needle, or of anything made by hands; but it will be the falling of a tree with limbs and branches and leaves under which we have rested and played, and in which we have heard the music of the breezes and the songs of the birds. Mr. Lincoln was once asked who was the greatest man in America. He hesitated a moment and then answered: "Henry Ward Beecher." So he was, not only in Mr. Lincoln's time, but has continued to be for more than a quarter of a century since.'

"I can not in the brief and imperfect form of an interview give all the eloquent and touching tribute paid to Mr. Beecher by Dr. Parker. More than once tears filled his eyes, and if the dying man had been in the adjoining room he could not have appeared more deeply concerned. 'You see we remember him here,' said he. 'You see a picture of him there in the corner. There is another on the easel in the sitting-room, and one in the hallway just as you come in at the door. Did any man ever have such a noble brow? If God were going to make a perfect face how could he improve it? I saw him coming down the stairway one morning just before he left. I was at the side and only had a glimpse of his side-face. His long white hair was streaming back, his eye was kindly and brilliant, and I felt as though I had a

vision of an angel. We did not agree fully in everything. At least, we did not always express ourselves
exactly alike, but I said: "That man is the living
exponent of religion; I like his religion, which is my
religion." I shall never forget the moment he parted
from us. Putting his arms about me, he simply said:
"Old fellow, I love you!" When he reached Liverpool he wrote me a characteristic letter, saying among
other things that he sometimes forgot things when
traveling, now that he was old, and that he had left his
heart with us. That heart was big enough to take in
us and all mankind besides.'

"I asked Dr. Parker if Mr. Beecher had any
thought of an immediate prospect of death when he
left England. 'He often talked of death,' said he,
'and always with perfect composure and serenity. He
said he hoped to die while at work in the midst of the
busy life he had lived. He hoped he would not have
any prolonged suffering but go at once, and in this
his wishes seem to have been met. He spoke one day
of the hymn he wished to be sung at the last service
over his body. It is one by Dr. Watt:

"'When I survey the wondrous Cross
On which the Prince of Glory died,
My richest gain I count but loss
And pour contempt on all my pride.'

"With this I took my leave of Dr. Parker feeling
that Mr. Beecher left at least one friend in England

who has both the heart and mind to do adequate honor to his memory. As I passed out I saw the life-sized portrait of Mr. Beecher that hangs in the hall of Dr. Parker's house. It was a speaking likeness, and it was made the more impressive by having a silken United States flag flung over one corner of the frame."

The following letter from England reached a New York lady shortly after the death:

My Dear Mother: All things of an earth-earthy character, pursuant to a predetermined infinite decree, have to pass away. The great, as well as the small; the strong, as well as the weak; the majestic, as well as the frivolous; the good, as well as the bad; all come within the scope of one unyielding, prophetic law. The age in which it has been our lot to live has been upheld and sanctified by a swelling tide—superlative in degree, and incessant in action — of intellectual greatness and moral force, unparalleled in the annals of our race. The majestic preservers of our nation; the Spartan heroes in the field and in the Cabinet and in the legislative halls—those who were the leaders in the greatest drama known to history—have all bowed to the unalterable decree. On either side of the sea, the past quarter of a century has noted the remarkable swath cut by the scythe of death. It was during the Ides of March that the conspirators slew the "greatest Roman of them all." It is during the Ides of March that conspiracy of disease will accomplish the greatest havoc in intellectual power that has been known to this century. A prodigy is about to fall! The greatest of the Beechers, the foremost American, the most advanced religious teacher and gospel expounder, either living or dead, is, if reports be true, about to "fold the drapery of his couch about him, and lie down to pleasant dreams." It may be true, and, in my opinion, probably is true, that not enough is said when we state that the greatest intellectual product, taken all in all, that this age has known in America is about to die. I am constrained to believe that the most versatile genius, the most apt and qualified man, in all the departments of life, with loftiness of purpose, with a capacity in any direction, possessing a lion's courage and a lamb's tenderness; having more marked, before unfound, and, after his day, unknown great qualities than are or have been possessed by any human being in either hemisphere during the time in which he lived, to do us honor by his work, and lead us by his example, and teach us by his thought. In the minutiæ of life neither a philosopher nor a logician, yet, abstractedly, great in either school. The mathematical problems of this world, worked out to a last result, cramp men's minds, and make them lose in scope and power. He belonged to no school of ethics, metaphysics, politics or religion. He was the leader of schools. He rose above them as the tide rises above the common level of the sea. More like the Pacific than the Atlantic, storm tossed at times, as tempestuous as the Western ocean when not at peace, and yet, like that ocean, most always at peace. The rule was a quiet, even, placid way. The exceptions brought out the stronger character, and deeply impressed the rugged make-up of the man. A leader at his will upon the political platform; a master of creeds and ceremonies; a scholar with a rare gift of poetical genius when holding the novelist's pen, he could, in the midst of his fancy and flight, map out a campaign, fight a battle, draft articles of peace, and equal, if not superior, to any American, practically determine the results of war. Engaged in writing "The Life of Christ," a pause could be made at any time to perform a marriage ceremony, deliver a funeral oration, write a squelching letter to a political foe on a political subject, mount the platform and clasp hands with the greatest atheist of the age, lead the vast multitude of Plymouth Church on to a better and higher life, indulge in any fancy or speculate with any fact, and do it all, or any portion of it, better than any contemporary.

He was Gladstone's friend, because Gladstone was a friend to the poor and the oppressed. He mourned oppression and despised the oppressor. He obeyed the promptings of a great and good heart, and followed sublimely the leadership of a massive brain and a glowing nature. He was good; he could not have been otherwise but by accident; then the act would have been but sporadic, as accidents constitute the exception, not the rule of life.

Henry Ward Beecher has performed more practical brain work than any man living; he underwent a most exasperating and undermining ordeal; with an even poise and a masterly bearing, he withstood assaults that none but he could successfully have encountered; the only ruining effects being a probable shortening of his days and a lessening of his inestimably valuable labors.

Time bestows rewards. Intellectual greatness must be recompensed. An eternal fitness clasps hands and joins hearts with an eternal justice.

I am reminded of Gilfillin: Beecher rises above other men, not as one limb of a tree rises above another limb, but as the sun of heaven rises above the tree itself.

Our age will not see his equal. His place may never be filled. The great light will probably never be relighted. He who strung the lyre that Mrs. Stowe played for the freedom of the bondsmen will be known while our race endures, so long as the Anglo-Saxon tongue is known or spoken.

Dust he is, and unto dust he must return. As he has been just and brave and true, so will the infinite God be just to him. We should not mourn, except in our loss. No! Not even in our loss, for such mourning would be selfish. Not for him or his. No! His work was bravely, nobly done. His — they can live proudly — as kings and queens can not live — in the memory of a beautiful, resplendant, and growing individuality; a luminous sun of intellectual light, closed to the eyes of a finite world to open in a gorgeous realm of eternal bliss; in the name of a foremost nobility of greatness, and an unranked majesty of mental force. His — they can live for generations in the reflected rays of the departed light — dream sweet dreams of him by night and follow, as best they may, in his footsteps by day, ever proud and ever joyful!

Henry Ward Beecher! Peace to his ashes! Honor to his name! Glory to his works!

As ever, most affectionately,   YOUR SON.

CHAPTER XXVIII.

The most striking, and the predominant characteristic of Mr. Beecher was his vitality. It was obvious in his person. No one could see his big frame, the strong limbs and deep chest, the broad and slightly rounded shoulders surmounted by the great head, the loose hair thrown back from the full forehead, the large eyes unsheltered by the brows, and the heavy yet mobile lips, without feeling that the tide of life with him was ample and constant. He was capable not only of bursts of energy, but of prolonged and exacting exertion. He was wont to say that the brusque changes of our climate made stimulus unnecessary, and with him they did. Any purpose that interested his feelings found an ardent and sustaining response. Any purpose that did not arouse this impulse left him dry and uninteresting. He was as famous as an after-dinner speaker as he was as a preacher or a public orator, and his humor, wit, and eloquence were awakened as promptly and freely by his glass of water as those of others by the most exhilerating wines.

But, unlike many others who have trusted to occasions for their inspiration, his range of sensitiveness was very wide. He was a passionate lover of nature, responsive to the suggestions of intellectual intercourse, at once tender and vehement, but he was dominated more than by all other things by his conception of the human soul—its capacities, its rights, its hopes, its dangers.

It was this that made him religious, with the profound fervor, the varied sympathy, that now touched, now aroused the hearts of his hearers. It was this that made him the champion of freedom, the untiring foe of slavery from his seminary days in Cincinnati to the moment when the civil war ended slavery. It was this that made him for nearly a half century a writer and speaker the most read, the most nearly worshiped, and the most blindly beloved of his time. He might also say, with Browning: "I was always a fighter," for his curious and comprehensive nature was singularly aggressive, not narrowly or selfishly so, for he was too broad for that, but with the spirit that knows "the delight of battle" and forgives and forgets with that greatness with which it conquers. His life in Plymouth Church, which was necessarily the larger share of his life, was marked by the same features as that in which he was more widely known. It was a long fight in

which he strode above rather than encountered ani-
mosity, and in which his magnanimity made itself
felt even more than his superb courage and his irresistible force.   Those who remember the crisis of now
twenty years since, when he turned against the tide of
patriotic passion he had aroused with a plea—essentially weak in reason but fine in motive—for a policy
of conciliation toward the South, will recognize Mr.
Beecher at his best.

It is not without difficulty that the greater number
of his countrymen now living can form a just estimate
of Mr. Beecher's work in the days when his work was
of the greatest service to his country.   Of the men,
who sowed in the heart and conscience of the people
that love of liberty and that steady hatred of slavery
which made the war for the Union possible and victory in the war certain, none did more than he.   His
labors with pen and voice were incessant.   There was
no faltering, not a moment of weakness, and there was
no doubting.   He was as confident that the right
would prevail as he was sure that it was the right.
And his influence was felt in every quarter of the
Union, hardly less in the South than in the North,
not less in the centers of free society that New England had established in the West than here where was
his immediate field of activity.   When he spoke or
wrote on this subject his inspiration never failed him,

for his heart was always aflame. And, curiously, it was in his anti-slavery addresses that his shrewdness, his rugged sense, his intimate sympathy with the common life of the farmer and the workman, his homely yet biting wit, were shown and were effective, even more than in his other utterances.

Mr. Beecher was hardly a theologian. He found it too difficult to accept any authority to become learned in a science which rests primarily on authority. His religion was a strange combination, in which it was not hard to set one idea against another, to see suggestions from the Hebrew prophets contending with suggestions from Herbert Spencer, and to find the tender sentiments of the pietists contradicted by the impulse of the warring reformer. It was enough for him that he felt the inspiration of each; he did not stop to reconcile them. But of one element of all religion—the sense of the brotherhood of men, the fatherhood of God—he never failed to give evidence. It was a natural consequence of such a nature that he was always a speaker rather than a writer, or even a thinker. He wrote much. Apart from his reported sermons, his published works — chiefly essays, prepared lectures, and articles for the weekly journals — are very voluminous. But they will scarcely survive him long. His own life, his own voice, were the conditions of his influence. In the

same connection it may be said that his personal conduct was in a sense independent of his work. He had
the defects of his qualities, or he never could have
permitted his reputation to be clouded by the scandal
of 1874, in which his part, whether innocent or not,
was most pitiful. But those who know what he was
and what he did for the people of the United States in
the course of his long life will not hesitate to say that
it was much, nor to pay to his memory the tribute of
grateful affection.

Mr. Beecher's personality was not hampered by
parsonality. He was not straight-laced in demeanor.
His vital forces continually overflowed and, like the
internal fires of a volcano, melted the snow of formal-
ity. His sensuous nature would have suffered a worse
fate than St. Anthony in the chains of asceticism.
The study was not his place — but the world. He
needed events. Beauty in any form was not only a
luxury but a necessity. Color intoxicated him. He
carried at one time in his vest pocket four little unset
gems. I think they were two rubies and two emer-
alds. I have seen him take them out, unroll the bit
of paper, and, turning them into the palm of his hand,
watch the play of complementary colors, as if it
linked his mind with some occult harmony beyond all
human discords.

One does not have to think long to know that a

man with these strong elemental characteristics would be stifled in the wrappings of ecclesiasticism. We feel instinctively in looking over his career that he was not so much an Erasmus or Melancthon as a Martin Luther. And like Martin Luther he needed the stimulus of great events.

It is absurd to say, as has recently been said, that he was a brilliant after-dinner talker. He never was. He did not bend to that persiflage with the willowy grace of a Depew or the sesquipedalian volubility of an Evarts.

But make him the champion of millions, let the issue be a nation's life, bring him face to face with a howling English mob, and he rose to the occasion like a Webster.

His generous disposition led him to comply with all kinds of requests, and to go and speak whenever he was wanted. And I have heard him at club receptions and dramatic fund benefits when he had nothing to say, and said it prosaically — standing desolate in his great good-nature.

He presents himself to me not as a casuist, but as a captain, and I have often speculated as to what he might have been, with his forensic gifts, in the Senate Chamber or anywhere abreast of great events.

The large diapason of some instruments will not answer to æolian touches.

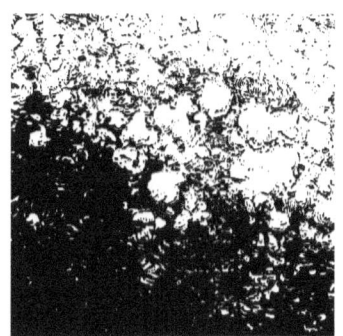

THE LAST LOOK.

389

Doubtless the quiet rectories of the world have held some of the noblest heroes, who served their Master uneventfully and faithfully, drinking their afternoon tea with the sisters in slippers, and weighing forever with sober duty the trivial cares of the sheepfold. Let us not disparage them. They kept the great distracted world with its momentous issues beyond earshot, but they paced their little round of individual sorrows and losses with self-sacrificing fidelity.

It is only here and there that a pulpit rose to a national forum and the sword of the Lord became the sword of the people. ·

There never was any hush of seclusion in Plymouth Church. Mr. Beecher may have struck back viciously at New England Calvinism, and now and then imitated Colonel Ingersoll in trying to stamp out hell, but he could not quite cut away from the New England spirit. The New Hampshire granite would outcrop in spite of the professional chair, and the blood that flowed at Lexington and crimsoned bright Champlain bubbled up both in the pulpit and in the congregation.

They did not shut their doors to the events of the time; they invited them in and wrestled with them.

It is in the white heat of events that we see Mr. Beecher now. He does not live for us in the pallid glow of pastoral duties. We take up his. twenty volumes of sermons and the vital iridescence is gone.

Loved, almost worshiped, by one of the richest, stanchest congregations in the East, filling every measure of duty and love to his charge, we still find it difficult to recognize in him the clerical shepherd. In spite of the great bulk of his work, which was pastoral, he appears to us now as a pioneer made for special and not general duties. Endowed with a puissant vitality that must have brought its thorns with it, Mr. Beecher stands at this moment, silent in his immortality, of strangely heroic proportions.

It is not the fashion just now to admire wholly vital men. The ideal man is a disembodied affair.

But we must not forget that some of the grandest types were magnificently vital, with large appetites and surging impulses.

Your Shakespeares and your Goethes were powerful furnaces that shook by the violence of their combustion the delicate machinery they propelled.

Your Handel was like an oak whose roots are in a morass but whose branches are in heaven.

And from St. Paul to John Knox we shall have to follow the events of history by the great vital captains that helped to make it.

I leave to æsthetic pietism to say, if in its efforts to

establish the purely psychic man it is not in danger of abolishing the cosmic man.

We must not regard Mr. Beecher's death as the extinguishment of a taper; rather let us think of it as the explosion of a meteor that throws a sudden light upon the world and reveals many noble deeds and a few crawling and obscene creatures.

But it also fell upon Court and Cathedral, touched the Bourse with a sad arresting ray, stopped the Legislature, dropped the national emblem, and shot its myriad pencils of pathos into countless human hearts from the hierarchy of religion to the lowest drudge of labor.

Grand contemporaneous tribute and verdict. He was human, but he was great and we loved him.

For some of us in the dusty highway, where the rose of Sharon can not bloom for the soot, and the voice that was heard in the cool of the evening is drowned in the iron clang, it is inexpressibly sweet to think that this oak, planted in a Calvinistic conservatory, burst through the roof with abundance of sap and cast its grateful shadows over our pilgrimage and wooed the birds to come and sing in its branches.

For more than half a century Mr. Beecher spoke in public. His addresses were on divers subjects — political, religious, educational, agricultural, charitable and other. He was gifted with a massive frame, a fine presence, a powerful and well modulated voice, and an impressive demeanor. Whatever he said bore the mark of earnestness. He threw himself into a subject impulsively. His diction was something marvelous. Although he never spoke from manuscript, and in his most polished addresses relied only on the briefest of captions, he was never at a loss for a word, never failed to get the most apt expression.

He had above most orators the power to sway an audience as he saw fit. He could touch and arouse, could move to tears and inspire to enthusiasm. In his lighter and more genial mood he would bring out smiles and bursts of most hearty laughter. His quaint conceits would often appear in his pulpit utterances, and on such occasions his enemies accused him of buffoonery, solely because of some garbled extracts which found their way into print. Read, however, with the context as they were uttered, their true meaning and purpose were at once perceived. He dealt less in imagery or word painting than in illustration and analogy, and rarely indulged in quotations. His appeals were to human feeling no less than to human reason.

Ordinarily he spoke slowly and with deliberation, but he would now and again indulge in passionate outbursts in which the words came like a torrent. Stenographers and other reporters of his addresses never felt quite sure of him. He would proceed for some minutes at the rate of about 120 words a minute, and then would suddenly rise to double that speed. The reporters, however, had one compensation. Mr. Beecher never found fault with their reports.

Nearly all of his addresses were extemporary in the sense that he had little or no notes to guide him. In his ordinary addresses, where he was one of several speakers at a meeting or assemblage, he would listen to those who preceded him and, taking as a text some one utterance would construct an address upon that. He had to a very marked degree the ability to "think upon his feet," and as a consequence was not ruffled by interruptions. In fact he often did better after being interrupted than before. An outside remark would spur him on and he would often use it to the discomfiture of the person uttering it. Most effective instances of this were had from time to time in Plymouth Church itself.

He prided himself on having made the pulpit of his church a free platform. From it spoke the heroes of the old anti-slavery fight with Wendell Phillips in the van. There it was that they raised money to buy the liberty of slaves. It re-echoed with a welcome to Kossuth and with appeals for the oppressed abroad and at home. From it came urgent calls for charity, for education, for freedom, and for humanity. No good cause ever found Mr. Beecher remiss. His heart, his purse, and his voice responded in no uncertain or half-hearted way.

His doctrinal addresses, including his famous Yale lectures, were gems in their way. The thought was couched in vigorous language, the illustrations were most varied, and the logical sequence was perfect. He could dress an idea in most intelligible as well as striking garb, and his comparisons were fitting as well as admirable

He was in great demand as a lecturer all over the country, and was always sure of a large and attentive audience. People would go to hear him deliver the same lecture again and again. But it was never the same lecture. The topic was the same, but the language, the illustrations, and the methods of reasoning were different. He never committed a lecture to memory, but relied on the inspiration of the moment to guide him in his manner of viewing or discussing his subject. The lecture would not be the same on two successive evenings. He kept abreast of the times, took a lively interest in current topics, and would weave in his discourse illustrations or incidents suggested by the occurrences of the day.

It was on festive occasions that his genialty in discourse found full vent. At public dinners, notably those of the New England Society in this city for many years, he was looked upon as the especial guest. He would at one moment set the tables in a roar, and next minute would thrill them to the quick with an appeal to their sympathy. It was a tribute to his ability that the dinner committee generally managed so that Mr. Beecher was the last speaker. Every one waited to the end in order to hear him speak. Presidents, Governors, and political magnates would precede him, but his advent would be anxiously waited for. He had no set speech for such occasions. At one time the burden of his talk would be good-natured raillery; at another it would be some earnest plea for progress or for charity. Whatever it was it was well said and well received.

In his political addresses Mr. Beecher rarely ventured on the domain of statistics, although when he did so he showed great art in his handling of figures. His appeals were usually to the feelings and the consciences of his auditors. He spoke in every Presidential campaign and in many of the minor contests, among them that for municipal reform in his own city. In recent years his most noted addresses of the kind were the memorable one in the Garfield campaign, in which he fairly flayed by his sarcasm the brood of culminators whose argument consisted in chalking the figures 329 on pavements and cellar doors; that in the Cooper Union, wherein he urged the renomination of President Arthur, and his Brooklyn Rink speech in favor of Cleveland.

Mr. Beecher had no fixed formula for beginning an address. He would sometimes open up his subject with his conclusion, and gradually show the train of reasoning leading to it. At other times he would begin by announcing certain undisputed facts and lead by easy stages to the result. He bound himself by no set of rules, and he followed none. He used few gestures.

His play of feature and his mimetic skill were so remarkable that it was often said of him that he would have been a wonderful actor had he chosen that calling. He felt too strongly what he said, however, to have simulated a passion. When he pleaded for a cause he did so with his whole being. His voice would grow husky, his frame would tremble, and tears would follow one another down his cheeks. His audiences, listening with rapt attention, would feel as he did, and be drawn the closer toward him. His spell was magnetic.

Henry Ward Beecher is already as historical a character as Patrick Henry, with the exception that, whereas there are multitudes living who have seen and heard Mr. Beecher, and many who knew him personally, there are few, if any, who can remember Patrick Henry. Mr. Beecher was the most versatile and ready orator this country has ever produced, a kind of Gladstone in the pulpit. He was a master of every style; could be as deliberate and imposing as Webster, as chaste and self-contained as Phillips, as witty and irregular as Thomas Corwin, as grandiloquent as Charles Sumner, almost as dramatic as Father Taylor, as melodramatic as Gough.

To attempt to analyze the sources of his power is like exhibiting the human features separately in the hope of giving the effect of a composite whole, for whether he moved his finger, elevated his brow, smiled, frowned, whispered or vociferated, each act or expression derived its power from the fact that it was the act or expression of Henry Ward Beecher. His oratory was marked by the entire absence of trammels of rhetoric, gesture, or even grammar. Not that his style was not ordinarily grammatical and rhetorical, but that he would never allow any rules to impede the expression of his thought, and especially of his feelings; nor was he restrained by theological forms, and always appeared independently and courageous. He stimulated the intellect by wit; he entered the heart and mind by humor; he melted the heart by unmixed pathos. The strange power of creating an expectation with every sentence he uttered always characterized him, and though he might on certain occasions, when not at his best, close without meeting the expectation aroused, no dissatisfaction was expressed or apparently felt by his hearers.

A metropolitan in the pulpit; a magician upon the platform; a center of life and good cheer in the house; a prince in society; possessed of exhaustless vitality, warmth and energy, he suggested to many who gazed upon him the apostrophe of Hamlet to the ideal man: "What a piece of work is man! How noble in reason! how infinite in faculties! in form and moving, how express and admirable! in action, how like an angel! in apprehension, how like a god! the beauty of the world! the paragon of animals!"

Such a piece of work was Henry Ward Beecher when in the prime of active life. He had no predecessor and can have no successor till a similar ancestry and life, the one coeval with the birth and the other running parallel with the lusty youth of such a nation, and a similar life-and-death struggle, born in a conflict of moral principles fought out under a democratic form of government, shall combine to evolve a similar career. The course of human history does not furnish a probability of another coincidence of elements so extraordinary.

CHAPTER XXIX.

SELECTIONS FROM WRITINGS.

Mr. Beecher never delivered a discourse in which there were not many gems. A hasty glance through a few of his published utterances discloses these epigrammatic thoughts upon every page. A few of them are culled and presented below, but they of necessity lack completeness and serve better to show Mr. Beecher's originality of expression than the breadth of his mind.

His ever exuberant and joyous nature was a constant protest against the ascetic in religion or in daily life:

"Don't mope. Be young as long as you live. Laugh a good deal. Frolic every day. A low tone of mind is unhealthy."

"A lawyer who works ten months in the year, and then for two solid months amuses himself, will last twice as long as if he took no recreation."

"Men have come to think that tears are more sacred than smiles. No! Laughing is as divine as crying."

"Humor usually tends toward good nature, and everything that tends toward good nature tends toward good grace."

"If laughing's a sin, I don't see what the Lord lets so many funny things happen for."

"Having wit and buoyancy of spirits, let them flash out in services of religion. Don't consider it necessary to rake them up and hide them."

"Humor is the atmosphere in which grace most flourishes."

"I say when a person becomes a Christian that he loses nothing that he should not be afraid to keep. If ever you are going to be a Christian, don't set out to be a gloomy-eyed, twilight-faced, bat-like Christian."

His struggle for the abolition of slavery provoked him to many beautiful and stirring utterances, of which the following are not the best types:

"That gospel which sanctions ignorance and oppression for three millions of men, what fruit or flower has it to shake down for the healing of the nations? It is cursed in its own roots, and blasted in its own boughs."

"Whether the Africans are an inferior race or not, it is evident that our destiny in some respects is bound up with them, and the study of their interests is the study of our salvation. This African race, in the Omnipotent hand, may be the instrument for our destruction, if we are to be destroyed. They may cling to our feet and entangle us in their final miseries."

Love, motherhood and the family were favorite themes with him:

"Oh, that men could be kept courting all the days of their life! What a school the school of love is!"

"A mother's heart does more in the bringing up of children, a million times, than a mother's hand, though the hand is sometimes quite busy."

"I think love grows between husband and wife by expressions of affection. I know there is a stately dignity in vogue. Husband and wife sit over against each other like those great statues of Memnon in Egypt; there they are, vast, stony and hard."

"You that live long enough will see women vote, and when you see women voting you will see less lying, less brutality and more public spirit, heroism and romance in public affairs."

"Robert Burns — A true poet, made not by the schools, brought up with no external culture or assistance. He came as a flower comes in spring. We say that he was a man of the people. No; he was far above the people. He was ordained to be an interpreter of God to his kind, then and forevermore."

"Of all the American novelists who have passed away the author of 'The House of the Seven Gables' seems to me the greatest."

"Grant had the patience of Fate and the force of

Thor. He has left to memory only such weaknesses as connect him with humanity and such virtues as will rank him among heroes."

"John Brown's name will travel through the ages as an illustrious example of what a man may do who is willing to suffer for a great principle."

"Emerson, the calm, the observational, not an enthusiast in religion, but with patriotism and humanity to make him a brave witness. It took seven generations of ministers to make one Ralph Waldo Emerson."

"It is a noble thing to see a man so in sympathy with his time and work, as Tennyson is, that even with expiring strength he still tries to chant the truth of God to the age in which he lives."   '

"Peter Cooper — a manly man, who lived for his fellow-men. May God increase the procession of such men! He will increase it. It is a tendency."

"Though slow, Abraham Lincoln was sure. A thousand men could not make him plant his foot before he was ready; ten thousand could not move it after he had set it down."

"Grover Cleveland, like Washington, has the great faculty of maintaining his own personality and enlarging his own knowledge."

"I would not weaken one single sinew in the sturdy arm of Bismarck."

"God raised up a Cromwell to wrest Liberty from

the King's hands and set it firmly upon its feet before the nations of the earth."

" Charles Sumner was a republican statesman because he sought the welfare of all, and not of a privileged class."

" Spencer will be found to have given to the world more truth in one lifetime than any other man that has lived in the schools of philosophy."

He was a champion of temperance upon occasion, but never made a hobby of it.

We once heard him in one of his marked efforts in this cause, when he appeared on the platform of the Cooper Institute, New York City, how well we remember the opening of his oration, in these words, "*I am a son of Lyman Beecher*,"—Lyman Beecher who had been the great head and front of the cause of temperance. Thus it was that the son throughout his career was ever a ready-full-armed combatant for the cause that his mighty sire had brought to the front among the great questions of the century.

" We drink, not to gratify the palate but for a business purpose. That being the case, we may begin with the milder beverages, just as we begin our fire with pine shavings, not only because we can light them so easily, but also because we want them to set on fire something solider. And wine is stepstone to brandy. Beer is stepstone the other way. It does not lead up to brandy, but it leads down to drunk and beastly drunk."

"Intemperance is the fertile source of crime. Have you done anything about it?"

At another time he wrote on the training of children:

"I thank God for two things—yes, for a thousand; but for two among many: First, that I was born and bred in the country, of parents that gave me a sound constitution and a noble example. I never can pay back what I got from my parents. If I were to raise a monument of gold higher than heaven it would be no expression of the debt of gratitude which I owe to them, for that which they unceasingly gave, by the heritage of their body and the heritage of their souls, to me. And next to that I am thankful that I was brought up in circumstances where I never became acquainted with wickedness."

In the closing paragraph of this letter of advice to parents, he said:

"Keep your children at home at night. There is many a sod that lies over the child whose downfall began by vagrancy at night, and there is many a child whose heartbreaking parents would give the world if the sod did lie over them."

Another letter speaks of the evils of night work and late amusements:

"I think the judgments formed at night are never so solid and fresh as judgments formed in the morning. If in the morning a man is without charity, if he is despondent, if he is dull, if he is unnerved, you may be sure that he is living wrong. For the order of nature is, that a man should rise from his bed in the morning as birds rise, singing and in perfect health. A man rises buoyant and has his best hours in the early day. For although perhaps the fancy may not be so brilliant in the early day, the judgment is better. The conclusions and determinations which a man forms in the early day are apt to be sounder and safer than those which he forms at night. Fancy for the night, judgment for the day. . . . If our nights could be shortened at one end and lengthened at the other it would be better for us. Get up early; breakfast early; work early. Use the day for the works of the day, and the night for the works of recuperation and not for works of darkness."

The observance of the Sabbath was the subject of another letter:

"The Sabbath is every man's day — especially every man's who wants to be stronger, higher, purer, nobler than he has been or is. It is a day made on purpose to elevate men. It is not a day designed to enable the church to get a hitch on folks. It is not a day on which ecclesiastical authorities are to watch men with jealousy. It is the common people's great liberty day; and they are bound to see to it that work does not come into it. Not because work is dishonorable, not because there is a special stigma to be attached to working on Sunday, but because they can not make it what it ought to be for them if they do suffer work to come into it."

The misconceptions of religion and the quarreling of the sects were frequent topics with him:

"Religion is a very slim, lean, gaunt, poor, ill-fed thing as it is ordinarily conceived of in this world."

"Men sit around a tool-chest quarreling about saws and planes and chisels. They are not building anything; they are debating about tools. They are fit to be a theological seminary."

"That kind of revival preaching which seeks to drive men into heaven by the fear of hell is not Christianity. It is the worst form of Paganism."

"Sects are candlesticks, and a man or woman that is big enough to be good for anything is too large for any sect."

"Why is it that men think it incumbent upon them to be cats and dogs in religion and gentlemen in everything outside of it?"

Sunday with him was not a day of gloom, and he took frequent occasion to show the needlessness of being sombre on that day.

"I esteem the awfulness that is attached to Sunday, and church, and pulpit, the greatest mistake of Christendom."

"The prevalent idea of keeping the Sabbath is that it is a day on which certain things must not be done.

To the majority of people, Sunday is a day full of *nots*."

"I am in favor of any movement that helps any-body to appreciate Sunday as a day of rest, of health-ful and pure pleasures, and that will gently lead men, women and children from the things of low estate up to the higher."

Some of his utterances on the question of death and the future life are peculiarly appropriate at this time:

"To one who is living aright, no death can be sud-den and no place unfavorable. One step and all roads meet."

"Dying is the best part of life to one who knows how to live worthily."

"If the life that has gone out has been like music, full of concords, full of sweetness, richness, delicacy, truth, then there are two ways to look at it. One is to say, 'I have not lost it!' Another is to say, 'Blessed be God that I have had it so long!'"

. "When we comprehend the fullness of what death will do for us, in all our outlook and forelook, dying is triumphing. Nowhere is there so fair a sight, so sweet a prospect, as when a young soul is passing away out of life and time through the gate of death—the rosy, the royal, the golden, the pearly gate of death."

"Death is as sweet as flowers are. It is as blessed as bird-singing in spring. I never hear of the death of any one who is ready to die that my heart does not sing like a harp. I am sorry for those that are left behind, but not for those who have gone before.

"As I grow older and come nearer to death, I look upon it more and more with complacent joy, and out of every longing I hear God say: 'O, trusting hungering one, come to me.' What the other life will bring I know not, only that I shall awake in God's likeness and see him as he is.

"Beat on, then, O heart, and yearn for dying. I have drunk at many a fountain, but thirst came again; I have fed at many a bounteous table, but hunger returned; I have seen many bright and lovely things, but while I gazed their lustre faded. There is nothing here that can give me rest, but when I behold thee, O God, I shall be satisfied."

How well he understands the ministry of grief!

"A Christian man's life is laid in the loom of time to a pattern which he does not see, but God does; and his heart is a shuttle. On one side of the loom is sorrow, and on the other side is joy; and the shuttle, struck alternately by each, flies back and forth, carrying the thread, which is white or black, as the pattern needs; and in the end, when God shall lift up the finished garment, and all its changing hues shall glance out, it will then appear that the deep and dark colors were as needful to beauty as the bright and high colors."

He loved children and the boy still fresh in his manhood.

"When your own child comes in from the street, and has learned to swear from the bad boys congregated there, it is a very different thing to you from what it was when you heard the profanity of those boys as you passed them. Now it takes hold of you, and makes you feel that you are a stockholder in the public morality. Children make men better citizens. Of what use would an engine be to a ship, if it were lying loose in the hull? It must be fastened to it with bolts and screws before it can propel the vessel. Now a childless man is just like a loose engine. A man must be bolted and screwed to the community before he can begin to work for its advancement, and there are no such screws and bolts as children."

He had a most Christ-like contempt for the hypocrite, whom he scourged with heavy evangelical whips, but the tenderest Christian love for earnest men struggling after nobleness.

"I think the wickedest people on earth are those who use a force of genius to make themselves selfish in the noblest things, keeping themselves aloof from the vulgar and the ignorant and the unknown, rising higher and higher in taste, till they sit, ice upon ice, on the mountain-top of eternal congelation."

"Men are afraid of slight outward acts which will injure them in the eyes of others, while they are heedless of the damnation which throbs in their souls in hatreds and jealousies and revenges."

"Many people use their refinements as a spider

uses his web, to catch the weak upon, that they may be mercilessly devoured. Christian men should use refinement on this principle: The more I have, the more I owe to those who are less than I."

He valued the substance of man more than his accidents.

"We say a man is 'made.' What do we mean? That he has got the control of his lower instincts, so that they are only fuel to his higher feelings, giving force to his nature? That his affections are like vines, sending out on all sides blossoms and clustering fruits? That his tastes are so cultivated, that all beautiful things speak to him, and bring him their delight? That his understanding is opened, so that he walks through every hall of knowledge and gathers its treasures? That his moral feelings are so developed and quickened, that he holds sweet commerce with Heaven? Oh, no! — none of these things! He is cold and dead in heart, and mind, and soul. Only his passions are alive; but — he is worth $500,000!

"And we say a man is 'ruined.' Are his wife and children dead? Oh, no! Have they had a quarrel, and are they separated from him? Oh, no! Has he lost his reputation through crime? No. Is his reason gone? Oh, no! it's as sound as ever. Is he struck through with disease? No; he has lost his property, and he is ruined. The *man* ruined? When shall we learn that 'a man's life consisteth not in the abundance of the things he possesseth?'"

Mr. Beecher's God has the gentle and philanthropic qualities of Jesus of Nazareth, with omnipotence added. Religious emotion comes out in his prayers, sermons, and lectures, as the vegetative power of the earth in the manifold plants and flowers of spring.

"The sun does not shine for a few trees and flowers, but for the wide world's joy. The lonely pine on the mountain-top waves its sombre boughs and cries, 'Thou art my sun!' And the little meadow-violet lifts its cup of blue, and whispers with its perfumed breath, 'Thou art my sun! And the grain in a thousand fields rustles in the wind, and makes answer, 'Thou art my sun!'

"So God sits effulgent in heaven, not for a favored few, but for the universe of life; and there is no creature so poor or so low, that he may not look up with childlike confidence and say, 'My Father! thou art mine!'"

"When once the filial feeling is breathed into the heart, the soul can not be terrified by augustness, or justice, or any form of Divine grandeur; for then, to such a one, *all the attributes of God are but so many arms stretched abroad through the universe, to gather and to press to his bosom those whom he loves. The greater he is the gladder are we, so that he be our father still.*

"But if one consciously turns away from God, or fears him, the nobler and grander the representation be, the more terrible is his conception of the Divine Adversary that frowns upon him. The God whom love beholds rises upon the horizon like mountains which carry summer up their sides to the very top; but that sternly just God whom sinners fear stands cold against the sky, like Mont Blanc, and from his icy sides the soul, quickly sliding, plunges headlong down to unrecalled destruction."

He had hard words for such as get only the form of religion, or but little of its substance.

"There are some Christians whose secular life is an arid, worldly strife, and whose religion is but a turbid sentimentalism. Their life runs along that line where the overflow of the Nile meets the desert. It is the boundary line between sand and mud."

"Many of our churches defy Protestantism. Grand cathedrals are they, which make us shiver as we enter them. The windows are so constructed as to exclude the light and inspire a religious awe. The walls are of stone, which makes us think of our last home. The ceilings are sombre, and the pews coffin-colored.

"Then the services are composed to these circumstances, and hushed music goes trembling along the aisles, and men move softly, and would on no account put on their hats before they reach the door; but when they do, they take a long breath, and have such a sense of relief to be in the free air, and comfort themselves with the thought that they've been good Christians!

"Now this idea of worship is narrow and false. The house of God should be a joyous place for the right use of all our faculties."

"There ought to be such an atmosphere in every Christian church, that a man going there and sitting two hours should take the contagion of heaven, and carry home a fire to kindle for the right use of all our faculties."

"The call to religion is not a call to be better than your fellows, *but to be better than yourself.* Religion is relative to the individual."

"My best presentations of the gospel to you are so incomplete! Sometimes, when I am alone, I have such sweet and rapturous visions of the love of God and the truths of his word, that I think, if I could speak to you then, I should move your hearts. I am like a child, who, walking forth, some sunny summer's morning, sees grass and flowers all shining with drops of dew. 'Oh,' he cries, 'I'll carry these beautiful things to my mother!' And, eagerly plucking them, the dew drops into his little palm, and all the charm is gone. There is but grass in his hand, and no longer pearls."

"There are many professing Christians who are secretly vexed on account of the charity they have to bestow and the self-denial they have to use. If, instead of the smooth prayers which they *do* pray, they should speak out the things which they really feel, they would say when they go home at night, 'O Lord, I met a poor curmudgeon of yours to-day, a miserable, unwashed brat, and I gave him sixpence, and I have been sorry for it ever since;' or, 'O Lord, if I had not signed those articles of faith, I might have gone to the theater this evening. Your religion deprives me of a great deal of enjoyment, but I mean to stick to it. There's no other way of getting into heaven, I suppose.'

"The sooner such men are out of the church, the better."

"The youth-time of churches produces enterprise; their age, indolence; but even this might be borne, did not *these dead men sit in the door of their sepulchres, crying out against every living man who refuses to wear the livery of death.* In India, when the husband dies, they burn his widow with him. I am almost tempted to think, that, if, with the end of every pastorate, the church itself were disbanded and destroyed, to be gathered again by the succeeding teacher, we should thus secure an immortality of youth."

"A religious life is not a thing which spends itself. It is like a river, which widens continually, and is never so broad or so deep as at its mouth, where it rolls into the ocean of eternity."

"God made the world to relieve an over-full creative thought; as musicians sing, as we talk, as artists sketch, when full of suggestions. What profusion is there in his work! When trees blossom, there is not a single breast-pin but a whole bosom full of gems, and of leaves they have so many suits that they can throw them away to the winds all summer long. What unnumbered cathedrals has he reared in the forest shades, vast and grand, full of curious carvings, and haunted evermore by tremulous music! and in the heavens above, how do stars seem to have flown out of his hand, faster than sparks out of a mighty forge!"

"Oh, let the soul alone! Let it go to God as best it may! It is entangled enough. It is hard enough for it to rise above the distractions which environ it. Let a man teach the rain how to fall, the clouds how to shape themselves and move their airy rounds, the seasons how to cherish and garner the universal abundance; but let him not teach a soul to pray, on whom the Holy Ghost doth brood!"

He recognized the difference between religion and theology.

"How sad is that field from which battle hath just departed! By as much as the valley was exquisite in its loveliness, is it now sublimely sad in its desolation. Such to me is the Bible when a fighting theologian has gone through it.

"How wretched a spectacle is a garden into which the cloven-footed beasts have entered! That which yesterday was fragrant, and shone all over with crowded beauty, is to-day rooted, despoiled, trampled, and utterly devoured, and all over the ground you shall find but the rejected cuds of flowers and leaves, and forms that have been champed for their juices and then rejected. Such to me is the Bible when the pragmatic prophecy-monger and the swinish utilitarian have toothed its fruits and craunched its blossoms.

"O garden of the Lord! whose seeds dropped down

27

from heaven, and to whom angels bear watering dews night by night! O flowers and plants of righteousness! O sweet and holy fruits! We walk among you and gaze with loving eyes, and rest under your odorous shadows; nor will we with sacrilegious hand tear you, that we may search the secret of your roots, nor spoil you, that we may know how such wondrous grace and goodness are evolved within you!"

"What a pin is, when the diamond has dropped from its setting, is the Bible when its emotive truths have been taken away. What a babe's clothes are when the babe has slipped out of them into death and the mother's arms clasp only raiment, would be the Bible, if the Babe of Bethlehem, and the truths of deep-heartedness that clothes his life should slip out of it."

"There is no food for soul or body which God has not symbolized. He is light for the eye, sound for the ear, bread for food, wine for weariness, peace for trouble. Every faculty of the soul, if it would but open its door, might see Christ standing over against it, and silently asking by his smile, 'Shall I come in unto thee?' But men open the door and look down, not up, and thus see him not. So it is that men sigh on, not knowing what the soul wants, but only that it needs something. Our yearnings are homesickness for heaven; our sighings are for God, just as children that cry themselves asleep away from home, and sob in their slumber, know not that they sob for their parents. The soul's inarticulate moanings are the affections yearning for the Infinite, but having no one to tell them what it is that ails them."

"I feel sensitive about theologies. Theology is good in its place ; but when it puts its hoof upon a living, palpitating, human heart, my heart cries out against it."

"There are men marching along the company of Christians on earth, who, when they knock at the gate of heaven, will hear God answer, 'I never knew you.' 'But the ministers did, and the church-books did.' 'That may be. I never did.'

"It is no matter who knows a man on earth, if God does not know him."

"The heart-knowledge, through God's teaching, is true wealth, and they are often poorest who deem themselves most rich. I, in the pulpit, preach with proud forms to many a humble widow and stricken man who might well teach me. The student, specta-cled and gray with wisdom, and stuffed with lumbered lore, may be childish and ignorant beside some old singing saint who brings the word into his study, and who, with lens of his own experience, brings down the orbs of truth, and beholds through his faith and his humility things of which the white-haired scholar never dreamed."

He has eminent integrity, is faithful to his own soul, and to every delegated trust. No words are needed here as proof. His life is daily argument. The public will understand this; men whose taste he offends, and whose theology he shocks, or to whose philosophy he is repugnant, have confidence in the integrity of the man. He means what he says, — is solid all through.

"From the beginning, I educated myself to speak along the line and in the current of my moral convictions ; and though, in later days, it has carried me through many places where there were some batterings and bruisings, yet I have been supremely grateful that I was led to adopt this course. I would rather speak the truth to ten men than blandishments and lying to a million. Try it, ye who think there is nothing in it ! try what it is to speak with God behind you,— to speak so as to be only the arrow in the bow which the Almighty draws."

With what affectionate tenderness does this great, faithful soul pour out his love to his own church ! He invites men to the communion-service.

"Christian brethren, in heaven you are known by the name of Christ. On earth, for convenience sake, you are known by the name of Presbyterians, Episcopalians, Methodists, Congregationalists, and the like. Let me speak the language of heaven, and call you simply Christians. Whoever of you has known the name of Christ, and feel Christ's life beating within him, is invited to remain and sit with us at the table of the Lord."

And again, when a hundred were added to his church, he says :

" My friends, my heart is large to-day. I am like a tree upon which rains have fallen till every leaf is covered with drops of dew; and no wind goes through the boughs but I hear the pattering of some thought of joy or gratitude. I love you all more than ever before. You are crystalline to me ; your faces are radiant ; and I look through your eyes, as through windows, into heaven. I behold in each of you an imprisoned angel, that is yet to burst forth, and to live and shine in the better sphere."

Here are extracts of that peculiar humor which appears in all his works:

" Sects and Christians that desire to be known by the undue prominence of some single feature of Christianity are necessarily imperfect just in proportion to the distinctness of their peculiarities. The power of Christian truth is in its unity and symmetry, and not in the saliency or brilliancy of any of its special doctrines. If among painters of the human face and form, there should spring up a sect of the eyes, and another sect of the nose, a sect of the hand, and a sect of the foot, and all of them should agree but in the one thing of forgetting that there was a living spirit behind the features more important than them all, they would too much resemble the schools and cliques of Christians, for the spirit of Christ is the great essential truth; doctrines are but the features of the face, and ordinances but the hands and feet."

Here are some separate maxims:

"It is not well for a man to pray cream and live skim-milk."

"The mother's heart is the child's school-room."

"They are not reformers who simply abhor evil. Such men become in the end abhorrent themselves."

"There are many troubles which you can't cure by the Bible and the Hymn-book, but which you can cure by a good perspiration and a breath of fresh air."

"The most dangerous infidelity of the day is the infidelity of rich and orthodox churches."

"The fact that a nation is growing is God's own charter of change."

"There is no class in society who can so ill afford to undermine the conscience of the community, or to set it loose from its moorings in the eternal sphere, as merchants who live upon confidence and credit. Anything which weakens or paralyzes this is taking beams from the foundations of the merchants' own warehouse."

"It would almost seem as if there were a certain drollery of art which leads men to think they are doing one thing to do another and very different one. Thus, men have set up in their painted church windows the symbolisms of virtues and graces, and the images of saints, and even of Divinity itself. Yet, now, what does the window do but mock the separations and proud isolations of Christian men? For there sit the audience, each one taking a separate color; and there are blue Christians and red Christians, there are yellow saints and orange saints, there are purple Christians and green Christians; but how few are simple, pure, white Christians, uniting all the cardinal graces, and proud, not of separate colors, but of the whole manhood of Christ!"

" Every mind is entered, like every house, through its own door."

" Doctrine is nothing but the skin of truth set up and stuffed."

" Compromise is the word that men use when the Devil gets a victory over God's cause."

"A man in the right, with God on his side, is in the majority, though he be alone; for God is multitudinous above all populations of the earth."

"A lie always needs a truth for a handle to it; else the hand would cut itself, which sought to drive it home upon another. The worst lies, therefore, are those whose blade is false, but whose handle is true."

" It is not conviction of truth which does men good; it is moral consciousness of truth."

"A conservative young man has wound up his life before it was unreeled. We expect old men to be conservative; but when a nation's young men are so, its funeral-bell is already rung."

" Night labor, in time, will destroy the student; for it is marrow from his own bones with which he fills his lamp."

"I never was sullied in act, nor in thought, nor in feeling when I was young. I grew up as pure as a woman. And I can not express to God the thanks which I owe to my mother, and to my father, and to the great household of sisters and brothers among whom I lived. And the secondary knowledge of those wicked things which I have gained in later life in a professional way, I gained under such guards that it was not harmful to me."

"I think to force childhood to associate religion with such dry morsels (as the Catechism) is to violate the spirit not only of the New Testament, but of common sense as well. I know one thing, that if I am 'lax and latitudinarian,' the Sunday Catechism is to blame for a part of it. The dinners I have lost because I could not go through 'sanctification,' and 'justification,' and 'adoption,' and all such questions, lie heavily on my memory. I do not know that they have brought forth any blossoms. I have a kind of grudge against many of those truths that I was taught in my childhood, and I am not conscious that they have worked up a particle of faith in me."

In the following selections Mr. Beecher's power of description is illustrated.

"The doctor drew near the now cast-away gutter, and stooping, plucked two or three of the weeds, and putting them under his hat-band, laid down his hat on the well-stone, while he unrolled the rickety old windlass and sent down the remnants of a bucket for water. It was an old-fashioned well, of mysterious depth. If

you looked down its narrow and dark throat, you saw
nothing. If you still looked, and dropped a pebble
down, a faint light was reflected from the crinkling
water far below. Four or five feet at the top, the
stones were lined with moss. Up, after long winding,
came the bucket, spurting out its contents on every
side, and filling the well with a musical splashing
sound, reserving hardly enough, at last, to serve for a
good drink. 'Well, Biah, I understand the old proverb—truth is at the bottom of the well. If I was to
go down after the water, very likely there is foul air
enough down there to put me out like a candle, and if
I send a bucket down the greatest part leaks out before I can reach it. Much work and little truth do
men get in the wells they dig now-a-days.'"

"The hall of a dwelling gives you the first impres-
sions, Sometimes on entering you fear that by some
mistake you have got into a clothes closet; at others,
you enter upon a space so small that it is only by a
dexterous interchange of civilities between yourself
and the door that you can get in or the door be shut.
In some halls, so called, a man sees a pair of corkscrew
stairs coming right down upon him, and fears lest by
some jugglery he be seized and extracted like a cork
into some upper space. Often the doors are so arranged that what with the shutting of the outside
door, and the opening of inside ones, the timid
stranger stands a chance of being impaled on the
latch, or flapped front and rear, for vigorous springs
attached to the doors work with such nimbleness that
one needs to be an expert, or, having opened the door,

before he can dash through, it will spring back on him with a 'now—I've-got-you' air quite alarming."

"When I walked one day on the top of Mount Washington,—glorious day of memory! such another day I think I shall not experience till I stand on the battlements of the new Jerusalem—how I was discharged of all imperfection! The wide far-spreading country which lay beneath me in beauteous light, how heavenly it looked, and I communed with God. I had sweet tokens that he loved me. My very being rose right up into his nature. I walked with him, and the cities far and near of New York, and all the cities and villages which lay between it and me, with their thunder, the wrangling of human passions below me, were to me as if they were not."

"Have you ever stood in Dresden to watch that matchless picture of Raphael's, the 'Madonna de San Siste?' Engravings of it are all through the world; but no engraving has ever reproduced the mother's face. The infant Christ that she holds is far more nearly represented than the mother. In her face there is a mist. It is wonder, it is love, it is adoration, it is awe; it is all these mingled, as if she held in her hands her babe, and yet it was God! That picture means nothing to me as it does to the Roman Church; but it means everything to me, because I believe that every mother should love the God that is in her child, and that every mother's heart should be watching to discern and see in the child, which is more than flesh and blood, something that takes hold of immortality and glory."

"There came to me last week one whose bad ways I had known, and whom I had avoided, supposing that he was but a sponge; but having since January last maintained a better course, he came to me, and, to my surprise, said, 'The kindness that some friends have shown me has been very comforting and very encouraging.' As I sat there my heart trembled. I rebuked myself that I had ever had any other thought than that he might be rescued; and as he went on my heart went out towards him. I longed to take him up in my arms, and out of the entanglements and temptations that beset him, and make a man of him."

"I am angry when I hear people talk of the awful responsibility of being a minister. People sometimes say to me, 'I should think you would shudder when you stand up before your congregation.' I shudder! What should I shudder for? Do you shudder when you stand up before a garden of flowers? Do you shudder when you go into an orchard of fruit in October? Do you shudder when you stand up in the midst of all the richness and grandeur of nature? I shudder in your midst? 'But the responsibility!' I have no responsibility. I am willing to do my duty; and what more is there than that? I will not stand for the consequences. I will do the best I can. I will say the best things I can every Sunday; I will bring the truth home to you; and I will do it in the spirit of love. Even when I say the severest things it is because I am faithful to love. 'But your care!' I have not a bit of care. I forget the sermon a great deal quicker than you do. 'Your burden!' I have no burden. I take up the battle, and I lay the battle aside again as soon as it is over. And I shall sleep to-night as sweetly as any man that is here. And every man that is in the ministry, and is willing to love men and be faithful to them, will find joy in it from day to day."

"I linger, and yet I know that it is in vain by added words or by intenser expressions to reach the heart. My dear brethren and friends, I am joined to you to-night in sympathy, I am joined to you in love. We are pilgrims together, we are moving on — of this we are conscious. My sight grows dimmer, whiteness is coming on these locks, and you are keeping company ; I observe it. Those who were little children when I came here are now carrying their little children in their arms. The young men with whom I took counsel are now speaking with their grand-children."

"Because our acquaintance with vital intelligence, sentient life, is limited, because the class of beings with which we are familiar exist in unity — unity and diversity as far as faculty is concerned, but unity without diverse personality — we are not to suppose that this exhausts all possible modes of being."

CHAPTER XXX.

The Atonement.

" If it be impugning the character of God to teach that there is a doctrine of substitution and vicariousness, by which the just suffer for the unjust, then it is a doctrine which strikes clear through outward creation. Who pay for vice ? Not the vicious. The virtuous pay for it. Who pay the taxes of the community ? The men whose vices are the leakages ? This community is a vast hull, and at every seam there is leaking and leaking. Whose work is it to caulk it up ? Why, it is the industrious man that pays for the waste of the shiftless man in the long run. It is the vice of the community that is the tax-gatherer of the community. If it were not for good men, communities would break down under the vices and crimes of bad men. . . . And if you say it is against the idea of divine benevolence that God should let just men suffer for unjust men, then your idea of divine benevolence was a false one. It is not in accordance with past reason; it is not in accordance with the facts of human life; it is not in accordance with your own ideas. . . . When you call to mind your own feelings as a father, and when you take lessons from the household, then your conception of a being that is true to the laws of the universe must recognize the principle of suffering one for another. What would you not do for a child ? How much would you not suffer ? How long would you not bear with him if only through your instrumentality he might be saved ? Now lift that sublime form of parental life which is familiar to you up into the sphere of the Infinite. Crown it, and enthrone it, and call it God, Savior, and how glorious it becomes ? Is it not adorable and praiseworthy when it rises to the proportions of divinity, and becomes typical of the character of the Creator himself ? "

Regeneration.

"A man goes to the minister, and says, ' What must I do to secure eternal life ? ' ' You must repent,' says the minister. So the man cries, and cries, and cries, and feels bad, and feels bad, and feels bad, and feels bad. That is the way he pays for his insurance. By-and-by he feels better, and he tells the minister. ' You have had your bad state, and you have come to your joyful state, and now you have your hope.' And the man goes home, and says to his wife, ' My dear, I

have passed from death unto life; and, come what
may, I am going to be saved. I may wander, to be
sure; but I have my evidence, my hope, my assurance. Oh! is there any heresy comparable with this
spiritual indifference and spiritual security!"

"Sometimes men complain of the doctrine of a
regenerated life, as if it were a requisition; it is not,
it is a refuge. Oh, what would not a criminal, who at
thirty-five years of age found himself stung with disgrace, and overwhelmed with odium, give, if in the
policy of human society there should be any method
by which he could begin back again, as if he had not
begun at all, and with all his accumulated experience
build his character anew! But in the economy of
God in Christianity there is such a thing as a man at
fifty and sixty years of age — hoary-headed in transgression, deeply defiled, struck through and through
with the fast colors of depravity — having a chance to
become a true child again. God sets a partition-wall
between him and past transgressions, and says, 'I will
remember them no more forever.' "

The Bible.

"There is no theory or philosophy of inspiration
propounded in any part of the sacred books. It is
manifest that it is a divine influence, an inbreathing
of God upon those who wrote; but the theories of in-

spiration are modern and human. We may take it as
stated in general that the sacred books were composed
and given to the church under divine direction or
influence."

"Bishop Colenso thinks he has shown that there
are mistakes in the writings of Moses. Very likely.
And suppose it should be shown that Moses never
wrote them at all? What then? It would be shown,
that is all. And suppose they should be taken out of
the Bible, what then? They would be taken out, that
is all. And how would it be with those that are left?
Why, they would be left, that is all. Cipher away
about Moses, fools! *I* will cling to the hope of Christ
and salvation by him."

"I declare that Christian instruction is more
profitable than anything else in the whole Bible.
The doctrines of humility, meekness, gentleness, non-
resistance under injuries, the whole schedule of Christian dispositions which were marked out by the
Savior, shine as though they were so many gems and
jewels brought down from the bosom of God." .

The Church, Sects and Sacraments.

So far from objecting to sects, he highly approved
of them. He says they are like flowers, all born of
the sun, and brought into their life and power, and
yet they are widely different in their structure and

appearance. "Would you," he exclaims, "reduce them all to one, and have nothing but daisies, nothing but tulips, or nothing but violets?"

"I believe in the organization of Christians into churches, as I believe in the forming of churches, by elective affinities, into sects."

"I do not see any harm in denominations. I would just as soon see twenty more as twenty less. . . . But sects are not Christianity, they do not represent the whole of it. . . . The specialties which distinguish one from another usually are specialties that have in them a truth which is nowhere else developed with such breadth and force. . . . Christianity is represented by the sum of all the sects —not by any one of them."

"I do not object to bishops; I dare say I should like to be a bishop myself."

"When we come to be released from the narrowness of our own church or sect, how joyful is the brotherhood of good men, and how strong are we!"

Infidelity and the Devil.

"The devil is distributive in our days—some of him is in governments, some of him is in judges," etc.

He condemns "the roystering infidelity of vulgar

men," and also "the cold indifference of educated materialism."

"Unbelief," he says—such unbelief as abounds amongst the intelligent young men of our days— "unbelief is the drifting of sensitive natures, famished and hungering and searching for something that shall feed them."

Secular Truth.

"If I know my own business—and the presumption is I do—it is to hunt men and to study them. . . . Do you suppose I study old, musty books when I want to preach? I study *you!* When I want to deliver a discourse on theology, I study *you!* When I want to know more about the doctrine of depravity, I study *you!* When I want to know what is right and what is wrong, I see how *you do;* and I have abundant illustrations on every side!"

"I know that there are operations in railway management that outrage every law of prudence. I know that when mighty capital is combined and capitalists are joined together, a fraternity of villains, they shall be able to swamp legislatures, and sweep whole communities to destruction. And when this accumulation of peril begins to globe up and fill the very horizon, I know it is my business to sound the alarm and say to men, 'There is no prosperity to society so long as

such gigantic swindles and frauds as these are going
on.' And when I do say it, they say to me, 'Are you
a railroad man?' 'No; but I am after railroad men.'
'Do you understand this business?' 'No; but I
understand the men that are in this business.' Is it a
part of your parochial affairs to meddle with such
matters?' 'Yes; it is a part of my parochial affairs.
I am a citizen of the United States; and you are my
parishioners; and I see that you are criminals, pursuing culpable courses which violate honesty, and purity,
and conscience, and though you are not honorable
men, and do not pass for such before God, though you
may before men; and it is just my business to tell
you these things.' And when it is said, 'No one can
give advice in regard to the affairs of any given
department unless he belongs to those affairs,' I say
that a cock does not need to be in bed with you to
know that morning has come and crow! It is because
he is out of doors, and sits aloft, and sees when the
sun is coming up, that he becomes the clarion of the
morning, and gives you the signal for waking up."

Marriage.

"Young men just beginning life need what they
can not have. At no after period, perhaps, in their
life do young men need the inspiration of virtuous
love and the sympathy of a companion in their self-

denying toil, as when they first enter the battle for their own support."

"Early marriages are permanent moralities, and deferred marriages are temptations to wickedness. And yet every year it becomes more and more difficult, concurrent with the reigning ideas of society, for young men to enter upon that matrimonial state which is the proper guard of their virtue, as well as the source of their courage and enterprise. The battle of life is almost always at the beginning. Then it is that a man needs wedlock."

"Society is bad when two can not live cheaper than one! And young men are under bad influences who, when in the very morning of ' life, and better fitted than at any later period to grow together with one who is their equal and mate, are debarred from marrying through scores of years from mere prudential considerations, and the heart and life are sacrificed to the pocket. They are tempted to substitute ambition for love, when, at last, over the ashes and expiring embers of their early romance, they select their wife. It is said that men who wait till they are forty or forty-five years of age select prudently. Alas for the wife who is not first a sweetheart!"

"Sister! sister—that is a sweet word, but exceedingly mischievous, too, in the realm of love! It is a

word for devout enthusiasm, for unselfish love, for un-
blushing friendship, for faithfulness and honest intimacy, for friendship without passion, for love without sultry ardors. Brother and sister! That is the
most simple and beautiful confluence of the sexes!

"But that word sister is the covered way of love!
It is the mask which bashfulness wears before it gains
boldness enough to say love. It is a gentle hypoc-
risy, under which souls consent to remain and dream,
in hope by and by of a rapturous waking! It is that
is July; and then love, which is August; but July
and August are so much alike that no one can tell
when one stops and the other begins!"

Women.

"The increasing intelligence in women is destined
to have an important influence upon the American
family. It is in vain that men cry out against the
emancipation of woman from the narrow bounds of
the past. It is destiny; it is God that is calling, and
women must obey. The world has unrolled and
unfolded until the time has come. It is a natural law,
and not the turbulence of discontended fanatics that
calls for a larger development and culture. The
world's history has traveled in one direction. Woman
began at zero, and has through the ages slowly unfolded and risen. Each age has protested against

growth as *unsexing* women. There has been nothing that men have been so afraid of as *unsexing* women. Ah! God's work was too well done originally for that. In spite of centuries of unsexing, women retain their sex, and they will. Every single footfall forward on that long journey which they have already pursued has been a footfall you should take to Turkey or Greece, that which every man in his senses allows to be proper in woman, it would be considered monstrous. And still, in earlier ages through a hundred degrees of development, woman has been met with the same cry, that they are stepping beyond their sphere. It is the cry to-day, as woman, taxed, punished, restrained in all higher industries, asks that vote which carries with it control of circumstances. It is unsexing woman! A citizen in our day without a vote is like a smith without a hammer. The forge is hot,' the anvil waits, the iron is ready, but the smith has nothing to smite with. The vote is the workman's hammer to-day."

"A woman's nature will never be changed. Men might spin, and churn, and knit, and sew, and cook, and rock the cradle for one hundred generations, and not be a woman. And woman will not become a man by external occupations. God's colors do not wash out. Sex is dyed in the wool."

"In the new years that are coming a nobler womanhood will give to us nobler households. Men seem to think that the purity of our households depends upon their meagerness and their poverty; but I hold that that household is to be the strongest not only, but the purest, the richest, the sweetest, and the most full of delicacies as well, which has in it the most of power and treasure. Augment the thinking power of woman-hood. You detract in no wise from her motive power. Is the heart cheated by the husband's head? Nay, it is rendered stronger. The frailty of the fair sex will cease to be the theme of deriding poets, one day, when women learn that strength is feminine, and that weakness is the accident of sex, not the beauty nor glory. That will be a wholesome and happy period when men and women alike will be left to follow the call of God in their own genius The time will come when there will be liberty for all who are ordained artists to become artists without rebuke, when scholars may become scholars, and when orators may be orators, whether the⁻ be men or women."

Children.

I have been called to give up dear ones, not once, nor twice, nor thrice alone, but many times I have sent my children on before me. Once, wading knee-deep in the snow, I buried my earliest. It was March, and dreary, and shivering, and awful; and then the doctrine that Christ sat in an eternal summer of love, and that my child was not buried but had gone up to One that loved it better than I, was the only comfort I had."

"When the child, a little animal greedily seeking to eat, drink, and warm itself, comes under the care of the parent, and is taught that it must not feed itself at the expense of its little brother, it is learning to love. The parent says, 'You must be generous, my child. Why! will you not let poor little brother have anything?' And his great big stomach says, 'No; I want it all myself.'"

Speaking of the recklessness of modern marriages, he condemns many of them as highly foolish, and even criminal.

"When a man wants a flock, he doesn't say, 'Sheep, sheep!' he says, 'Give me Saxon, or Spanish, or Southdown.' When it is a wife or children he doesn't care; when it is a horse the kind is very important; when it is an immortal soul—anything will do."

"How beautiful is religion in an honest man! We often hear it said, 'That is a good Christian, but not a very honest man.' People say it is censorious. It is true, nevertheless. The world sees it better than you are willing to see it, and declares it to be a fact. The man has many aspirations, and longings, and struggles, and repentances; and yet these are all of them rooted in a temperament and in an education that is being swept this way and that by the force of temptation. And men see that he is selfish, though he prays beautifully; that he is proud, though he is devout; that he is vain, though he has a great deal of religious sensibility; and they pronounce him a hypocrite. The trouble is that his religion was planted in bad moral soil. If he had been educated in boyhood to conscience, and honor, and truthfulness, and his religion had been planted in these as a soil, the world would not have seen the inconsistency which he exhibits."

"It seems impossible to say of that royal woman, as serene as the evening sky, and as glorious and pure as the stars which are in it, that she gave signs and tokens of the utmost depravity in youth. But she did. It was, however, only a fitful manifestation; it was scarcely to be distinguished from a morbid state of the body, and after the patient waiting of a few years, when all the faculties began to get the mind regulated, this depraved tendency disappeared."

"I think truthfulness and openness of conduct is the first qualification, and the first foundation of the kingdom of God and the kingdom of man in the human soul. The older I grow the more I believe it. · · · The next element is self-respect, or the habit of acting, not from what others may think, but from a sense of what is befitting to you. · · · The man who is only restrained from wrong-doing by the influences around him will, when he goes away from home, when he is not under the operation of those influences, find his powers of resistance too weak to withstand temptation. The last element is conscience. Truthfulness, honor, and conscience; train for these three qualities. Talk with your children about them. Interpret them to them by your own conduct."

Money.

"So men that will at all hazards and at any rate, be rich, give up honor, faith, conscience, love, refinement, friendship, and sacred trust, and having given all these up, God blesses and blasts them — blesses, for they are rich, and that is what they call blessing — blasts, because it is not in the nature of God himself, without an absolute change of the laws by which he works to make a man happy who has, for the sake of gaining wealth, divested himself of those elements in which happiness consists. · · · Wall Street is my commentary — Broadway is my commentary!"

"Almost every crime that fills our jails has money at the bottom of it. To-day the whole Atlantic seaboard is covered with smuggling—money. The whole land is a pandemonium of swindling—money."

"It used to be raised up as an objection against revivals of religion that they set men crazy, that religion addled thin heads. Ah! ten men go crazy after money where one goes crazy in religious excitement, and yet nothing is said in the papers about that."

"There are many men belonging to business circles in New York who 'step out,' and what is the matter? Softening of the brain. Hardening of the heart is very apt to end in softening of the brain. There are many whose business goads them on — whose troubles harass them to such an extent that some latent tendency, induced or inherited, is developed in them, and they become insane. And shall nobody mark these things? Is it enough to say of a man, 'O, he is gone crazy!' Shall nobody say, 'How?' Shall nobody take young men aside in the streets and say, 'What is the matter with that man?'"

Dwelling upon the slowness of honest gains and the quickness of dishonest speculation, Mr. Beecher said: "One said to me, who had spent some forty years in honest and ordinary toil in commercial life, and who went into speculation during the war, 'I have been all my life fumbling and blundering, and I have just learned how to make money, and now I

can make just as much as I want;' and to-day he is
bankrupt — thank God."

Politics.

"Citizens that stay at home pay the expenses of
politicians that go racketing about the country and
doing nothing but mischief."

"The growth of liberty in England is one of the
most important studies for a Christian philosopher. I
regard no one feature of our time as so striking as
this; and no one event in our age is more striking
than the fact of our great war and the result of it, in
the development of the spirit of liberty, and of faith in
it among the nations of the earth. . .. . No
crowned head, not even the Czar himself, could have
put a million men along a base of a thousand miles,
and sustained them with ever growing strength through
four years of war.   No exchequer of any monarch
could ever stand the drain to which the treasury of
this government was subjected, and which was sup-
plied by the taxation and labor of a few people.   All
Europe predicted our bankruptcy — my own ears heard
it. Manchester, and Liverpool, and London, said to
me, 'Oh, your money is but paper; besides you are
only a democracy, and what is property in a democracy?   Do you suppose your people will bear taxation?'   I said to them, 'There is no people on earth

that will bear taxation as a people that tax themselves. Your government comes down to your people, and they do not like it, and they do not like to be taxed to support it, and the life of your government depends on light taxes; but our people do like their government, and are willing to be taxed, if necessary, for its support. Our government represents the living wants and the present judgment of our people, and they shrink from no self-sacrifice that may be required for its preservation.' "

"As long as a man thinks of what he is going to say, he can not be a public speaker. His speaking must get ahead of him, and he must go on behind it and find out what he has said, as it were. That is the sensation he has."

Beecher in three of his many powerful moods; the first rugged and forcible:

"How is it, brother? I do not ask you whether you like the cup which you are drinking; but look back twenty years. . . . What has made you so versatile? What has made you so patient? What has made you so broad, so deep, so rich? God put pickaxes into you, though you did not like it. He dug wells of salvation in you. He took you in his strong hand, and shook you by his north wind, and rolled you in his snows, and fed you with the coarsest food, and clothed you in the coarsest raiment, and beat you as a flail beats grain till the straw is gone, and the wheat is left. And you are what you are by the grace of God's providence, many of you. By fire, by anvil-strokes, by the hammer that breaks the flinty rock, God played miner, and blasted you out of the rock, and then He played stamper, and crushed you, and then He played smelter and smelted you, and now you are gold, free from the rock, by the grace of God's severity to you."

This is Mr. Beecher in one of his most delicate poetic flights:

"Is it because seeds have failed in the south that birds begin to flock north? Is it because summer has ceased to warm the fields there that they are flying hither? Near the time appointed by God for their migration the birds begin with their peculiar instinct to yearn and long, and they abstain from their wonted food, till, by and by, at a given signal, they lift themselves up, and move in throngs through the air toward the land where there is new summer.

"Now God breathes a spiritual, migratory instinct into the hearts of men. Not because they are not well off here, not because they would be unclothed; but because beyond and above them there is something better and nobler than this life. They long for perfectness."

Mr. Beecher could be stately on occasion, and at

times the majesty of his rhythm had quite a Shakespearian ring about it. We might select many passages in illustration of this, but the following must suffice; it closes a fine sermon on "Self-control Possible to All:"

" Now they do it to obtain a corruptible crown, but we are incorruptible," and the two garlands are there, for the last time, as it were, held up before us, whilst we are called upon to contrast once more the newness in the earthly and the heavenly arena:—

"While yet they live, the leaves grow sear upon their brow. Their very footsteps with which they sound the dance, shake down these withered leaves; and they are discrowned in the very wearing of their crowns. But around about our heads that follow Christ, invisible leaves there are; or, if they are visible, men call them thorns, as they should be called, since we follow Him that wore them; but as the angels behold them, they are those imperishable flowers— that amaranth which never blossoms to fade or to fail. And our crown shall be bright when the stars have gone and the sun have forgotten to shine!"